GENER

HUMANITY

DAWN OF HUMANITY

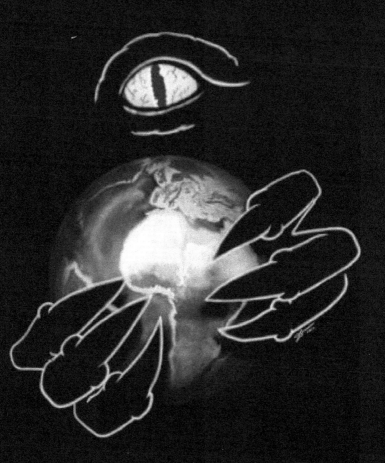

K. KALOR

Generations of Humanity
Dawn of Humanity
By K. Kalor
Published by Tea, with Coffee Media

Printed in the United States of America

First Printing, 2022

ISBN 978-1-957893-01-3

Tea, With Coffee Media

7181 Durant Ave NE

Leland, North Carolina, 28451

www.teawithcoffee.media

Chapter 1:

"My Lord," hissed a reptilian voice. "The Trinary System that we are currently exploring will not be suitable for our needs, despite the candidate planetary bodies in proper orbits. However, there is a system less than four light-years away that appears to be suitable. It is a young star with multiple planetary bodies orbiting within the prime zone. It appears to be a young system, unlike this one. Our records suggest it formed less than five billion cycles ago."

Standing before his Lord, Sa-Tan Enki moved his long, scaly fingers, each tipped with a long claw, along a dotted line in a projected image. The image showed the current star system that would later be named Alpha Centauri, with a purple dot next to Proxima C. The line led to the closest star, a yellow dwarf.

The Sa-Tan was a bi-pedal creature that stood about a meter and a half high; his reptilian skin was pale green and his eyes had a faint yellow glow. His snout extended slightly from his face while his upper incisors extended somewhat below the lower jaw. When he spoke, his forked tongue flicked out occasionally. His tail reached out nearly half a meter, allowing him to stand at a slight angle. As befitting a member of his station, Enki wore a blue cloth draped over his neck. Hanging on the left side were icons that looked like two snakes twisting around a pole and an atom. On the right was a mark that looked like a flying craft and a dragon in flight.

"I would recommend, Lord Anu, that we send a team to observe the system directly. I suspect they will determine it is suitable. In that case, they can prepare for the rest of the blessed ones' arrival," Enki said as he tilted his head to the reptilian creature standing on the dais in front of him.

Upon a golden dais stood three reptilian creatures, the Anunnaki Lords, each standing over two meters tall. Lord Anu was the eldest-looking one and stood in front of the other two. In the elder's right hand was a gold scepter that showed his power. The head of the staff was shaped like an eye, the iris glowing as it darted around in every direction. He wore a red cloth over his shoulders, embroidered with gold ankhs along the edge while the mark of the Anunnaki hung over his heart. On the left side was a coat of arms that identified him as head of the Anu family.

Behind the elder stood two reptilians. One was a lighter green, much like Enki's own coloring, while the one on the left of Lord Anu had soft grey scales. They both wore purple cloths over their necks; the green Lord's left side had the crest of the Anu in silver, while the right side had the mark of the Anunnaki. The silver mark held two sapphire gems in the center that marked Lord Enlil as the Anu and Anunnaki's primary Heir. The second in command of the Annunaki had a silver staff in his hand, the head shaped like Lord Anu's own.

The Grey Scaled one's markings had scythes in gold, identifying him as Lord of his House. On the right side was the mark of the Anunnaki in silver like Enlil's coat of arms, but missing the gemstones. The emblem marked Chronos as the secondary Heir but the head of his family, representing the lineage of Mazda. Ahura Chronos's staff was in his left hand, a skull with horns, a square jaw, and raggedy teeth adorning it.

"What is our provision status?" asked Sky Lord Anu.

Enki reached out to touch the hologram, gave a few taps with his three-fingered and thumbed hand, and a list scrolled. "We are low on water, hydrogen, industrial oxygen, multiple fertilizers, along with some ores such as gold. The latter is the most pressing need for our technology if we wish for the Spirit Mother's blessing."

Lord Chronos stamped his staff on the ground, causing a loud crack. "Why can't the blessed harvest meet our needs here?" he demanded. "The Titans are tired of wandering in the realm of the Mother."

Enki's eyes flicked over to the Grey Lord. "Because the planets in this system lack an atmosphere. As you are aware, since your caste lost control over the few remaining Ama-gi, we cannot leave the confines of the Nibiru."

"You dare talk to us like that, Sa-Tan," spat Chronos.

Enlil placed his hand on the Grey Lord's shoulder. "Sa-Tan makes a point; we are unable to walk within the Mother's cold embrace due to how the Great Mother created us, even with her blessed cloth. Perhaps this exhibition might be the sign from the Great Mother that we have searched for these past tens of thousands of cycles. We felt drawn to this system because of our connection to the Great Lady; perhaps she is directing us to our new home."

The Sky Lord of the Anunnaki closed his eyes as he whispered words of power. His eyelids glowed slightly before the head of his staff glowed. A spark flew from one statue of the Great Mother into the staff's gemstone eyes. The Lord's body stiffened as his snout lifted and his hand twisted the rod, breaking the conduit of power.

Behind the Lords, each statue's eyes lit up with power in them. Slowly, each figure moved from its standing position to a seated one. Several sat crossed-legged; two sat with their feet hanging over their podiums. One fell backward, blue blood leaking from a hole in the chest. Another was holding a youngling.

Turning, Lord Anu looked over the Great Mothers, his eyes widening. "The Mothers agree but warn that we might lose all."

"Then we shall find our rightful home," said Chronos.

"We should settle if it is possible. We are dying as a race. After the last of our slaves, the Ama-gi, died, we lost the ability to harvest resources past the shell of the Nibiru. Even if this system provides a simple rest stop, we should take the time," replied Enlil.

"What good is resting if it kills us? Do you lack the strength to stand?" Chronos asked. "The risk is too great for us."

"Die in the icy embrace of the Mother now or possibly die at some point later; I say we throw the astragali and see where they fall," Enlil retorted.

Chronos slammed his scepter against the ground. "You dare evoke Lady Chance when it comes to the Gods?"

"Peace, Brother," Lord Anu interrupted. "The signs are clear; the Great Mother wishes for us to settle this system. She is merely warning us not to allow our arrogance to rule us once more. Sa-Tan Enki, you will take a team to the system and determine its suitability for us."

Enki bowed his head. "Yes, my Lord," he said before sharply turning and walking out of the chamber.

Anu's body sagged as he turned to face the two Lords. "We have followed the pillar of light for eons. When we were removed from the lands of An, the seers of the Gods saw that I would see the new home of our people, but I would not live beyond setting foot upon them. I am old; my time as Sky Lord wanes. Soon this power will be yours, Enlil. I leave the choice to settle in your hands. Chronos, you will advise him as the will of the Great Mother."

"Yes, My Lord," they said together.

"Do not worry, my child, I shall not die until I lay eyes upon the land flowing with gaábkùga and lal," Anu promised. "It's only at that time; I lay down my burden."

Chapter 2:

Space was vast. The distances between stars became so abstract that most sentient beings shrugged and thought, what's a few trillion kilometers?. They thought that it couldn't take that long to travel. Four years at the speed of light came across as a short distance, but when it came time to traverse space, years turned into decades. Often centuries.

Time passed onboard the long cylindrical research vessel. Its diameter was two kilometers, while the length was four kilometers. The outer shell was a hollowed-out asteroid they had captured a millennium ago for resources. Its inner core rotated around a central axis, providing gravity to the travelers. The inside had layers from vast fields and hills that provided a sense of natural life among the void of space, to the research labs and offices.

Enki looked up as he entered the command center due to the alarms that blared at the flight control station. The pilot hissed loudly, "just another micro ice chunk pinging off the barrier."

"Silence the alarm," said the Officer of the Deck, or OOD. Moments later, the impact alarm ceased. That Annunaki stood more erect than others. His stature was similar to the Lord's. "If something bigger strikes us," the officer's lip lifted as he shook his head, not finishing the thought. "Is there damage beyond the Sheg Barrier?"

"Rolling in a replacement ice block now. Two blocks have to be removed from the system for reforming," reported the engineering liaison.

The OOD turned, his teeth slightly bared. "Sa-Tan, how much more damage will we take?"

"There are only a few hundred thousand kilometers before we reach the main solar system. From there, I wouldn't expect much micro-debris. Set course for the third planet. If the orbits allow, please see about any other planets for a fly-by," ordered Enki.

"Yes, my Lord," said the OOD. "We shall have a flight path ready in forty-eight hours."

Enki waved his hand dismissively. "Make sure it is accurate," he instructed.

Snapping a quick salute by pressing his claw to his chest, the OOD bowed his head before turning to his navigator to discuss his orders. Enki left the command center; he found his way to the throne room. He entered a code for the quantum entanglement holo projectors and knelt, waiting for the connection. Ten minutes later, three holograms appeared.

"My Lords, we have the early reports. We have passed through the cloud of debris that wrapped the solar system. The ice and dust are remnants from when the system formed billions of years ago and marked for harvesting later. Perhaps the automated systems of the Nibiru will be able to harvest if they still work. We are now entering the system that has eleven planets of varying size and composition.

"Starting with the Primary, it is a yellow dwarf, roughly four billion cycles old. The innermost planet was a lifeless rock that was almost tidally locked. There is an apparent metallic composition that would work well for future projects, requiring much deeper exploration.

"The second planet is a lush green world, gravity nearly perfect for our race. The biosphere, however, is running much too warm for us. We would have to cool the environment, which would require a constant power draw. My Lords, as you know, we cannot repair our equipment, thus removing it for now. Settling this planet would require a native that could be modified into a new species of Adama.

"Thankfully, the third planet is near perfection for us. While the tropical zone might be on the warm side, the size should allow for cool nights, much like our old home. There is plenty of land in the sub-tropical zones that are perfect for us. This planet is almost identical to our homeworld. It is as if the Great Mother gifted this planet to us. It is effectively one astronomical unit (A.U.) from the star.

"Coming to the fourth planet, it is roughly half the size of the prior two. Because of the distance from the solar primary, it doesn't have a tropical zone but a broad range of sub-tropics before moving into a tundra. Both poles have temperatures well below anything that we could survive, even with our suits.

"Almost inhabitable, the next body is nearly three A.U. from the system's star, a frozen fifth planet. Same size as the fourth, but even the equatorial zone was a tundra landscape with a very narrow band. This planet has nothing for us, but perhaps we could use them to gather resources after creating an Adama species.

"Sitting two and a half A.U. from the fifth planet is the first gas giant, complete with a massive storm that looks like an eye. Around the planet are dozens of moons; some could almost be considered a planet of their own. The rest of the planets are not inhabitable, aside from a possible moon here or there. There are, however, a plethora of resources we could harvest at some point.

"One planet of note is the eleventh. While it is a rocky planet, double the size of the third planet, it has a massive orbit. Stellar cartography projects suggest that the second and third plenary orbits might shift as the planet passes through the system. Another irregularity is the inclination of the orbit of eighty-two degrees. It is most likely a captured exo-planet," Enki concluded his speech.

Enlil's tongue flicked as he looked over the holographic images. "Very well. The third planet clearly is the gift we have been looking for."

"The third is to become the home of the Gods. The throne, the mountain that watches all. The Gift of the Great Tiamat, our Great Mother. It is clear, this planet is the focal point. The outermost planet allows the flow of power to be redirected back within the system. It is in the same shape as the Obium Particle that the Mother Ninmena forged into our blood," Chronos said, his voice becoming pensive. "Perhaps we will require less Dimethyltryptamine in our Ambrosia?"

"The Nibiru will arrive in four decades. Enki, you shall land upon the third world. It is the most like our old homelands. Research the system as you see fit. Ensure there is a home for us to rest in," Enlil said, not looking at his brother.

Enki bowed as he spoke, "As you command." He turned sharply and broke the connection.

Chapter 3:

A holographic Enlil stared at a hologram of the largest planet in the solar system. It was on the edge of being considered a hot gas giant. Its bands of milky white, yellows, browns, reds, and other colors were nothing short of breathtaking. He felt his soul connect as they surveyed it on their way past. The eyes of his staff seemed to track a massive storm of red hues, bigger than the inner planets. The storm reminded him of the all-seeing eye of Anu, the eye of the Sky-Father.

The door opened with a hiss, allowing the Sa-Tan to enter. Enlil's head turned slightly to look at his son. "Have we completed the orbital survey of the planet?" he asked as his holographic body turned to face them.

"We have identified several possible landing zones," Enki replied, his fingers tapping on a tablet.

The image of the gas giant changed to the third planet. One side of the planet had much of the land. There were seven major land masses. A thick ice sheet entirely covered the southern pole. A mountain range on the western side ran along the coast until it merged into the ice sheet. The northern two-thirds formed a peninsula, letting the ocean reach deep within. The eastern side looked like it slotted right into the continent's western coast, a few thousand kilometers across the sea.

The middle continent crossed the equator, most of the western bulge was above that line. Covered in a desert down to the planet's center, reaching into a savannah surrounding a rainforest. There were mountain ranges around the southern tip. The orbit would likely shift the rainforest to desert and back every twenty-three thousand years, partly due to the trajectory of the captured exoplanet. A few hundred kilometers away from the southeastern coast was a large island that would be the perfect way to hide from any pandemic.

Crossing east a few more hundred kilometers was another dart-like continent, but much smaller than the first one. It was about a third of the other masses. From orbital observations, there was a rainforest that covered the eastern side of the island.

Attached to the southern ice sheet was a massive tropical mass. It was coming out almost like a cell dividing. One could expect that it would eventually pull away. Several islands dotted the ocean for a few thousand kilometers east and north of the mass.

The northern continents were split into three masses with an ice cap of several kilometers connecting them. The first mass reminded Enki of a bird of prey trying to land on the southern continent from the image or perhaps swooping in to eat the land in the middle.

There was a large island on the western side of the northern center continent, with a claw-like mass trying to grab the bigger land. It was connected to the boot via a thin isthmus. Above the boot was a bulbous mass that led to a large but shallow gap between the second and third land masses.

As continents go, the northeastern seemed bland. It wasn't shaped like a delta as the southwestern one, a gun like the center southern one, or the birds of the other two northern ones. That one looked like someone opened a lid on a box. One side was longer than the other, giving it an odd shape. There was a small delta-shaped island below the box.

The ice covering the south pole made the landmass difficult to identify. On the eastern side, there was a protrusion the size of another continent. That landmass was a few hundred thousand years from separating into a bigger lonely island.

Between the middle two land masses were a series of islands, providing a sub-tropical environment. Many of the islands had towering mountain peaks that attracted a lot of the storms.

Enki looked at his father as he launched into the report. "The planet seems to be ideal for our kind. The northwestern lands have plenty of forests, in which our scouts have seen large creatures. We've found many species from the middle gun lands, including what look like hairless apes. These creatures have progressed to where they live in small cities, as you can see by the marked locations.

"There is an issue with the system's primary that it is a highly active star. It goes through high and low cycles. Even these cycles have their own highs and lows. During busy times, the void around the system will not be travelable due to gamma rays. Even our own ark would suffer. The Magnetosphere of the third planet is the strongest of the inhabitable planets and moons."

Enlil slowly had the image spin to act like him walking around it as Enki spoke. When the Sa-Tan finished, the future Lord of the Annunaki tapped a land mass. "There is where we will land," he ordered. His claw touched the island chains that separated the middle two land masses. There was one city nearby, but they should have plenty of time to make first contact. "As per your suggestion, we shall build the Ekur here."

"The assembly of the gods?" Enki asked. "Why not the Hearth?"

"The Great Mother has shown me the future. We return as the rightful representative of Tiamat," Enlil answered.

"Father, have you interpreted the visions correctly? While I am no Chronos, I am the En of our clan; perhaps I could help with what you saw," Enki suggested.

Enlil turned to look at the younger Annunaki. He thought about it for a few long moments before nodding. "Before we entered the system, my dreams were full of stepping foot on the planet below, a feeling of rightness in my heart. A sense of returning home overwhelmed me as I fell to my knees. The landscape changed, showing a great battle in the heavens and upon the land. Anunnaki, Titans, and Adama fighting among themselves. I saw our forms melting away into the ground.

"Giant bi-pedal creatures grabbed the lighting, the oceans, the earth, even the very air, manipulating them to their will. I saw a massive explosion in the sky before a great shadow grew in the wake of the fireball. The ground shook, causing the Giants to run while the shadow loomed over them.

"Shadows covered the ground; screams, terror, joy, and love came from the dark. There were flashes of light before a great tower rose. It reached through the darkness, touching the sky. Great balls of fire struck the ground multiple times, with the last strike causing a massive rush of water from the great dark.

"The ground rose from the waters before mud hills grew. These hills turned into stones of many kinds. Soft rock, hard stone, gemstones formed. A black speck appeared in a hard stone. The dots appeared on the other stones. Soon the rocks started touching, allowing their colors to mix. Still, the black specks turned into a sickly ooze before forming lines that grew into a gooey sheet covering the entire mass. It touched a warm stone, the last to be felt. The rock must have been liquid as it recoiled from the black tar before the vision went white in a flash of light.

"It is at this point I awake. Every time," Enlil whispered. "Since we left the last system, the feeling of a mother wrapping her arms around a lost son that has wandered home has replaced the dream. I see myself sitting on a throne, my hands pale. Those around me remind me of hairless apes. They are celebrating my ascension on the throne.

"My wife sits at the same time as I do. She is dressed in a gown that sheens like scales, reflecting the light as our scales do. She glows as the representation of Tiamat is blessed by the great Mother. Lady Gaia steps back, her hands lowering from placing the crown upon my head, glancing at my wife. Lady Gaia's eyes, however, look sad, warning my wife of something to come."

Enki's staff leaned forward as his tail twitched. The researcher and spiritual adviser shook his head before speaking. "Father, can you describe the others in the throne room? Perhaps the throne itself?"

"The faces of my retainers were smoothed as if I was not allowed to know them yet. Even my wife. Her golden fur flowed from her head. It framed her face, making her shine as the goddess of motherhood should. She wore a scabbard that looked like it held a short sword. The runes carved into the hilt said the weapon was named Laevateinn.

"Lady Gaia's skin reminded me of the ochre color of the Ahpap'la. Her dark eyes carried the weight of the planet. Her hair was the color of charcoal. She wore an outfit that almost glowed a pale blue that slowly turned into Anunnaki green and Titan grey-ish blue. The smile she had radiated the pride that a mother has for her children as they achieve greatness."

"Laevateinn is the name of the Sky-Mother's blade. It awaits someone worthy to claim it but held in guardianship by our Claim. This is clear that our clan will remain as the Sky-Lords," Enki stated.

"That is my viewpoint as well, my son," Enlil agreed. "There is a third dream that I've been having. You and I are walking past a broken wall, the bodies of those hairless apes scattered around. Our fellow Anunnaki laid on both sides of the fight as if we had a civil war. Most seemed to be defending the apes. You were twisting your staff, words of power on your tongue. My arms lifted, grabbing the wind to provide aid. I felt desperate to defeat whoever it was."

"Of the three, the last is the clearest. We are going to settle upon the third world. At some point, we will have a sundering. The only reason that we haven't had one yet is that we are all trapped upon the Nibiru," Enki explained. Closing his eyes, he whispered a few words as he tapped the staff to the deck in time. The head glowed purple with a blue streak rising from it. Inhaling, he drew it into his body. As he exhaled, his tongue flicked, forming shapes from the smoke.

"The wandering one returns while Sol wanes," Enki said, before waving his staff through the smoke. "We are blessed, Father. The Great Mother gives her blessings for us to take the planet."

Chapter 4:

"Open the hatch," Enki hissed. He stood at the rear of the shuttle, his tail flicking slightly in irritation over the fact that warriors would be the first to step foot on their new planet. The door popped open with a hiss and sank into the sand of the beach. The carbon monoxide and oxygen levels were not perfect for them, but it was close enough. They were used to CO_2 levels over four hundred parts per million. Even the air pressure at sea level was perfect. His free hand came up to shield his eyes from the light emanating from the local star.

Gasping at the local fauna, he could see tall trees, taller than anything he had seen in his life. Then again, when your whole life was spent inside a metal sphere, everything was more prominent than expected. Enki took another moment to breathe the air. It smelt pure, a sense of home filling him.

A pair of warriors exited the landing craft and darted forward, sniffing the air; their tri-toed feet left claw marks in the sand. Birds that had returned after the landing screamed in terror. After walking around the shuttle a few times, the two warriors returned to the hatch.

"Sa-Tan Enki, the smells are overwhelming. The smell of salt hangs in the air along with many plants. We can smell many creatures in the area, covered in the stench of fear," reported one warrior.

The hunter's head snapped to the right, sniffing the air.

Crouching, he dug his toes into the sand. With a roar, he launched forward, jaws snapping around the neck of a tiger. With a twist of the head, the feline's neck snapped. The hunter returned to Enki, dropping the creature.

"Native for you, milord," said the hunter. He looked like he was struggling not to devour the feline.

"How long has it been since you've had meat? I am talking about real meat, not that meat grown from plants we have," Enki wondered.

"Many cycles, milord, since before the trinary system," the hunter admitted.

"Go hunt, make sure you take images before you eat," Enki said as he poked the feline with a clawed toe. Saliva dripped from his lips, tongue flicking out, tasting the blood in the air. The hunters darted into the forest, sending the local wildlife screeching in fear. The academic knelt as he ran his fingers over the gashes in the neck. He closed his eyes, letting out a few breaths before gathering the blood in test tubes.

"Tan Ninurta, I want the DNA sequenced. If this is going to be our home, we need to know everything about the wildlife," Enki said as he handed the vial to his assistant.

"Yes, milord," Ninurta said.

As he stepped out of the shuttle, Enki felt his foot sink into the sand. The coarseness surprised him. Enki used his staff to inscribe a rune in the sand. His eyes closed as he began pushing, reaching out to grab the magic of Tiamat. A whispered word caused the rune to glow purple. As it faded, shapes appeared in the grass.

Several felines were crouched a few dozen meters away, perhaps part of the same pride. In the subtropical forest, Enki noted the shapes of many creatures in the forest canopy. Creatures were slithering in the sand and on the ground of the woods. The Annunaki Lord turned slowly, sniffing and attempting to put smell to shape. His jaw dropped at the amount of life in the water along the shore. Deeper into the water, several large shapes swam around a school of fish.

"This planet is so full of life," Enki said.

"The Great Mother has blessed us," responded a female Anunnaki.

"Lady Inanna." Enki tilted his head slightly, noting that his fellow Anunnaki held a scribe pad. She came up to Enki's shoulder, her snout elongated, her eyes on the sides of her head. "The ease with which I cast the scrying rune was surprising."

Shaking her head, Inanna waved her clawed fingers at the water. "Beyond that. The blessings of food from the land, sea, and air. This place holds a beauty that I have never felt so drawn to. When I stepped off our shuttle, I connected with this planet. Kulla and I will work everlasting wonders to show off Lady Gaia's true wonders," she said.

"This is not the first time someone has spoken of this Lady Gaia. This is yet another sign that this is to become our home," Enki replied.

"It is a shame that we will mar her beauty within the first hours of landing, but shelter and a landing pad are required. The engineering chief is rather upset at the pilot landing in the sand; he will have to take the engines apart to clean them. He can't do that because he needs the lift on the ship, since gravity is at the Olympian standard. He is very adamant that the pilot's name shall forever be stricken from the Gods," Inanna explained.

"That sounds like him when anyone messes with his work," Enki said with a shake of his head. "Where shall we start then?"

"I need a survey to know exactly what stone we have available to us. Lady Ninhursag is preparing to send Kulla to conduct some penetrating scans. Kulla has pulled up plan Theta," Inanna replied as she handed Enki the scribe pad.

"I see. Won't this destroy the beauty?" Enki asked as he took the pad.

"We will provide an enhancement to the beauty of this place. Don't worry, milord," Inanna reassured him.

Enki signed the scribe pad and handed it back to her. "Approved. Get the hunters to unpack. Tonight, we dine as the Gods of old. That is, if they haven't lost their skills while trapped in the heavens for so long." A roar of frustration tore through the air, as if to confirm Enki's statement. "They have," he said dryly.

Inanna bowed her head. "By your leave."

Enki distractedly returned the bow with his head. The water was calling him, somehow. He started walking along the shore, just above the wave line in the sand. After a few hundred meters, he stopped and placed the end of his staff into the water. The eyes glowed as Enki's head snapped up. His eyes glazed over as he processed the sensations. He intuitively knew the location of every life form within a few kilometers of him.

'Who?' 'What are you?' 'They have returned!' 'fleeeeeee!' and other phrases filled his brain/head as the inhabitants reacted to the brush against their minds. Enki fell to his knees, his hands gripping at the sand. Claws left long lines in the ground, his breathing labored as he went into shock as his own mind created new pathways to handle connection. His blue blood dripped from his nose.

Enki felt something touch his shoulder. Spinning, he snapped the staff's head towards the person's knees behind him while a word formed on his lips. His attack stopped as Inanna deflected the blow with ease.

"Are you ill, Sa-Tan?" calmly asked Inanna.

"No. Well, maybe. Perhaps being overwhelmed would be more accurate. Our connection to Tiamat has been growing since we entered the system. I can feel the creatures in the sea. I can touch their minds, and they can touch mine, even without the staff. I'm the Lord of Magic, not Oceanus, for Anu's sake. I shouldn't be able to feel them clearly," answered Enki.

Inanna shifted, her eye ridges twitching in confusion. "But our staffs were forged from celestial bronze to enhance our lost connection. It amplifies the power of Tiamat from the background. We physically can't cast magic without one."

"That is the question," Enki replied just before loud explosions went off in the forest. He turned to look at the Tan, his head tilted.

"The Builder is clearing parts of the forest," Inanna explained.

"Very well. Let's get the camp set up," Enki said.

Chapter 5:

The pack felt dirt under their feet for the first time in thousands of cycles. The lead hunter lowered his head, sniffing the ground. "Many scents. Fear of our presence," he grunted.

"Ninurta, there are climbers near," said the huntress as she sniffed a tree.

"Gula, are they a threat to us?" asked Ninurta.

"Perhaps. I need to spend more time here," Gula answered. Her head tilted to the side, her tongue hanging out slightly. "There, large mammal in that tree," she said as she stretched out a claw.

A shaft of wood suddenly shot out of the tree canopy. The third hunter snatched it out of the air. He sniffed the straps of leather wrapped around the center and around the weapon's edge. His head shot back when he reached the tip. "It is covered in a foul substance."

"Rundas, what kind?" asked Gula.

"How should I know? I'm not Enki, but probably meant to kill," replied Rundas.

Ninurta lifted his tail, causing the other hunters to stop talking. His head slowly moved back and forth, sniffing the air. He darted to the left as his jaw opened for a strike. He was not rewarded with flesh, but with another shaft of wood. A large creature dived out of the way before rolling behind a tree.

Gula darted around, but the mammal was climbing up a rope. She dug her claws into the dirt to get a feel like a cat preparing itself before she lunged. As she flew through the air, her jaws opened wide to bite hard, but was denied her catch by the simple act of her target lifting his legs out of the way. The creature grunted something before continuing up the rope and into the canopy. The huntress slammed into the ground, causing the air to rush out of her lungs.

"Get it!" snarled Ninurta.

"What do you think I'm trying to do?" Gula spat before scrambling to her feet. Without checking her footing, she leaped a few meters up the tree. Snarling, she tried to climb up, but the bark gave way.

Lady Gula's target observed the actions of the mighty hunter from his perch on a branch. It wore leather clothing with a rope around the waist. Tied to its calf was a leather sheath with a knife. It only had fur around its head and face. A second one appeared in another tree, making a loud sound that the first one responded to.

It grabbed a horn from its belt. The second target's face seemed resigned to death. He gave three short bursts, followed by a long sound three times. The first creature shouted at the second, who moved his hands to the side before putting the horn back. It shouted its intelligible nonsense while the two hunters circled the first creature's tree.

Ninurta was standing between the two, looking back and forth. He looked at the second creature's tree, noting that it was thinner. He lowered his head to add to his speed as he broke into a run. He had reached nearly his top speed before jumping into the tree, causing it to shake. The second creature wrapped his arms and legs around the trunk, holding on through the swaying. As the tree moved, the creature yelled something, causing the first to tie himself to the tree.

Jaws wide, Ninurta let out a scream of frustration. He spun, slamming his tail into the trunk. The sound of wood splitting ripped through the air. The other two hunters hurried over to help knock the tree down. The head hunter dug his claws into the ground and smashed over and over into the tree. Their target tied a loop into his rope before flinging it across to a thicker tree. Pulling the rope, he dropped out of the tree, swinging across to the thicker one.

"Come down here, primitive!" snarled Gula, but the creature simply brought up his hand and raised a single digit as he spat some sound.

"Screw the old ways," spat Rundas. He grabbed a daihkish thrower, a long rod that had a green glow near the trigger. He lifted the rod to point at the forest.

The head hunter slammed his tail into Rundas. "Waste not the holy daihkish! You know we can't create more plasma!" Rundas' face was rammed into the ground with a crunch.

"Yes, milord," groaned Rundas, blue blood dripping from his snout.

Gula lifted her head as distant horns sounded. The second creature grabbed his horn, responding with three long blasts. There was a single long sound in response. The three hunters glanced at each other before turning as one. They bolted from their prey, heading back to the beach.

"We might have upset the natives," Rundas grumbled.

"They smelt like fresh meat; how were we to know that the apes were that smart?" asked Ninurta as he ducked under a low branch.

"So much for the apex hunter. Running from a group of tree climbers," Gula said.

"Not running away. We're gathering data for the hunt," Ninurta corrected.

The trio kept their high speed up as they ran back to the landing site. They quickly entered a clearing where their fellow Annunaki were moving trees with their staffs. Through the manipulation of magnetic fields, they were able to float heavy items.

Coming up to Enki, Ninurta bowed to his Lord. "We have discovered that there are intelligent natives."

Enki's staff stilled as he tilted his head to look at the Lord of the Hunt. "Were you not instructed not to run afoul of any potential intelligence?"

"Yes, milord. We were tracking a large feline when a pair of hairless apes attacked us. They attacked from the forest canopy. When we trapped the pair in the trees, they called for reinforcements," Ninurta explained.

"Just how were a pair of primitives able to make a remote call?" asked Enki.

"They used a horn, which suggests that the reinforcements were close. We only know of two, but we heard at least one other horn."

Enki closed his eyes as he let out several slow breaths. "Lovely. Not only did you start some nonsense, but you also have no idea how badly you stepped into dung. By Lord Anu, the three of you are the very ones I'd place in charge of rebuffing the primitive attacks. Nergal! Take these three. They are to take point."

"Yes, milord!" Nigral answered.

Returning to the shuttle, Enki called out, "Nabu, can we leave the island?"

"I'm pretty sure I had word sent that we can't return to the

Nibiru," spat Nabu from under the engines.

"Is that what I asked? I asked if we could leave the island, as in go somewhere else on this planet," Enki said.

"No milord, we sucked too much sand into the air intakes. Everything is clogged up," Nabu reported.

"We have landed on so many planets before. Why is this one a problem?" Enki demanded.

"We had to strip parts from most of the shuttles to keep a few up. The dust covers were removed well over a thousand cycles ago, and then we repaired the Carbon Dioxide scrubbers. We told Zababa not to land on the beach, but the fool still dropped us here," Nabu explained as he slid out from the engine.

"Thus, we can't leave. Any kind of power?" asked Enki.

"No, it would take a lot longer to reconnect the fuel lines," Nabu answered and wiped the grease from his claws. "You could try runes."

"I would rather not enter torpor for a week," Enki said.

"Looks like we might not have a choice. Only you can wield the Sharur of Cthulhu), one of three that can transfer that kind of energy from the background. At least, that is what the old technical manuals said. We've been unable to repair the other staffs."

"Very well. I shall prepare myself," Enki replied as he stepped back out of the shuttle and walked over to Inanna. "Lady Inanna, we are about to perform a shielding ritual. I haven't actually cast this before, so after completion, you will assume command, with the orders to prepare for landing."

"Of course, milord. Will you require assistance in preparing the runes?" asked Inanna.

"Yes, we do not have a lot of time before the natives arrive. If we knew how many were coming, then perhaps we wouldn't need this. Better safe than dead."

The two of them drew a circle in the sand around their landing area and equipment. Then the pair drew three shapes that repeated around the outer line. Finally, they drew four sets of runes to make a block for Enki to stand in. As they finished, horns blared. Enki looked up to see several hundred creatures moving at them.

He stepped into the center of his command runes. The creatures coming at them moved on two legs, clearly fully upright. Most of their fur appeared to be around their heads and they covered themselves in the flesh of other creatures. They held spears and knives while projectiles flew from behind them.

Enki sliced his palm with the blade he'd had ready. "Lady Tiamat, lend us your power to protect your servants. Through this servant, your power shall prevail," he chanted. He smeared his blood before his claws started to tap the staff, causing the eyes to glow purple. Its mouth opened, electricity arcing between its teeth. Slamming the rod into the ground, he screamed, "SHIELD!"

Chapter 6:

Lines of purple power shot out from the base of the staff. The inner runes flashed red before shifting to a dark green with the runes flashing . The outer ring of runes had a line of red fire flash through and then began glowing navy blue. The outer circle glowed white before the sky darkened. The head of the staff split, the skull separating from its housing. Crystals glowed iridescent as they drew in energy from Enki's reserves. He dropped to his knees, gasping.

Above the staff, the sky turned green and red in curtains of light enveloped by a ring of purple. Slowly rotating, the colors stretched down. Lightning burst across the sky as the lights entered the lower atmosphere. The cracks of thunder were enough to drive the primitives to a halt, at least the ones that hadn't noticed the sky event yet.

The bolt of lightning slammed into the staff, sending arcs of electricity into it. Lightning wrapped faster around the staff as it reached the runes etched into the ground. The runes flashed a blinding white light before the circle became a solid bubble of the same. It broke the connection, but the runes held the charge. Enki fell to his side, his right hand blistered from the deep burns he took due to channeling that much power. The staff had split in half, exposing the circuitry within. Many of the power amplifiers had burnt out, identified by the blue emanating from it.

"Enki, you let the magic blue smoke out!" Inanna exclaimed, her voice full of awe. The other Annunaki were looking at the shield.

One engineer tossed a bolt at the white bubble. It bounced off with a soft thud. Several softer thuds sounded from weapons striking above them.

"How? What? What?" Nabu gasped.

"Tapped planetary energy," groaned Enki. "The staff was never designed to handle that much power."

"By the Great Mother, that sounds like the old stories," said Nabu.

"Those are fables carved on rocks from our homeworld. Stories of Gods and their powers arriving from the sky. Nothing but a fantasy that we left behind eons ago. If it were real, our souls would have remembered it," Inanna replied.

"Perhaps, perhaps not. Sixty-five million cycles is a very long time, even among our long lives. Bring me the medical bag," Enki requested. He was holding his blackened hand close to his chest. A hunter ran off to grab it.

"What do you think happened, milord?" asked Inanna as she knelt to inspect Enki.

"I felt the spell drawing upon my reserves to turn the sand into a wall to absorb the arrows and the first attack when I felt the power reaching from the earth itself through the sky. I was able to let go, but not quite in time," Enki explained. He hissed in pain as Inanna poked at his burns.

"That's all well and dandy, milord, but what about the natives?" demanded Nabu.

"If they are primitives, we just harnessed the power of the Gods.

Any successively advanced technology will look like magic. While we know that simple biology and technology allowed me to shape the energy, they don't. Open a hole in the dome, and we'll probably have offerings, or at least nothing to worry about," Enki said as they rubbed burn cream into his hands.

Nabu snorted as he grabbed the two halves of the staff. "Are you really trying to say that the Gods didn't do this? Their Lords could object to us taking this planet."

"They couldn't have Lords. Don't you feel you've returned home? That means something. However, that could be simply due to how young the system's primary is. Before, it was like taking a drink from a trickle of water versus drinking from a river. We all have felt more energetic since entering the system. Thanks to how active the star is, we can boost our own. Even now, I know where every water creature is within a hundred kilometers. I've always had an affinity for water. It's one reason I am my clan's Priest, but this takes it to a whole new world, so to speak," Enki said.

"I have found the stone to be as malleable as clay. The landing site is almost complete thanks to this. It even has Lord Anu's statue in place," Kulla informed them.

"Already? That is impressive," Enki responded, his hand being wrapped in a healing bandage. "Are you using a staff?"

"No, the stone responds to my touch. I can feel the power within," Kulla explained.

"Does anyone feel a connection to the earth? The shell is ceramic; it should be easy to cut through even if no one here is an earthmover," said Enki. When no one said they could touch the dirt, the Lord of the Water looked at the Engineer. "Well, I need to be on the other side of this wall. Please cut me a door before taking it down. Perhaps it will protect the ship from this blasted sand."

"Yes, milord. We'll have you on the other side in a few moments. Girra, get the grinders out; we need to make a door," Nabu instructed as he turned and walked to the back of the shuttle.

Enki rose, his eyes closing from a jolt of pain coursing through him. His unburnt hand lifted as he seemed to lose his balance. He shook his head, trying to clear it, but the fog just wouldn't lift. His muscles felt like he could burst into a run and make it around the island in less than thirteen seconds. He flexed his clawed toes into the sand. He felt something brush against his mind. It made Enki jump, looking around, trying to find the person who touched him. Nothing, absolutely nothing, should be in someone's mind, yet as sure as he stood there, he felt something. Even with their magical powers, they still never could solve the psionic barrier.

The Annunaki Lord stepped forward, his left hand shooting out a word of power. Flames appeared a few centimeters from the tips of his claws. He could feel the pent-up energy draining from his muscles, drawing down his arm. He let out a grunt as he pushed his power into the flames. Scorch marks rolled up the barrier he had made.

"Stop that!" yelled Inanna. "You'll use up all the oxygen."

Closing his hand, Enki caused the flames to come to an abrupt stop. He staggered as his body reacted to the sudden flow of power being removed. A warmth started from the sand before flowing up his body, restoring his vitality. His burnt hand itched under the scales.

"By the Goddess, what were you thinking?" demanded Inanna.

"No idea. It just came to me to try. I felt the need to test my theory to convert the background energy through the pituitary network. The solar primary is so active, I can taste the power in the air. We'll have to find the limit of this new power," Enki answered.

Inanna snorted. "Who do you think you are? The God of Magic?"

"Yes," Enki said.

"Wait, what?"

"We are Gods, and this planet has connected with me," Enki explained. Both turned as the sound of grinding tore through the dome. The pair walked over to watch Girra and Nabu cutting their way past the ceramic. A few minutes later, both Girra and Nabu spun, slamming their tails into the center of the door. There was a popping sound followed by a soft thud.

Enki stepped through the door, only to find a dozen of the hairless apes on the ground, with their faces touching the sand while prostrating their bodies. Their weapons laid next to the dome. A pair of the creatures were dragging a dead animal. They appeared to be in quite the hurry.

The newly minted God of Magic had an idea. He needed to communicate to the natives, but how? Thankfully, he had already felt the brush against his mind. This let him replicate the effect, waving his hand, whispering a word. A purple mist settled over the assembled ones.

Chapter 7:

"I am Lord Enki, of the Annunaki. We come from the Heavens, looking for a home. We have many things we can share with you in exchange for a few simple things. I wish to discuss this new future with your chieftain. You will take your new Gods to your leader," hissed the Lord of the Annunaki. Thanks to the connection he established, they understood the intent of his words, even if they could not understand them exactly.

One stood and walked over to Enki. They knelt before their new lord. "I can take you to the Chief."

"Take us," Enki said after a few long moments as he studied the intent. He motioned for Inanna and Ninurta to follow. The creature stood, barked out something that caused eight others to form a box around the Reptilians as an escort. He waved his burnt claw to remove the translation.

"They might not be proper Adama, but they will make an excellent template to work from. Their form lends to climbing, which could mean that they can dig what we need. Regardless, having a local tribe under our control should make the locals more compliant," Enki explained.

"Yet we are surrounded. The natives could attack us in a moment," Ninurta replied.

"After I called the power of the Gods from above? No, we are above them, and they know it," Enki said. He flicked his tail near one of the creatures, who stepped out of the way.

"Do you think it is far?" asked Inanna.

"Probably on the other side of the island. Then again, as there were about two dozen hunting, they could be a simple hunting party," Enki answered.

"As hunter/gatherers, two dozen seems like a large tribe," Ninurta said. "We are told that we hunted in packs of three back on An. Thus, we still hunt in the holy trinity."

One of the hairless creatures grunted at them, its face primarily devoid of any hair. A voice softer than the others made a few more noises. Enki waved his hand again to return the mist. The creature spoke again.

"We track by smell," Ninurta said. "How does your tribe hunt?"

A string of sounds came forth, the creatures' hands gesturing wildly. Fingers moved, making the motion of someone walking, pausing to look at tracks. Then their hands showed the action of pulling bows and throwing spears. The Lord of the Hunt nodded, his posture shifting slightly to show respect for these smaller hunters.

"These small hairless apes understand the chase. The art of running a creature to exhaustion. They will teach us much about the local food, milord," Ninurta informed.

"Why do you think we are even speaking with them over having them for dinner?" Enki asked with a look. The creature gave him a sideways glance. "What? Growing meat isn't as easy as it sounds." That earned him a look of disbelief. He shook his head. "I'll just have to show you later. How long will it take?"

The creature pointed at the sun and then pointed to where it would be in the sky. The point was nearly at the other horizon, while the sun was a quarter way into its daily trip. The trip would take most of the day, it seemed. Perhaps by the end of the day, they could figure out a better translation system besides conveying ideas.

The party stepped out of the forest and onto a stone pathway with evident cart ruts laid before them. A small trading center, or perhaps a hunting camp, judging by the gear around the clearing. There were wheeled carts and another group of hairless apes hanging their kills to drain the blood. The hairless apes that hadn't seen the Annunaki froze at the sight of three giant lizards with very sharp teeth being escorted by their own. There was a lot of noise between the two parties, with the new group bothered by the latest arrivals.

"For the love of Anu," Enki grumbled before pointing his burnt claws away from the groups and grunted the power word. Flames shot into the air. This had the desired result of cowing the hunt cleaners. More noises between the two groups before a pair of runners started down the path. The head of the Annunaki escorts bowed to Enki with his arm outstretched, lowering his head.

Heat beat upon the group, but a western breeze tempered it. The system's star slowly crossed the sky, passing several groups of hunters. Those groups gave them a wide berth. Once the star reached nearly its resting point, they had arrived at the group's settlement.

Protecting the settlement was a stone and wooden wall. Tree trunks were laid between pillars that kept most of the wildlife out. There was a gate that was connected via ropes to the wall, but it was open. Inside contained a few hundred mud huts covered in straw. The homes wrapped around a large cooking pit. Half a dozen of those apes moved around, preparing the evening meal.

The Annunaki Lord was led to a horseshoe-shaped table where there were six more apes. At the head of the table were two near hairless apes, one with long grey hair on his face and head. The softer featured creature had long grey hair as well. It had become clear that the softer ones were the females of their group. The female Enki had spent the day talking with spoke to the elders before bowing her head at Enki.

Chapter 8:

A spear flew from the rear right side of the group, slamming into Ninurta's left thigh. A bellow of pain tore through the air, his tail slamming into the rear guard. The Lord of the Hunt grabbed one native before smashing it into the roofline of a nearby hut, a sickening snap cutting through the air. Ninurta snarled at the escorts, who were jumping away from the enraged lizard.

The two natives at the head of the table sprang to their feet, the male shouting something. Enki wasn't sure if he was giving orders or trying to end the attack. Both leaders looked quite angry at the attack, but they couldn't stop the others. Ninurta lunged forward for another native, his jaws gripping an arm before a simple head twist removed the appendage from its owner.

Enki's head fell back, his burnt claws reaching out as he grabbed the energy in the air to form a barrier. A round column of air slammed into the ground, drawing from the cold reaches of the stratosphere. The massive cooking fire went out from the impact while jugs of water steamed. Food on the spit roast slammed into one of the cooks while the cooking pot was knocked over, instantly cooling the coals. It blew steam into the face of one of the hairless ones as he tried to hold his position. His hands covered his face as he screamed.

Almost as quickly as the wind started, it ended. Enki stumbled as blue blood dripped from his nostrils. His eyes had blood spots from where the vessels had exploded. Gasping for air, he panted out, "Let's not do that again."

"Let's not," agreed Inanna. Her eyes narrowed as she searched for the one who threw the spear. "We might be Gods to these creatures, but there is a limit to what your mortal form can do."

Enki looked around the village. He shook his head and blinked his eyes a few times to process the carnage. He had obliterated the camp. The mud-brick dwellings looked like someone had slashed a scythe through them. The hairless apes were tossed throughout the remains, their corpses shattered. Steam wisped from the ground, and bits of straw had embedded itself into the bodies, walls, and pottery.

"Good job, Enki, you killed them all. Fresh meat. Thanks," said Ninurta before dropping his head to tear flesh from the creature under his clawed feet. "Do we kill the runners?" he asked between tearing flesh.

"They will tell stories to the others. The ones at the shuttle are enough to start with," Enki replied before his head snapped to look at the source of a sound. Someone was trying to unbury themselves from the mess. Inanna and Ninurta moved over to clear the rubble. The hairless ape female had no covering of her flesh. "Search the devastation for others who still live. We will bring them back to our camp. Hopefully, the worshipers have brought offerings of food. Short term, we will need shelter tonight."

"Why not just sleep on the ground?" asked Ninurta while his tail lifted a board from a nearby body.

"We are reptiles," answered Enki.

"So?" pried Ninurta.

"Do we produce enough body heat?"

"Uh, no?"

"When our ancestors were the size of a house, our mass produced enough heat. Now? It's one of the many reasons we can't handle space repairs. We will need a fire and something to protect from the wind," Enki explained as he moved over to the fireless fire pit. While the wind attack scattered a good portion of the wood and coals, there was a small bed of heat from the stone lining. He threw some of the roof rubble into the pit, the straw caught fire almost immediately. He went around, throwing more fuel into the fire, letting it build to about a quarter of the last bonfire.

Around the restored fire, a half dozen of the hairless apes that survived the wind assault gathered. Each of them looked dead in the eyes. They sat on the ground, their legs crossed, staring into the flames. Inanna had handed each a cup of water, the vessels carved from wood by the natives. She glared at Enki every time he looked at her.

"You made a mistake," Inanna said without malice.

Enki's head dropped. "I know. I wanted to push them away so we could leave."

Inanna shook her head. "You used powers you don't understand as a weapon. You snuffed out a hundred and forty lives in seconds. You caused frostbite on the ones closest to us. They would have died if the impact hadn't shattered their bones. You then crushed the remaining when their homes slammed into them. The very place they felt safe, protected from harm. Think about what happens when we have a decompression on the ship." That earned a look of shock from Enki. "How does the rest of the crew feel?"

"It is a loss, but no one is truly gone. They will return from the arms of the Great Mother," Enki said.

"You are a first-generation soul, Enki. You understand the abstract, but you haven't had your first death yet. You have never felt the terror of being sucked out of your home in the middle of your rest where you were safe from harm. The feeling of your hopes and dreams being ripped away as you try to remember your training. Forcing all the air from your lungs so you don't get the terrifying feeling of your lungs exploding from the pressure differential. Then the feeling of your brain screaming 'I want to live' as the remaining oxygen is used up." Inanna shuddered.

"Never, ever forget the first time your lungs explode," Ninurta whispered. He slammed his tail into the ground, causing the hairless ones to jump. "I'm going to take a walkabout. Junior here took out the walls, so I need to make sure we won't be eaten in the middle of the night," he growled at Inanna.

Inanna sighed as she looked at the younger God. "To be honest with you, Enki, the only reason you are your clan's En is that no one else in your line can still connect to the Great Mother. The En Council gave Lord Anu special dispensation for your admittance when you were but a hatchling. However, your powers are still weaker than the older Generations.

"Without you, the clan would fade away once your father returns to the Great Mother. Your sister wouldn't have been re-born unless someone had a random child, which none of the clans continue to do unless they are in the direst of positions, as your own is. Your own twin sister, Iškur, wasn't blessed with enough of a connection to the Tiamat particle to reach the Great Mother.

"You are the strongest in your Generation, yet you are a first-soul. This shouldn't be possible. You are stronger than a lot of the ones near the end of their rebirth cycle. We know what is happening; we are not producing enough Dimethyltryptamine. Perhaps the background radiation that we use is simply too much for our bodies. Despite this, why this is happening, we do not know. Perhaps the Great Mother is simply telling us we've learned what we need to, and it's time to ascend to a new level, free from her," Inanna finished.

Enki took a bite of a local animal that the apes had in pens well enough away to avoid significant damage. "Are you passing Judgement upon me?"

"You have committed a crime here, no matter your intentions. You will discover how you hurt the natives. You will train to master your powers. You must never let your control slip again. It is a harsh lesson that we all learn. Perhaps not as harshly, but we all need to learn. While they are not Adama yet, our laws protect them as Adama. So says the Great Mother." With Inanna's last words, a slight purple glow appeared around Enki. It twisted into a mist that sank into his scales. Inanna's head tilted, her eyes narrowing as she felt power leave her body.

"By her will," Enki whispered.

"Good, we shall not need to speak of this again. We will walk back to our ship at first light, and we will take them with us. We owe them care and protection as we ruined the locals' view of safety," Inanna said. A beeping from Enki's belt interrupted her.

"Lord Enki, this is Haya," came from the communicator.

"This is Enki. Is there a problem up there?"

"You could say that. We've detected a massive plasma flare heading this way. Projections show it will envelop the third planet in twenty hours or about nightfall in your current location. It will strike the fourth planet ten hours after that," reported Haya.

"How much plasma was ejected?"

"Enough to run Nibiru for a hundred years. We have sent a message to Lord Anu that we will move closer to the planet. Also, as per protocols, disconnect any external connections and move to the dihydrogen monoxide shelter. You will want to seek shelter from the storm."

Enki glanced at Inanna. "We might have just the thing already. The Natives also might have something, depending on how often this happens. Activate Theta-Kappa just in case."

"Already active milord, we didn't want to take any chances if we all perished."

"Sounds like you have this under control. Report when the skies are clear again. Enki out."

Inanna had been handing out cooked meat for hairless apes. "Enki, what is going to happen?"

"Well, the system's primary had a large coronal mass ejection, and it's heading this way. The planet's electromagnetic field will get stretched out to where the bands will snap. When this happens, plasma might strike the ground if my planetary theory is correct. My little show of power before might just save us from this storm. Ceramic doesn't conduct currents well and should protect us from most of the heat. Or we might get fried and cooked as if we were in an oven. Either way, we should leave at first light. Rest. I will take the first watch." Enki said as he added another set of logs onto the fire.

Chapter 9:

Enki stood facing the East as the night sky lightened in the pre-dawn light. He watched the sunrise for the first time. The mix of orange and red in the sky struck him with awe at its beauty. Colors reflected from the clouds; long wispy ones started blood red, stretching into orange before fading into a dark grey on a black background. The moment the star broke the horizon, Enki felt a surge of power rush through him. Starting at the tip of his nose, a flash shot through to the tip of his tail.

The new God turned before walking back to the sleeping group. The hairless apes, Enki really needed to name them at some point, were huddled together to conserve body heat along with animal skins laying over themselves. The two Anunnaki had curled themselves into a ball with their tails covering their eyes. They were laying on a layer of straw that they took from the roofs. Under the straw was hardened dirt. He took a deep breath and let out a long bellow. This caused the apes to roll out of bed with shouts, their hands going for spears. The two lizards simply lifted their heads, sleep still in their eyes.

"Time to get up. We have a long walk ahead of ourselves," Enki said. "The apes will need food before we move. Inanna, get the fire going for them to cook."

There was some grumbling as the apes stopped moving for weapons that were lost in the airburst. After the morning meal, the sun had risen fully and the party left the ruined town. It didn't take long to return to the hunting camp. Only a few had stayed behind to prepare the camp and the evening meal. One of Enki's group shouted something that caused the hunting group to scramble for spears and bows.

"What did you tell them?" snarled Ninurta.

Inanna stepped forward, power laced in her voice. "Stop. We have passed judgment on the mistake. Reparations for what was done shall be given. There is a storm coming; travel with us so we may provide shelter."

Her words had the desired effect. The two groups briefly exchanged words before the eldest female grabbed the horn and gave three long blasts, followed by two short ones. The natives started packing their hunting camp, putting out the cooking fires. There were kids in harnesses on the back of the females while the men lashed large packs to their own shoulders. A runner took off for the next camp. By the time the hunters had returned, the small encampment had been taken down, save for a few permanent items and the hunters quickly gathered the bundles.

The sun had risen to its zenith when the next encampment came within sight. They had already prepared to leave, thanks to the runner. The new group was sixty-three of the hairless apes heading back to the shuttle landing site. By the time the sky changed colors, the group had arrived.

It looked like the Annunaki had been preparing all day. They had covered the dome with sand so that it looked like a natural hill. There was an entrance passage that had a large room at the start of the path. The side doors had several of both species that were moving food and other supplies inside. The dome had several openings on the upper side of the hill, while the bottom only had two, one on each end of the oval mound.

"Lord Enki, thank Anu that you have returned. The flare is going to strike within the hour. Thanks to the Great Mother's powers providing a translation for us, the locals said that the Lord of the Sky often has temper tantrums like this. They hope that it's only a display to show he's stronger than you, not his anger over borrowing their Lord's power. That is why they are helping us prepare. They are terrified of his anger. At least that's the impression we get," explained Nabu.

One native broke out in a run for Enki's group. She made a lot of noise, pointing at the sky. Nabu watched the woman for a few moments. He gasped when he looked up at the sky. Glancing at Enki, Nabu told him, "she says their Lord is arriving and we should seek shelter immediately. The waves of green in the heavens are his heralds. Their Lord will soon appear at the bottom of the ether. I can say that the bands are quite beautiful." The sky had long, wavy streaks of purple, green, and teal colors in the darkening sky.

"I wish to observe the Sky Lord, one Lord to another. Perhaps I will even speak with him," Enki replied.

The woman shook her head; her noises sounded very panicked. Enki shook his head as well before waving his hand over her, muttering a few words. "Will strike the ground, and everything close to it melts!" cried out the woman, her language clearer to him now that he'd spent the day with their kind.

"You were here when I called upon the same power, yet nothing happened to me. I am not worried about his wrath. But I assure you, if your Sky Lord gets too angry, I will seek shelter," Enki promised.

This seemed to calm the woman down slightly. She bowed her head as she backed away. "By your word."

Enki glanced back up to the sky and noted that there were more bands of those lights in the darkening sky. There were several dozen streaks versus the prior four. "Nabu, get a visual record of tonight. This is not likely a one-time event if the locals worship the star and fear his wrath. Is there any way we can monitor the electromagnetic fields on the ground? If the flare is powerful enough, then the field might stretch to a breaking point. I am not a planetary engineer, but the data from space and ground might help us build structures to harness this power."

"We do have sensors on the landing craft that can help with that. We use it for surveying for minerals. I should have them laid out in a few hours," Nabu answered.

"Have a runner bring me a tablet; I wish to take notes," ordered Enki.

"Yes, milord," Nabu said before walking away.

Enki observed the sky. He noted that the light streaks came from the southern hemisphere. About five minutes later, a runner brought Enki his tablet while engineers moved around him. "Stay by my side, Inara. I wish to ask you questions as we observe," explained Enki.

As the system's star sank below the horizon, the skyline filled with hues from the entire spectrum. As Enki made notes, his head shot up. "Inara, have one of the hunters join me," he ordered. She hurried off to find one and She returned with a hunter in tow.

"My Lord?" asked Gula.

"Your branch has retained sight in the ultraviolet and infrared spectrums. What do you see in the sky?" Enki inquired.

Gula studied the sky before answering. "It is beautiful. The bands of light are stretching and warping as the plasma interacts with the planet. It looks like a sea with visible bands as waves. The heat behind the plasma is still intense. It must still be in the thousands of degrees. Ah, there goes the first magnetic band."

Above the landing party, a spark of light appeared, causing the pair to wince as the sky briefly lit up as if it was daytime. The light split into two bands of charged plasma following the charges of the planet. The southern pole attracted most of the plasma. Sparks cascaded out one side, almost as if the atmosphere itself was catching fire.

The southern sky glowed dual purple lights before stretching up. The center column stretched along the center of the sky. Branches arched out seven times before the upper tip split into a pair of horns.

"Is that one of your Gods?" asked Enki.

"That is the herald of our Lord. He is the world serpent, the bridge between the Lord and us. The longer Jörmungandr remains, the more peaceful our Lord tends to be," said the local woman.

Enki took a few more notes taking care to draw the sky exactly as he saw it. The serpent appeared to swim through the sky, the bands of light bathing it. The hours passed, giving the Engineer time to get the sensors up and heaters for the Annunaki. Daybreak was near, if the glow on the horizon was any indication. Nightfall was only five hours before.

"Inara, when is daybreak?" asked Enki.

"It is too soon for daybreak; Let me get a native to ask," Inara replied before she hurried off. She brought a young man with a long feather headdress.

"The Lord must be angry. His wrath will reign upon us harshly," the priest said with a hard swallow. "Fire and brimstone are coming; we must take shelter." Panic had crept into his voice and body.

"Everyone take shelter! The locals are calling for a storm of fire," Enki ordered. The Lord let himself be pulled back within the shelter. Inara and the priest rushed through the earthen tunnel, following the sharp turns to reduce any shock waves. Enki entered behind her, noting that most hairless ones were making sleeping quarters for both races. The cargo area of the shuttle was open, with rendered meat being loaded into the chillers. Freshwater was also being directed into stores for the long term. An Annunaki was leading them to show where things should go. His own race was going about making sure that the engineering side of their shelter was sound. Beams were being added to provide better structural support, along with living quarters for their own. Things were going to be a little rough in the short term for everyone involved.

Enki entered the shuttle and went to the command deck. He called the support ship in orbit. "Status report."

"Milord, this is a massive eje *static* It appears to be a sustain *static* expected to last at least fo*static*gh hours. We are sta *static* rk side, as the planet shields us from most of the storm," reported Haya.

"How much of a threat are we expecting?"

"Ground strikes, direct plas*static*ages, maybe something else. We need more time to stu*static*re."

"Report every shift, Enki out." The Annunaki Lord ended the call before checking the cameras. The shape in the sky looked like a ladder of bubbles that were stacked on top of each other remained despite the increased glow from the solar flare. A fireball cut through the atmosphere, passing the horizon before the sky turned white. A visible shock wave rushed across the water before impacting the island. The wave hit the sloped mound with a massive thud. Passing along the island, the trees exploded from the pressure, striking them before they passed out of sight.

Another firebolt cut across the sky, but this one was much farther away. It exploded in the upper atmosphere. The shock wave was visible as it rushed out. The impact made a softer thud but still was loud, and the cameras lost focus for a moment before returning the image.

"Status report," Enki commanded after pressing the internal communication.

"Nothing damaged, milord. The earthen works deflected the shock wave over us," reported Nabu.

"Do we have a planetary researcher? I want to know more

about these fireballs. I think they are bursts of plasma from the star. We didn't detect trojans around the inner planets, so I don't think it's asteroid debris," Enki said.

Nabu's brows furrowed for a moment. "Nuska might have an idea what's going on. I last saw him going over all the data. I don't think he's stopped drooling since this event started. We haven't seen an event from a planetary perspective before, only from outside the heliosphere. The last time this happened, that system's blue world died from the heat."

"I do hope that it won't happen here," Enki replied.

"That planet was much closer to the primary, at the inner edge of the habitable zone. Since then, if the star was less than three billion years old, we've avoided the system. They are just too active. Most G-Type stars like this one are too active if they are less than four billion. Clearly, we are going to have to adjust that since this star is older than that, but barely," said Nabu.

The plasma lines that looked like a ladder on-screen split. Bands of light explode as it shattered. Supercharged plasma arched outwards in all directions. A beam slammed into the ground beyond the horizon as the image above became a circle, with fifty-six columns around it. The center reached from the surface deep into space.

Enki noted that the waterline retreated from the shore. It left aquatic creatures behind, including larger ones. The Lord felt the sudden panic from the still-living fish. "Well, that probably isn't good."

Nabu moved over to the communications station. "Nuska, what's going on?"

"This is Adad. Nuska is busy with the plasma event, but this is my field. A tsunami is about to come. We have minutes before impact. I've already directed crews to seal the vents. We should be able to open the vents back up after it passes. Ereškigal says she can feel the very earth itself. She's been moving matter since the shock wave. The Magi of the Natives have lent their power."

"Wait, the natives can access the same power as us?" asked Enki.

"Apparently, milord. They say when the Sky Lord is angry, they have greater access to his gifts," answered Adad.

"My Lord, the water is coming back! I can feel the earth being smashed back down," shouted Ereškigal from the background.

Enki hit the ship-wide comms. "All hands brace for water impact. Everyone onto the ship, I don't care where. If that door fails while the ramp is down, we are all dead." Those working on the sleeping units dropped what they were doing, rushing for the ramp to seal everyone away in a protective shell.

Less than a minute later, a thirty-meter wave passed over them. The ground shook due to the weight of the water. Thankfully, the shaping of the hill protected them from the worst of the tsunami. He noticed several of the cameras go dark as they were ripped away. As the water retreated, it began to take the entry passage. The Lord changed the camera to an external view to look at the exit of the ceramic.

"Close the ramp," Enki ordered with a heavy heart. The ramp

started to close, leaving a dozen apes and three Anunnaki trapped outside. The head ape opened a box that he had brought, placing a long headdress on. He moved to protect the door, his amulet moving in time with his words. A glow appeared directly over the cuts, becoming mostly solid as the water pushed the door slightly.

Not wanting the shield to falter, the man chanted louder, his gear starting to glow. Sweat formed over his body as he pushed more energy into the spell. His fingers spread as he pushed back against the weight of the water. He gave a loud grunt before collapsing. Water exploded through the fading barrier, slamming ceramic into the Shaman. The cavern within the dome quickly filled with ocean water even as the wave retreated.

The Annunaki shuttle tilted before sliding into the wall, shattering the ceramic. Spiderweb cracks appeared, water flowing through them. It forced the cracks wider, expanding them until the shield exploded. The ship groaned as liquid slammed into the structure. The sound of metal tearing coursed through the ship as a landing leg was torn away. A horrifying scream ripped through the air as parts reached well beyond their limits.

Chapter 10:

Picking himself from the wall and floor, Enki groaned. The ship was at an angle, causing issues for his feet to grip the floor. Emergency lighting had kicked on as the landing generators had gone offline from the ship being thrown around. Water could be heard dripping beyond the broken door. The Lord stretched his burnt claw out, spoke a word of power, and blew out the broken door. Water rushed into the command center, but thankfully it was a light river versus a deluge.

Gripping the door frame, Enki pulled himself out of the command center. He could see the night sky through the broken hull. To his right, the ship was mostly level while he stood at an angle. The water had damaged the ship. He scrambled over to the level part, looking through the tear in the vessel. The sky looked clear in the limited view. A groan caused him to rush to the lab door, pushing it open.

"Ereškigal, Adad, or Nuska. Is anyone still alive?" asked Enki.

"We're alive. The storm has passed," answered Nuska as he pushed a monitor upright.

"Ereškigal passed out from exhaustion. She tried to hold the ship together from the water," Adad explained while he cleaned the blood from Ereškigal's nose.

"Perhaps metal is harder to manipulate than the dirt, or more likely we all need to practice our powers," said Enki.

"Water also could be a weakness to her power," added Nuska as he flicked the monitor back on. "The power that was produced from that pulse was off the charts. We'll have to find a way to harness this amazing energy. It's like having the entire lifetime of the core of the Nibiru at your fingertips. The total amount of power could have powered the planet ship at near the speed of light for the next five billion light-years if we could have harnessed it."

"What would we do with that much power?" Enki laughed.

"Wormhole. We know the mathematics to make the portals, but we lack the power to charge the supercapacitors. We could colonize the other planets and moons in this system, all connected to this planet with that power. By Anu, it might be enough to power wormholes to other solar systems," said Nuska.

"That is something to consider. We'll need to understand how often that event is. It must be sporadic. Prepare a proposal for the Sky Lord. I will include it in my own," instructed Enki.

"Unless it's our fault that the star had a coronal mass ejection. Your first use of magic disturbed the plasma," Nuska suggested as he showed a synced recording of the sun and Enki's magic. "Then the ejection happened the moment you created the barrier," he said, the video confirming it.

Enki watched the video, his eyes narrowing. "Then we shall have to set up protection from it. You know that there is no way we won't avoid returning to act like Gods, more so if we have to get powers that make us like the Gods of old."

Nuska changed the screen to show their DNA. "One more thing, milord. We've sequenced this blood sample from a feline six times.

Its DNA has a high percentage, about eighty percent, matching our own. As this shouldn't be possible, we then checked the plants and other wildlife with the help of the Natives. They handed us one of their domesticated birds they said could barely fly. We share ninety percent of DNA with these birds. I think this is our original world."

Enki's jaw dropped as he processed the bombshell. He tried to speak a few times before he found his voice. "By the Great Mother, the home-world, the home-world? Being from another world was one reason we became the gods of the last world. Why we left Olympus was lost to time. But if this is that place, then our return home might allow us to take the next step in the great cycle."

"We left seventy million years ago. I've done the calculations. Our year is the same as this planet. Even our perception of time matches a solar day. I would say that this truly is the home of the Gods," said Adad.

"Gather everything for the Sky Lord. I will deliver the report in person," replied Enki.

"Yes, milord," answered the trio.

"Was the landing pad finished before the flare?" Enki asked.

"We were working on the instruments in here for our planetary studies," said Adad.

Enki rolled his eyes. "A simple 'no idea' would have worked. Gather the data, select three of each sex of the apes to go with me. I am going to see what the damage is." He then headed to the back of the ship, where the ramp was.

'Used to be' would have been more correct, Enki felt when

he saw the hole where the ramp had been torn away. Water was dripping from the cargo area, but thankfully, nothing else looked broken. Both races were working rapidly to help several that were pinned under ramp parts. Two hairless apes were hanging onto a rope as the water retreated past them under the ship.

"This is a spaceship, not a boat. We don't have many remaining, and this one just became scrap," snapped Nabu.

"Can it still be used for shelter?" Enki asked.

Nabu tapped the wall behind him with his tail, causing the panel to fall off. "Not in any way I would trust. We'll have to slop the outside to protect from those waves. There are so many things to do, like protecting the landing pad, the defensive walls, digging out shelters, and developing food production."

Enki tapped the deck with his tail. "Focus on the here and now. What do I need to know right this second?"

"Call for a rescue ship; we'll clear the pad for it. Ensure our support ship is still fully operational and update Lord Anu. We'll have a town built for us, perhaps over the remains of the town you wrecked," Nabu said.

"That's a lot of water," Enki observed as he pointed out of the ship.

"Lord Enki, I can clear a path," offered one of the hairless apes. He wore a small headdress. "I am a priest of Nana-Buluka."

"Do it," Enki hissed as he grabbed his comm. "Haya, are you still alive up there?"

"We survived. We had to hide in the radiation chambers when

we were on the dayside of the planet, but we have a lot of data for review," reported Haya.

"I am most interested in that last plasma strike. It struck the ocean and sent a tsunami. Thanks to that massive wave, we have a wrecked shuttle. Load the secondary with supplies for long-term habitation and send it down," Enki commanded.

"We will prepare the shuttle, Haya out."

The priest started a soft chant, causing the earth to rise, forming steps into the cargo bay. He sang and danced his way down. Slowly, the ground rose above the water by half a meter before the liquid was drawn out of the mud and clay. He walked along the path he was creating and out of sight. Several followed the holy man, including Nabu. Enki spent the next few hours preparing for his report to his Lords. When the time came, he stepped into the Holographic Chamber.

"Report, Lord Enki," rasped the hologram of Anu.

"We have found Olympus," Enki stated.

"Impossible," snarled Chronos while Enlil said, "Amazing."

Anu raised an aged claw. "Silence, my hands. Lord Enki, explain your declaration."

Enki spent the next few hours going over pages of images and text that he had used to document the events on the third planet. He then showed the commonalities of their own DNA to the local fauna. He eventually stopped on an image of a bird that stood at a hundred centimeters, with red flesh on top of its head, a short-hooked beak, orange feathers, and spindly feet.

"The natives call it a chicken. They must keep them in small pens because they lack any kind of self-preservation. Our DNA has a ninety-five percent match to these creatures. These creatures clearly evolved from ancestors after we left Olympus. How this branch of our species evolved into this, I do not know. We only know the DNA evidence," Enki said.

"It is possible we left because of the solar activity, but as these apes evolved to become the intelligent species on the planet, it's not likely. Or if it is, it's not the only reason," suggested Enlil.

"Perhaps there was a planet killer event coming, so we departed. Our lore said that the Gods smote our decadence in fire and brimstone, causing us to flee from the great mountain in the great Nibiru," Enki offered.

"Oh, that legend. We have dismissed the 'asteroid impact' theory," snapped Chronos.

"Perhaps we shall find the truth," Enlil said.

Chronos had started to growl when Anu spoke over him. "Now that we've had a closer look, what of the other planets? Are they suitable for us?"

"The Third Planet is best suited for us. However, the Humans, as they call themselves, could survive on the second, third, fourth, and fifth planets. The Jupiter-like gas giant might have some moons that at least might have bacteria on them. Still, it would require a space station for actual inhabitation," Enki informed them.

"What of the solar storms? Are they a danger to us?" Chronos asked.

"It depends. Is it a threat to the Nibiru? Yes. It is half the size of the fourth planet, but without a magnetosphere, it would allow solar plasma to cook the hull directly. The support craft we had in orbit ended up with the port side partly melted thanks to the heat it faced on the last three orbits. In open space, the support craft can move out of the way within hours of detection, but it takes months to change the direction of the Ark," Enki said.

Chronos waved his claws at Enki. "Yes, but will it kill us?"

"Yes, but no. In a support craft, no. In our ark? Yes. If we get caught unaware and in the open on a planet, we will die just like the natives. Now, because we are aware of the possibility of the event, we can design buildings that will absorb the power and store the energy discharge," Enki replied. He brought up blueprints of a tall pyramid. The sides were white granite and smooth, while the capstone was solid gold.

"Nabu sent me this last night; I have not had much time to review the pyramid he has designed. He says the locals have shown him many building materials they would like to use but lack the technology to cut stone. The whole structure will store massive amounts of power."

"Enki, see to our grand return to Olympus, including necessary protections. I wish for you to see if our souls can inhabit these humans. Our current flesh is weak. We must improve upon it. We are the Elder Gods here and we shall rule over the primitives," Anu stated before slamming his Spector down, stopping Chronos from speaking again. "I have spoken."

"Your will be done," Enki said.

Chapter 11:

The Lord of Magic sniffed the air, flicking his tongue out to taste the particles in it. He could sample the scents of the Adama that were working in the field. He knew that half a dozen men were working in the acres with the new grain plant they had developed, just from the scents in the air.

They were being watched over by Ninurta, Enki's second, or Tan. His skin color was light green, with white-colored fingertips, and a shorter snout. His part of the family managed their food sources through agricultural methods. Thankfully, after landing on this planet, they could grow enough food to consider expanding their race. Enki looked for his Tan. He stood in the field with a group of Adama, who had seed bags draped over their shoulders.

"This is a barley seed," Ninurta said, holding up a handful. "In your packs, there are samples."

One of the shorter men reached into the bag in the back, pulling out a smaller bag marked with the barley symbol. After pouring some into his hand, he shoved it all into his mouth. "It's dry," he commented with a full mouth.

"By Anu's immortal soul," Ninurta grunted. "These seeds are not for eating," the Tan growled as he ran a clawed hand over his snout.

"Oh, so this one is for eating," the man said as he pulled out the bag marked wheat and poured it into his mouth.

"Gods damn it, Hulu!" Ninurta spat. "None of these seeds are for eating. They are for growing so everyone can eat."

Enki shook his head before starting on soil sampling to ensure that the crops would keep growing correctly. A few hours later, Enki checked the bacterial content with a microscope.

"My Lord." The Tan had returned from his duties and spoke to Enki.

"Tan Ninurta, I hope this crop of Adama is behaving better. Even if they want to eat everything," Enki said.

"Yes, My Lord. The addition of the new genes helped with their social dynamics. There has been less fighting on and off the field. I think we can add females to make them even more docile at night," Ninurta proposed, who was wearing a white lab coat.

"It has been several hundred years since we tamed that crop of locals. Since then, we really haven't experimented with introducing the two groups. I also need fresh DNA, primarily female," Enki stated.

"Perhaps we can just extract the female from the genome of the Adama?" Ninurta suggested.

"That could work, but I would rather extract from the natives. It makes it much easier to splice the proper segments into their code," Enki explained.

"Of course, My Lord. Perhaps you could capture a youngling then. I have observed that the old Humans are very protective of them," Ninurta offered.

Enki's tongue flicked out. "That would work. Bring me at least three without major harm to them. Oh, and target the Denisovans or Ethos races. You'll have some travel, but I'd rather not use the locals. My daughter would be upset with me."

The Tan tilted slightly to look at his Lord. "I will have it done, My Lord," Ninurta said as he bowed head.

Enki flicked his tail slightly, which Ninurta took as a dismissive move. Enki then started walking through the field, looking over the growth. Once that batch of Adama proved fruitful, they would grow more to dig for gold and other metals.

Taking a moment, he turned to look at the stonework that was built. They constructed the door in a trapezoidal shape, with the panel recessed into the stone. Enki's eyes lifted slightly to the next layer where the residences were, then the layer that would hold the Sky Lord, even if he remained outside the solar system. He spent the next few hours walking through the field, taking soil samples. That would be the first field to be harvested, providing the weather continued to be warm. The ground freezing and frozen water crystals falling from the sky had ruined their last crop.

After the sun had retired for the night, Enki retired to his lab. He spent the time examining the samples until Ninurta returned. "My Lord, Enki."

Enki turned quickly and saw Ninurta standing there. Behind him were five females, two were children, and three were mature females. Their hands and feet were bound. They looked terrified as they were led into the room by a leash connected to collars around their necks. That was much quicker than had been expected for him to snag a group like this.

Ninurta bowed slightly. "My Lord, I brought the youngling girls as well as mature females to provide you with the best genetic options."

"Tie them to the walls," Enki ordered as he rubbed his hands in glee at having new creatures to experiment with.

"If I may, My Lord, the females are quite protective. They would likely damage themselves to protect the young." Ninurta slightly bowed his head, his eyes on the ground.

"Indeeeed," Enki drew out the sounds as he appraised the women. They were attractive in their own way, animal skins covering some of their bodies to protect them from the elements. They had even wrapped their feet in leathers. The women stood over three meters, using their bodies to shield the two girls. The older woman had skin that was a dark color, reminding Enki of bronze.

The children were similarly dressed. They had longer foreheads than the current generation of Adama, along with much bushier eyebrows. They looked the size of a teenager, but how they clung to their mothers suggested they were still young. Enki took a few notes before he walked over to his primary terminal, pressing a button. "Bring the Adama food to my lab, ensure that they are laced with a mild sleeping agent." He turned back to look at the group as he released the button, not waiting for a response. "Perhaps they will be more docile after a meal."

The Neanderthal women felt fear, but they were mostly defiant. It was clear in their eyes that they would not break, nor would the younglings. Bending them to another's will would not be easy. The males of the species were defiant at first, but gave in rather quickly.

"Remove the bindings on their hands and feet," Enki said as he slowly paced in front of the women, looking them up and down.

"We will try another method to tame these humans."

Ninurta tilted his head before he complied, turning to the five females. The three mature-looking ones stepped in front of the younglings once more. The oldest-looking one snarled at them, trying to pull the rope out of the other's hand.

The Neanderthal woman kept screaming, "Jeetta!"

"Perhaps we should feed them first," Ninurta quipped. "Or, you could use a translation spell."

Enki snorted. "Perhaps. Just perhaps," he said as he thought for a moment. "No, the experiment requires them to be as unaltered as possible." Picking up a computer pad to take notes, Enki noted their behavior and, more importantly, their protection of the young after writing the no magic rule. "The males do not behave like this at all."

The youngest adult glanced at Enki before she sampled the food to ensure that it was edible once it was placed in front of her. After waiting for about ten minutes, she let the others eat, guarding them as they ate. They watched as the sedative took effect. After the women had fallen asleep, Enki drew blood from the group.

"You were right to bring them undamaged and awake. It provided some interesting points, such as they are fierce protectors. I think the females could be guards for us," Enki observed as he took careful notes.

"That would take much of the burden from us, My Lord," Ninurta commented as his tail slowly twitched right and left.

"Take them to the Adama pen. I wish to observe how they react to the new creatures, the females, but make sure that the three adults are awake and rearmed before you leave them," Enki ordered.

Ninurta bowed his head. "By your will, My Lord."

Enki watched the freshly appointed Tan of Agriculture call three Adama servants to pick up the females before picking up the children. After they left, Enki returned to the workbench to extract the DNA and other components of the blood. It was fitting that a former hunter would teach the planets hunter-gatherers how to farm grain.

It was morning before Ninurta contacted Enki. "My Lord, all five have awoken. I placed them in their own bedchambers, G-9. We provided food for them, but they refused to eat. They even stopped the younglings from eating. They located the exit, but we have not unlocked it yet."

"They remember what happened last night." Enki turned on the camera for the Gamma enclosure, observing twelve batches of grown Adama. He focused on one camera to watch the new female dwelling.

There were six of the Adama that ate their morning meal in the middle area. Ah, that was batch Gamma. They were one of the more advanced test subjects and likely would be the final design for the Adama. They were identical clones. "Unlock the door," Enki instructed as he ended the call. He turned up the sound on the feeds.

The door clicked open, popping ajar. Inside the bedchambers, the three eldest women pulled blades from their footwear. It was thoughtful of them to have backup weapons. The most senior pushed open the door slowly.

In the common area, one of the males heard the door open. He turned to the sound, freezing for a moment, when he saw the woman. He tapped the guy next to him to get everyone's attention. They slowly stood up.

"What are they?" the lead man asked.

"How should I know? I only harvest here," came the grumbled voice of another.

"They look kind of like us, just shorter," said a third one.

"Can we lick it?" asked a male in the back.

That got the attention of the other five, turning to look at the licker. "What?" The speaker looked a little confused.

"Hulu, what is your obsession with licking everything?" The first male shook his head.

"I have no idea, Whiz, but, hey, we need something to do." Hulu smiled at Whiz. "I don't think they are like those furry things with teeth. First, they are like the size of three of us. Second, they have flesh that looks like ours, maybe wrapped up in blankets of the ones that eat us?"

Whiz shook his head. "Wolves. We call them wolves." He was gesturing with both hands.

Hulu stuck out his tongue. "I thought we called them the fur of death. But wolves work, I guess."

The others shook their heads. Whiz turned to look at the women. He walked closer to them, his head tilted to the side. He didn't know to stop when the eldest female swiped the sharpened stone she had turned into a blade.

"Ja-Al ka!" snarled the blade welding woman, swiping the blade a second time.

This swipe sliced Whiz from the right shoulder to the left hip. He jumped as he howled, tumbling back as he experienced that kind of pain for the first time, trying to curl into a ball. His tears fell into the dirt.

Hulu froze, fear flashing across his face. "Aw, come on, not another thing that kills us," he pouted.

One of the other four darted forward to pull Whiz back from the women, but thankfully he was not attacked. The bunch of females backed up slowly from the other group. Whiz was slowly drawn back into the group of his brothers.

Whiz was curled in a ball, whimpering as if it were the worst thing he had ever felt in his short life. He was less than two years old, after all, so it really was the worst thing that had ever occurred to him. Thankfully, the cut was not fatal. The wound would scar but otherwise heal with little issue if untreated.

"The pain response is quite active in these creations. I should test some without pain, perhaps they will work harder. Possibly even alter them to explore under the saltwater. Could I make them fly?" Enki mumbled before pressing the call button to Ninurta. "Bandage subject W and send them out to work field seven."

"By your command," Ninurta intoned before he ended the communication.

Enki watched as Ninurta's workers entered the enclosure to remove the men for their next shift. Yes, it was early for them, but controlling the situation was better than letting it grow out of hand. He watched the females chatter back and forth in some language that they had developed.

The five women knelt, each one of them pulling stone knives and placing them in front of their knees. They started to chant in their native tongue. After an hour, Enki noticed that their hair seemingly glowed purple.

The female's knives lifted from the ground, glowing the same sparkling purple for a moment before they slammed into the ground with the blades sinking into the glass. The group slowly placed their foreheads next to the blades as they ended their chant.

As the group of natives sat up, they seemed visibly relaxed. The eldest stood up and started to explore the enclosure. Enki watched her enter each sleeping pod and explore the eating area before she returned to her family. She quickly explained what she saw.

The sun was near setting when the Adama returned to the enclosure. They were clearly tired due to the hard labor in the field. Hulu froze when he noticed the females still in their evening quarters.

"Hey Whiz, they are still here." Hulu looked confused. "They never leave newcomers around."

Whiz shrugged as he walked over to the food table and sat down, wincing in pain. He pressed at his bandages. "These things pull at the chest hair," he grumbled.

"Well, next time, don't let them do that," Hulu suggested as he sat while the rest of the group of males followed, sliding into their regular seats. They looked at each other, expecting the food to appear like normal.

"So, where's the food?" Gamma looked confused as he poured himself a glass of water.

Thetha shook his head. "What gives? We don't normally wait like this."

"What? No food now? First, we get a new thing that kills us, now, no dinner. Unless..." Hulu turned to look at the newcomers, tilting his head slightly. He started to wave at them, trying to call them over. When they didn't move, he began to mime like he was putting food in his mouth and waved at them again.

The females didn't join them. Pursing his lips, Hulu picked up the water jug that they had been drinking from, taking it to the females. He stopped well out of the range of the female with the blade. He placed the jug between his feet and bowed slightly to them.

"Water," he said, pointing to the inside of the jug. He mimed drinking and stepped back, watching the females.

The eldest stepped forward and picked up the jug, sipping at it. She carefully swished it in her mouth before swallowing. She bowed her head slightly, holding the pitcher to her right.

"Ja Ka'l," the elder snapped.

The young adult female stepped up and handed the water jug to the youngest, helping her drink before letting the others. Once they had finished the pitcher, she returned it to the elder female. The elder female placed the jug back where Hulu had put it. He smiled and bowed slightly to her.

"Come, eat." Hulu acted like he was putting food in his mouth.

The elder female nodded slowly. "Ja," she said as she slowly walked forward, the rest of the females walking with them to carefully sit with the males around the feeding area. Food was sent that included cooked meats, raw vegetables, some fruits, and several prepared dishes. Enki nodded in pleasure as he watched the group tentatively start to share a meal together.

Chapter 12:

Enki stood in a room that was filled with tanks. On the left side were opaque tanks to protect the objects within, next to each one as a holographic image of the younglings within. Several had prominent brow ridges, three others were triple the size of the others, while several other types of humanoids were growing within.

Across the room, some tubes had a red liquid flowing through them with a few transparent bubbles. Those tubes were filled with creatures with four arms, babies with wings growing, two had the tails of fish, another pair had the legs of a horse. The walls were made from a copper cage with turquoise-colored quartz squares that protected the room from external influence, and engravings of hieroglyphs that explained how to operate the cloning tubes.

Enki's primary terminal beeped, alerting him to the message. He absentmindedly opened the letter from the immunologist, Erra. He barely understood some of the jargon but came down to the part that said: enclosure C with DNA version G-Nine has the most robust counter to the plagues. White blood cell counts are optimal with this gene set. Subject Gaia is now ready for experimentation.

"Hello, father," greeted Enki as the door opened, allowing Enlil to enter.

"The Sky Lord would like an update regarding the development of our new pets," Enlil half growled as he walked towards Enki.

Enki walked to a display and activated the map. "We have discovered many variations of the genus Homo. The creatures in this area will be excellent at mining the massive ore deposits along the largest landmass in the polar area. Standing at three to four meters. They seem to have lower intelligence than their smaller relatives, which is fine for the simple manual labor we have for them. However, the lack of intelligence could simply be a translation problem, as they have large and complex brains. If I could teach them to read, they might comprehend more things, but I'll need to experiment with them."

The younger lord tapped on the runic keyboard. Two blue holograms appeared, showing both human sexes. "I took the smaller of the native specimens and played with their genomes. I was able to accelerate their evolution into what you see in tanks nine through fifteen. The other specimens are likely not viable, but I still wish to test how they perform when fully grown.

"Moving on to the specimens that I've tweaked the genetic code of the natives. Gamma-Nine appears to be the most viable. From the experiments, it's clear that having more limbs simply causes issues with how their spinal columns and bone structures form to support the weight carried during manual labor.

"I will provide details in a later report, but for the moment, I have the data on the rest of the Gamma series," said Enki as he handed Enlil the reports on the creatures.

"The Sky Lord will be pleased," Enlil replied as he glanced over the reports.

"We have confirmed that Ambrosia is produced in great quantities within their brains. This gives them the same access as our staffs allow when they reach for the Great Mother," Enki explained.

"What do they eat? Does the Ah-pap'la fruit grow here?"

"None of our searches have found any. Their Medicine Women use some vines when they wish to speak with the spirits. We might find another plant, but it will require more research to find or grow our own. It will take a millennium or more to explore everything." Enki changed the image. "If you will review the psi series, named homo-electi. They are a fusion of our DNA and their own. Their blood is blue, along with adding several organs from our own species. Subject Psi-Alpha has shown that he is quite powerful, even at the young age of a hundred."

"Is there a suitable candidate for Subject Gaia?"

"Yes, milord."

"Very well. Breeding restrictions have been lifted for those planet-side. Your sister requires the En of the family tonight for the Punarjanman ceremony. I wish to summon one of our line as an Elite."

"I will be ready, father."

Enlil nodded before leaving. Enki gathered what he needed to bring an incubation chamber with the fertilized egg to the ritual room. He then placed the data within a genetically locked safe that only he could access. On a whim, he grabbed a tube that contained fertilized eggs.

After departing his lab, Enki went directly to his quarters. He glanced out of the window to take in the ocean view before making the window opaque. He quickly removed his lab protection before walking to the auto mirror and red markings over his face. The paint was made from the leaves of their sacred tree.

Slowly, he marked an ankh on both sides of his snout. The outline of the ankh wrapped around his eyes, much like eyeliner being applied. That mark showed the connections of all aspects of one's life, encompassing physical life, death, and reincarnation. Slowly, he traced blue lines over his chest and arms, tracing the channels of power.

After completing the markings, he opened the ritual storage chamber to don his spiritual gear. The stole he draped over his neck was made from an auburn fabric, embroidered with symbols made with pure gold thread. The two gold markings near the shoulders held a circle, with four points representing the compass points from the center. Between them were wavy lines to show solar light. Depicted in the next row of the stole was the image of the first Sky Lord, Cronus. He was displayed on the upper left, the Great Mother was on the top right. The third marking closer to the ground on the lower right represented Tiamat and her will. The last marking introduced the current form of the Sky Lord, An. Enki then palmed the egg tube.

He walked from his chambers to the garden that contained all the fauna that was sacred to their race. Before selecting his flowers, he placed the tube in the middle of the pentagram. Moving to the wall of prepared herbs and plants, he picked gold flowers, green oval-shaped leafed plants, and another green plant that was oblong. Enki placed the plants on the obsidian stone altar that adorned the center of the garden. Inlaid on the surface were runes engraved with gold that helped focus the mind on the task ahead.

"Vilfac," Enki mumbled as he slipped into the language of the gods, allowing Tiamat to flow through him and light a small fire. He placed the flame in a small chamber full of water. "Blessed be the power of Tiamat," he chanted while placing the golden plants into a mortar with a pestle. "Long we have entrusted our lives into your embrace when you ask us to return." Enki's voice slipped into a ritual quality as he ground the flower. "We ask you to bless us as your chosen ones and restore one that has been taken." The idea was not to crush the items into a powder but merely break it apart to seep into the water.

The En of the family moved to a new bowl to grind the oval leaves. "Bless us, Tiamat, with one of our blood. Bless our blood with your gifts of life." Taking up the third bowl in his hand to grind the most crucial plant he'd collected. "The gift of the spirit that you have blessed us will provide the conduit to reach your depths."

Gathering up the three bowls, Enki poured the water from the gold flower into a small bowl. "With the flower that represents our souls, I call upon your will, sacred Tiamat, to bless us." He slowly sprinkled the oval leaves into the water. "Representative of the blessed flesh, please provide guidance for the lost souls."

Picking up the bowl that had leaves, he saw they'd turned into a dark green paste. "Tiamat, bless us with your lifeblood. Please give us your knowledge," came Enki's whisper as he placed the dough into the pot.

He went to a giant golden bowl engraved with trees. He had to reach much farther than he had in the past, finding that only six of the Ah-pap'la fruit remained. They didn't have the space to grow trees that reached over sixty meters in height, with trunks that were well over eight meters wide on their ships. Only the fully grown Pap'la provided seeds once every five solar cycles. They would have to find an appropriate area on the planet to grow.

Taking a silver blade, Enki placed the Ah-pap'la fruit in the center of the altar. He put the small bowl into an inset slot on the platform. "Spirit Mother, we thank you for the expression of your blood," he chanted before striking the blade into the Ah-pap'la. The fruit's sacred, red liquid flowed into a channel, then dripped into the ritual bowl.

The En did a ritualistic dance as he chanted. "Blessed be Tiamat and her will." With each word, he willed Tiamat to hear his calls for her blessing. He danced around the carved channels, the liquid within having an orangish glow. There was a chorus of voices chanting, "Blessed be Tiamat and her Will." As the newcomers entered, Enki's pitch changed, his chanting became faster and more focused. Two beings stopped behind the Lord while the other five stepped into equal points around the shrine.

The five points kept chanting as Enki stepped forward, his hands rising above his shoulders, reaching outward. "Beloved Spirit Mother; Tiamat. Dumuzid and Inanna come before you for a blessing to allow one that resides within your bosom to return to us for the next life."

Kneeling behind Enki, Inanna and her mate bowed their heads. "Blessed Spirit Mother, please bless us with this boon so that we may further honor the blessings that you have given us," he heard Inanna chant.

"Only by accepting the Blood of the Spirit Mother within you can you find her blessing," Enki said as he picked up the small cauldron that held a thick sludge. "Drink the blood of Tiamat," he chanted as he tipped the liquid into Inanna's mouth.

Inanna swallowed before she placed her forehead on the ground. "By the blood of the Mother, grant us your blessing," she chanted, her voice full of reverence.

Enki turned to Dumuzid. "Eat the flesh of the Spirit Mother. May it infuse you with her blessing." He tipped the cup into Dumuzid's mouth, allowing him to swallow what was left of the brew.

Dumuzid chewed the ground bits of the plant before he placed his forehead on the ground. "By the flesh of the Spirit Mother, grant us your blessing."

Placing the now-empty bowl over the fire, Enki reached to pick up a torch, lighting it with the flames. He made grunting noises as he spun the torch like a baton around the supplementing couple. Enki danced around his sister and her mate for the event for nearly two hours before they moved.

Inanna rose from the floor, her eyes seemed to have a glow behind them. "Blessed be the unbroken line of An," she said in a distant voice, sounding like it was from across a large room. "We call to those of thine blood to return to the physical."

As she spoke, Dumuzid moved over her form. "Blood of the holy Anu shall call forth to its own." He sounded just as far away as Inanna seemed. He pulled a blade from his stole and slit his forearm, allowing blood to fall over their bodies, the eggs that came out of Inanna, and into the incubation chamber.

The birth was over less than a minute later. There were three eggs on the ground and looked like they were absorbing the blood that had pooled under them. "Blessed Spirit Mother, bless us with known souls." Enki's hands hovered over the eggs. "May the lifeblood give the path home. Blessed be Tiamat and her will." The last sentence was given by the group.

The gathered ones chanted, "Blessed be Tiamat and her will" for another two hours until the eggs had absorbed the blood. They all bowed to the center altar before the eggs were covered with a straw-like plant. The couple curled around their eggs to incubate them, preparing to spend the next few months taking care of the eggs and another hundred years taking care of their young.

Casting a spell, Enki lifted his tube of fertilized eggs and floated them to his hand. The fluid that was suspended within glowed purple with streaks of blue. As he returned to his lab, the glow faded, as if it were being absorbed. He placed them into the incubator, ready for growth.

Chapter 13:

A child who looked about twelve years old placed her ebony hands on the back of a terminal. Her hair was braided into long cornrows, with multi-colored beads woven into them that hung past her shoulders. Besides purple eyes, the feature that set her apart from the natives was her elongated skull. She was hiding in Enki's lab, a sly smile on her face. When the door opened, she ducked under the table.

"Enki's going to kill me," grumbled Ninurta. He looked around the room, growling softly. He moved a few boxes, looking behind them. "Gaia, are you in here?"

Gaia snuck behind the bubbling tanks moments before Ninurta looked behind the terminal. She placed her hand over her mouth to stop the giggle from leaving her lips. Enki's Tan let out a growl before storming out of the room. It left the child alone to her own devices. She wasted no time finding a shiny button in the back to press. This caused a door to pop open, blinding her from the post-mid-day sun.

"Wow, these are where the fields are," Gaia whispered. From her view, near the top of the Royal Scribes building, she could see fields of grain and lambs. Working among them were several humans and Anunnaki. In the distance, she could see the golden top of the Exousía building. It held inner chambers of Enki, An, Enlil, Chronos, and the other leaders of the Annunaki. They resided in the golden layer, while red granite provided the outer shell. She quickly headed down the servant's stairs.

Entering the wheat field, Gaia broke into a run. She let out a giggle as she hopped through the rows of wheat. Her eyes glowed, purple sparks coming from the corners. Behind her, the wheat aged. It quickly moved to harvest age. A line of yellow-green followed her wake. Popping out of the far side of the field, Gaia slammed into the side of a dwelling. She landed with a loud 'oof', and shook her head as she picked herself up.

"Are you alright?" a young voice asked. Gaia turned quickly, but she lost her balance. The young girl grabbed her, stopping Gaia's fall.

"Yes, who are you?" Gaia asked.

"I'm Aamira," answered the girl.

Gaia looked at her new friend, a girl who looked her age, her skin a few shades lighter than Gaia's own. Aamira's black hair hung in long dreadlocks. She wore light clothes and leather shoes. "I'm Gaia."

"Where are you from? I know all the girls here, and I've never seen you before," said Aamira.

"Oh, I live there," Gaia replied as she pointed at the Pyramid of Science.

"But only the Gods can enter!" Aamira gasped.

Gaia straightened her spine, a wide grin on her face. "I am a Goddess."

"Sure, you are. You look nothing like the Gods. You look like me," Aamira stated as she poked Gaia.

"I am a new Goddess. I really am. Father was told by Lord Anu to see what he could do and made me," Gaia explained emphatically, her hands moving to either side as if to say 'ta-da'.

"Oh yeah? What are you the of Goddess then?"

"I am the planet," Gaia said with a bow.

"I've never heard of a planet, so you are not a Goddess."

Gaia stamped her foot. "No, I am."

"Nuh-uh," Aamira replied as she stepped forward, her hands making fists.

"I'm telling the truth!" cried Gaia. Her hair lifted slightly, her eyes flashing dark purple, lines of power sparking from the corners again.

"Woah, you are like the Medicine Woman," said Aamira.

"Medicine Woman? Is that like the En of your family? Papa is teaching me to become the En of all the Annunaki." The mention of the Medicine Woman quickly changed Gaia's emotion from anger to curiosity.

"But what does the En do?"

"We connect our family to the Great Mother. We ask for many things such as advice, blessings for a bounty for our crops, helping familiar souls return to the living for their next Yuga, and we also train those who are blessed with Tiamat's power."

"That's what our Medicine Woman does. You should meet her!" exclaimed Aamira, pulling at Gaia's hand. The pair cut between several houses, heading for a hut in the center of town. The young native girl burst through the door. "Grandma!"

"Child, what have I told you?" asked a woman with long grey

dreadlocks. She had skin the color of walnut and was dressed in white and red with long feathers hanging from the edges of her clothes. She stood next to a cauldron that had a light blue smoke hovering over it.

"Not to burst in like that, Grandma. You might have something that might explode," Aamira answered, her head slightly bowed.

"That's right, Aamira," Grandma said as she ruffled her granddaughter's hair. "Who's your friend? Someone from Carthage? No, they just left and won't be back until after the harvest."

"I'm Gaia. I live in the Science Pyramid," she said with a grin.

The older woman raised a grey eyebrow. "One of the God's chosen few then?"

Gaia shook her head. "My papa is one of the Gods."

"Which one, my child?"

"This one, Femi Meyeso," replied Enki as he entered the hut. He placed a clawed hand on Gaia's shoulder.

"Papa," Gaia said as she wrapped her arms around the God of Magic.

"Lord Enki, forgive my granddaughter. We did not know tha-," Meyeso started.

"There is nothing to forgive. There was no slight given," Enki quickly said. "My daughter loves to explore. Perhaps she should come down here and visit with you and yours."

"It would be my pleasure to watch over your daughter, milord," Femi answered.

Enki glanced at Gaia, seeing the hope in her eyes. "Gaia, call

Ninurta when you are ready to return home. You are not to travel without an escort. There are creatures and others that would love to harm you."

"Yes, Papa," Gaia responded.

"Femi, if an outsider can learn your private rites, I would welcome Gaia learning them along with your granddaughter," Enki said.

"She is one of ours. Of course, she may learn," Meyeso agreed.

"Thank you." Enki bowed his head slightly before leaving the tent.

"Femi," Gaia started, but was cut off by Meyeso's raised hand.

"Call me Meyeso, child. Femi is my title, Medicine Women of the Azalea tribe. When I rejoin the God that you call the Great Mother, Aamira here will become the next Femi," stated the older woman.

"Who can become the Femi?" Gaia asked as she sat on the ground, her hands tucking under her chin.

"The title normally passes mother to daughter, sometimes to the granddaughter, unlike the Anunnaki who pass their En through father to son. My daughter knows everything, but she chooses to work with the Gods, such as your father. Little Aamira here wants to become the Fermi," Meyeso explained.

"Do you want it?" Gaia asked the girl.

Aamira nodded with a grin on her face. "Oh yes. I feel the calling within my blood."

"Gaia, has your father discussed the Lord of the Sky?" asked Meyeso.

"Great-grandfather is the Sky Lord of the Annunaki," Gaia answered.

After grabbing a leather-bound book, Meyeso sat on the floor, forming a triangle with the children. She opened the book, showing several drawings. Images of a squatting man, a snake, a beetle, a shower of sparks, spinning sparks, and other markings. In the upper left corner was a mark for the sun glowing brightly. Around the sun was a shape that looked like an eye.

"The Azalea have observed the Lord of the Sky over the eons. We told our children about his wrath. Other tribes have their own name for him. We call him Ra, while others call him Inti, Sué, Aten, Tawa, Algao, or other names." Meyeso then tapped the corner outside the sun. "The all-seeing eye of Ra has watched us since he created all. His wrath manifests in the sky, which drives us underground."

Meyeso turned the page to show a small group moving animals and food into underground shelters. "When a civilization reaches its peak, Lord Ra strikes them down. We have to shelter within an ark, as Ra reminds us he rules over all." She flipped another page, this one showed a group of stick figures getting confused. "Over time in the ark, we forgot who we were before. We lost what we knew as we forgot how to read the holy texts. The meanings of words were lost, as they had no context. We were reborn from the great mounds in an altered world."

"Wow," Gaia whispered.

"Now, when the Anunnaki arrived, they tried to drink too much of Lord Ra's life-giving river. He let his displeasure known to us when he tried to smite Lord Enki and the later destruction of Ur. Since then, your clan has learned how to float upon the great river alongside us," explained Meyeso.

"When can we tell if Ra is getting mad?" asked Aamira.

"In the twenty-five thousand year cycle, we fear the Libra and the Scorpius. This is when Ra is awake, from the stories," Meyeso said.

"If it was lost, how do you know this?" Gaia asked.

"The priests made sure some stories were passed down by song. Aamira will practice the stories until she can recite them word for word. We do what we can to ensure the songs are passed from generation to generation as books can be lost," Meyeso stated.

Gaia frowned, her eyebrows furrowed. "What happens when language changes? Meanings of words shift as we grow."

Meyeso smiled at the young Goddess. "We make sure that the young ones understand the meaning, not just the words. They learn the reason we want them to learn. Those who have passion are the chosen ones. My little Aamira here wants to learn while my daughter thinks of it as just another thing to study."

"I want to learn alongside Aamira," Gaia said.

"You will have to catch up. She's learned a lot already," Meyeso informed her.

"Grandma, you said that we learn best by teaching someone. I can teach her. It will help me remember better," Aamira said, shifting excitedly.

Meyeso smiled at both of the children before checking her

teacup. "Why don't you start with how to make one of our teas?" she asked.

Aamira nodded before grabbing Gaia's hand. "Come on, let's start with the water."

Chapter 14:

"Are you going to see Aamira today?" asked Enki as he set a plate in front of Gaia.

The young teen pushed the food around with her spoon. "Aamira asked me to wed her to Ian," she said before she took a bite of egg.

"Are you going to do it?" Enki placed a plate full of raw meat across the table from his daughter.

Gaia looked up, shock on her face. "Wait, I'm allowed?"

Enki looked confused. "You have free will, don't you? The Femi and Aamira taught you their rituals, did they not? I taught you our own wedding rituals. That's two you can choose from. I'm sure we could find some Denisovans to ask them their rites."

Her fork dropped to the plate as Gaia launched herself at Enki, wrapping her arms around his neck. "You are an amazing dad."

Nuzzling his nose into Gaia's neck, Enki whispered, "I love you, little one."

"I love you too, dad," Gaia said as she stepped back. "Will Lord Anu approve?"

"Totally. He'll probably take a recording and send it to Chronos just to rub it in," Enki laughed.

Gaia wrinkled her nose as she sat back down. "Must you do that? Why would he care about a girl? He is over twenty thousand years old. Aamira is twenty-five and looks like it. I'm sixty and look like I'm thirteen. She will die of old age before I become an adult. Her Great-Great-Great Grandchildren will die before I can accept my inheritance, taking my place in the Pantheon.

"Chronos has lost sight of the mortals. I can see why. A hundred years might as well be a day for us. We don't even sleep like the mortals. We know the Annunaki can live between ten and twenty thousand years. How long will I live, father? The same? What about a hundred thousand? Half a million? Can I even die of old age?" Gaia demanded, her fist hitting the table.

Enki shook his head. "I don't know. You are the firstborn of the Humanaki. You are the bridge between the Annunaki and the Humans, giving you a foot between both worlds for all time. This kept the Annunaki alive and whole within your memory. Despite our abilities, our tech, and our knowledge, we can't stop the damage that comes from inbreeding."

The Lord of Magic paced as he talked. "I created the Humanaki as a stepping stone between the Adama and us. This sadly leaves you asking questions like that. I wish I could tell you something to soothe you. All I can say is that I will be with you as long as the Great Mother allows my return."

Enki placed his hands on Gaia's shoulders, looking her in the eyes. "I felt like you when I was your age. I had a feeling of hopelessness at being alive for tens of thousands of years, wondering what I was going to do. It left my stomach cold as I had no experience to draw upon. I hope that you will not have to experience that as well. In time, you will connect with your past selves. Also, don't worry, everyone loves you."

Gaia chuckled. "Well, not everyone loves me. The Titans loathe us and are constantly trying to piss off Khione and me. She's gotten great at giving the cold shoulder to them. I swear one of these days, she's going to turn them into a block of ice."

"We've had to move the nursery well away from the Titan's dwellings. They've tried to use the Humanaki as slaves as if they were Adama. They don't mess with you because they don't want to face the wrath of Anu, even if he's still on the Nibiru," Enki said before Gaia hugged him.

"Father, I'm going to spend the day with Aamira and Khione. I'll be back well after dark, perhaps not until the morning," Gaia stated. She stepped into leather shoes and slipped a purple shawl over her shoulders.

"Alright, I'll be in my lab tonight. Several tests are being completed," Enki said as Gaia left.

The young Goddess headed through the Annunaki living quarters. As she passed the golden doorway of the Titans, a slim Annunaki with pale gray scales hissed at the young Humanaki. "Watch your step, human," the Titan hissed, a blade appearing in their hand.

"Oh, look, it's a Phonoi. Taking a break from hunting the mortals?" Gaia demanded, her body shifting to one that suggested that she was the superior one. Her brown eyes changed as her pupils went white, and her irises changed to a rich purple, the white streaking like rays from a star.

"Would you like to find out how many I've dragged back? I have plenty of trophies I could show you," Phonoi almost purred, their words layered with several voices as they reached for the young woman.

Gaia rolled her eyes as she batted the reptilian hand away. "Does your murdering spirits that live within you really want to play this game? Do you think Lord Chronos would protect you from Lord Enlil's wrath?"

Phonoi's head jerked back as if they had been physically slapped. "Be gone, child, find another path to your pets." The Titan's lip curled as they stepped behind the Grey's entrance.

"Thought so," Gaia spat before she sharply turned and walked off. She refused to show any fear until she had left the complex. The moment the sun touched her face, the young goddess let out a breath of relief. She felt her body shift back as she shook her head, her eyes returning to their normal color.

"Gaia," called a young voice.

The Earth Goddess looked up and waved at the approaching girl, who looked about ten. Her hair was white like snow, while her skin was the color of alabaster. She had light grey eyes and was dressed in a light blue sundress. "Khione," Gaia greeted warmly.

"Aamira was making bottles of this year's harvest of those long green things. You know, so they can eat it in the winter? Yeah, she's soaking them in that sour sauce," Khione said as she wrapped her arm under Gaia's. The pair headed for the Fermi's area.

"Soaking in vinegar, and the plant is called a cucumber. She's making pickles," Gaia correced with an eye-roll.

"Pah, it's more fun my way," Khione laughed.

"You're only thirty. When you're sixty like me, you'll find it annoying," Gaia sighed as they ducked under a back awning of the

Human camp. "Hey Lath," she said, waving to the old man reclining in the window.

"Gaia! Khione!" exclaimed the bald man. "On your way to see Aamira?"

"Yes, we are, but we'll stop by for tea tomorrow," Gaia said with a wave.

Lath chuckled as he waved back. "I'll hold you to it. Tomorrow night's story is about the pride of the Ocuin and the wrath of Ra."

"That's the last cycle's major civilization, right?" Khione asked.

The old man nodded as he lifted his cup. "That's right, Lady Khione. I'll tell you more during story time."

"Bye, Mr. Lath. See you tomorrow," Gaia said as they kept walking. It took the pair a few more minutes to enter the Fermi's hut.

"Khione and Gaia, I was afraid you'd forgotten our lunch date," Aamira said. The girl used tongs to lift a jar out of a cauldron full of boiling water.

"It's not like you're ready anyway," Gaia replied as she grabbed a towel and another pair of tongs.

"The middle jars are ready," Aamira said.

"Do you need my help?" asked Khione before picking up tongs.

Aamira nodded. "Please. The sooner we remove them from the water, the sooner we can have lunch." The trio made quick work of removing the jars. "Thanks. Let me grab a lunch bag before we head out."

After grabbing their packs, the trio left the hut. The city was constructing walls to protect the town from plasma storms, but it was early in their construction. They were starting on the southern side by digging down to the bedrock. The trio walked a few kilometers into the forest, coming to a clearing with large boulders.

"This is the spot. We will set the tent up with the stones," Aamira said, pointing to the three stones. She knelt in the center as she pulled her pack off her back. Gaia and Khione stepped over to the far stone. The Earth Goddess found a hook while the younger girl removed a leather awning. She clipped it to the tall rock, taking each corner to the others. They lit the torches that were attached to the stones.

Aamira raised a pole in the center to provide covering from the elements. Brushing the dirt and other collected plant matter away from the stone, she uncovered a pentagram carved into the hard surface. The carving was at ninety degrees to true north, aligning four out of five points to the cardinal directions. In contrast, the top point pointed nowhere, but everywhere. As the night sky appeared, they worked to ensure the foundation of their ritual was cleaned.

"What does each point stand for?" asked Aamira as she removed a box from her pack.

"The upper-left corner represents the earth," Khione explained as she took the box. After opening the box, she placed the ritual dirt on the point. "The ground is always there, stabilizing us as we move through the world. All things living, even us, will grow old and die while the stone and earth will be here long after."

Gaia drew a book, some drawings, and a small horn from her

pack. "The lower left is for air. It is our thoughts, intelligence, and our arts," she said as she placed them inside the point.

Khione placed a water skin down. "Our emotions wash over us like water. We must have the intuition to understand how to flow around each other as represented by the lower right point."

After placing a few small pieces of wood down, Gaia whispered a word to light it on fire. "The upper right is our courage, our daring, cleansing the world for rebirth. Fire consumes everything within its path, but it leaves a whole new home for us."

"The topmost point, this is our spirit. How our souls connect to the Great Mother. She is everywhere but nowhere. The Great Father guides us, but we always return to her embrace," Khione said with a bow.

"Clear your thoughts. We shall begin," Aamira instructed. Shadows cast over her face, hiding her eyes as she grinned widely.

Chapter 15:

The two Humanaki bowed their heads. Gaia knelt at the earth point while Khione knelt between the bottom points. Aamira knelt at the point of the spirit before speaking. "Lady Tiamat, Lord Nammu, we beseech you for your blessing. We have lived with nature, striving for balance for all. We have lived by the creed 'It harms none, do what you want' as you commanded us in the eons past. Bless us, oh teachers, bless us."

As Aamira asked for blessings, the trio used a ritual knife to prick their fingertips. Blue and red blood dripped into the grooves. Moments later, each point lit up with a different color. Earth was represented by a dark brown, air was a light blue, water taking a dark blue, fire's grooves lighting up a rich orange, while the spirit glowed pure white.

The three stepped into the center of the pentagram. They stood with their backs to each other, shoulders touching. Aamira withdrew an obsidian knife from her waist and held it over her left hand as she spoke. "I freely offer my life blood to Gaia Enkisdottir to become my blood sister." She sliced her palm, letting a small pool form in her hand as she handed the blade to Gaia.

"I freely accept Aamira Kandottir as my blood sister. May we become flesh of our flesh, bound by blood and family," Gaia said, slicing her right hand. Blue blood pooled before she grabbed Aamira's cut hand. "Bound by sisterhood." Their hands flashed white for a second before they let go and their blood dripped onto the stone

Gaia turned slightly, slicing her left palm, "I freely offer my life blood to Khione Boreasdottir to become my blood sister."

Khione took the blade from Gaia. "I freely accept Gaia Enkisdottir as my blood sister. May we become flesh of our flesh, bound by blood and family," she repeated, slicing her right hand. Blue blood pooled before she grabbed the Earth Goddess's cut left hand. "Bound by sisterhood." Their hands flashed white for a second before they let go as well. Khione sliced her left palm and repeated the ritual once more. "I freely offer my life blood to Aamira Kandottir to become my blood sister."

After Khione sliced her left palm and returned the blade to Aamira's waist, Aamira grabbed Khione's left hand. "I freely accept Khione Boreasdottir as my blood sister. May we become flesh of our flesh, bound by blood and family."

As Aamira grabbed Khione's hand, the pentagram glowed brighter, the light blocking the trio from seeing beyond it. As one, the three chanted, "One becomes three. The flaws of the one are replaced with the best of the three. The power of three protects. Three shall act as one in perfect love and perfect trust."

Their heads snapped back as the five points flared. From Gaia's right hand, a flame wrapped around Aamira's arm. Reaching across the human's shoulders, it found Khione's form. The moment the flames touched the younger-looking girl, they turned into ice. Spikes of ice crawled up the young goddess's arm, across her shoulder, and down her other hand. As it reached Gaia's left hand, stone crawled up the ebony goddess's frame before completing the circuit with Aamira's hand.

The Human woman's hair burst into flames but didn't burn. Her eyes glowed white as another form overlaid her own for a moment. "Morimi," Aamira whispered. Her body changed shape as she let out a cry of pain, her body mass enlarging and her frame grew.

Khione's hair crystallized as if made from ice, but moved as freely as water. Her eyes darkened, becoming dark grey like a storm cloud. A cold wind bellowed forth from her open mouth, turning the water in the air to ice. Her voice let out a wrenching scream of pain as her legs elongated, her fingers growing longer and her shoulders growing wider.

Gaia's eyes glowed purple as her hair grew, glowing dreadlocks reaching the ground, white light emanating from the center of each lock. Her body shifted, growing, but not as dramatically as the other women. She winced from the growth of her limbs as she felt something settle within her. A sense of oneness with the world. She couldn't quite place it, but she felt more secure.

Aamira let out another cry of pain as her body grew to over three meters, her bones rapidly growing. Her skin tone lightened, an orange hue under her dark skin. The offering of fire before her roared to life and was consumed within moments. Dark ash fell to the ground, but cold winds wrapped around the trio, smudging the ash across their faces.

Khione clenched her fists as she heard a loud crack from her shoulder. Her face contorted in determination as she stopped herself from screaming. She lowered her head, her eyes narrowing. "I am Khione, Goddess of the Arctic Winds, Sister of Gaia, Sister of Aamira Morimi. This body serves me," she spat through gritted teeth. The water skin split, allowing the winds to lift the water across the snow-white-haired Goddess. The water froze upon touching her skin, then absorbed into her.

The Trio dropped to their knees, their clothing in tatters from the sudden growth and the light from the spell faded. Aamira sank to the ground, gasping in surprise from the size of her hand on the stone. "By the Gods," she whispered.

"By the Gods is right, for you die now for the crime of disturbing the will of the Great Mother," hissed a voice. Half a second later, the three were pounced on, their bodies being slammed to the ground.

"Phonoi," Gaia spat. She raised an eyebrow at the tone of her voice.

"Look at that, the little Adama found some mortal magic to make her all grown up," hissed the Annunaki in Gaia's ear.

"Let ussssss eats it," hissed the creature on top of Aamira, licking her ear.

"Not yet, Cold Phonoi," answered the one over Gaia in a similar hiss.

"But we wants to. We need to feel her writhe under usss," hissed the one on Khione.

"As we just told the Blue Spirit, Chronos wants them alive," reminded Gaia's Phonoi.

"A taste will leave her alive, just a hand. She won't need the hand," suggested Khione's attacker.

"Blood Phonoi, no. Tie them up," hissed Logical Phonoi.

"You tie them up," spat Blood Phonoi before licking Khione's ear. "I think I will eat this one rare. Chronos only wanted Gaia alive."

"Fine, kill her quickly," said Logical Phonoi.

Gaia twisted, her right hand snapping out as she cried out a word. The stone below her hand ripped out of the ground, slamming into Blood Phonoi's right side. He rolled a few times, gasping for his breath. Logical Phonoi arched his head back as he bellowed in pain.

The shifting weight allowed Aamira to twist free, her elbow impacting Phonoi's right ribs. The sound of bones snapping filled the air as the Annunaki rolled as he roared in pain again. "Kill the bitches," he spat, one hand holding his ribs, the other on the ground as saliva dripped from his jaw. "Chronos can deal with the body parts."

Blue Phonoi's jaw clamped down on Gaia's right shoulder, sharp teeth tearing through flesh. She arched her head back in pain; her face contorting in rage. She spat a word, causing the stone to leap from the ground, slamming into the Annunaki's shoulder. The shock of his victim fighting back caused him to let go as he was tossed from the Humanaki.

Their shoulders touching, the trio of women lifted their hands in a defensive posture. "Well, we have a bat-shit crazy Lizardman who wants to eat us," Aamira said.

"Thanks for that obvious comment," Khione snarked.

"Save it, you two," Gaia hissed. "Phonoi, you know I am going to kill you, right? Chronos will not protect you. Do you really think the Great Father will judge you worthy of returning to the great river? Do you think he won't punish you for the wicked actions you've taken?" she asked in a friendly voice.

"Why isn't it dead?" hissed Blue Phonoi. "The pale one should be frozen, and the black one should be dead."

"We don't knowssss. Our venom has always worked on the Adama. Why don't it work now, Smart One?" asked Blood Phonoi. "We bites them, and they die in our teethises. Then flesh-tearing wonderfulness."

The Logical Phonoi sniffed the air. "Enki hasn't allowed us to eat one of his precious experiments. Maybe they will die soon, or he made them immune to us. The other Adama, she is mortal. We've eaten her kind many times. She should be dead. Why are you not dead?" he asked as his head bobbed, sniffing at Aamira.

"A challenge presented to us," giggled Blood Phonoi.

"One we've not had since An," laughed Blue Phonoi.

"Wait, wasn't that like eons ago? How are you alive?" asked Khione.

Blood Phonoi gave a laugh that caused the hair to stand up on the woman's arms. "We take bodiesss. We eats them, or we take their essence and become our prey. Titan Lord found ussss after we ate one of his lines. We eat and take whom he wants gone; we live. Titan Lord always kept us hidden for this until we came here. We found prey, but nothing worthy of the chase."

Khione shook her head slightly, her lip curling. She flung her hands out, shards of ice flying from them. "You all talk too much," she spat. The bits ripped through Blood Phonoi's flesh. Holes appeared on his back while Logical Phonoi screamed in pain. The wounded one fell to the ground, gasping for air before dissolving into a cloud of black smoke that enveloped Logical Phonoi's form.

"You killed him! He was the first!" cried Blue Phonoi.

"You're next," growled Gaia as she grabbed the air at her waist, causing the ground near the blue Lizard to quiver. "You messed with the Goddess of the Planet," she snarled. The ground came up and swallowed the attacker.

Aamira lifted her right hand, flames appearing right above her palm. She gave Phonoi an evil grin. "And you're next."

The remaining attacker rolled to the right, taking him behind a support stone and into the darkness. It caused the fireball to miss him. Aamira darted forward, flames lighting up the surrounding area, but when she looked for Phonoi, he wasn't there. "Find him. He can't have gone far," she said.

Gaia had closed her eyes, looking at something only she could. "No, he hasn't, but that wasn't Prime. Prime is too much of a coward." She stopped talking and shook her head. "Oh, my, I feel lightheaded. Must be his venom," she murmured as she slumped to the ground.

Khione knelt next to Gaia. "Is there anything-" she was cut off as she felt a blade fly past her ear. Sparks flew as it deflected off the stone behind her. She turned to the thrower, frowning slightly.

"I'm fine," Gaia whispered. "Three of them. The middle is Prime," she groaned, her hand waving in the direction Logical Phonoi went. "Thirty meters and closing, that way." She placed her other hand on the ground, whispering in High Annunaki words of cleansing.

"Shall we bring light to the darkness?" Aamira asked, her right hand lifting into a throwing motion.

"Wait, I have a better idea. It's cooler than normal. Let's make them really cold," Khione whispered. Her hands moved in front of her face as she grabbed something only she could see. She let out a grunt as a column of air from the stratosphere slammed into the ground. The vegetation around the circle flash froze from the sudden temperature drop.

"Cold is a dear friend," called out a Phonoi. "Prey is easy to kill when cold," came the taunt.

"He lies, or at least isn't telling the whole truth. He's moving a lot slower," Gaia said, blue lines reached from her hand on the ground up to the bitten shoulder.

"This is downright balmy," Khione growled as she grabbed another burst of air from the upper atmosphere. "Try this for cold," she spat as she released the energy. One of the attacker's teeth chattered.

Aamira's lips curled as she flung a firebolt to her left. The light showed a chattering Phonoi twenty meters in front of her before it impacted the one on the left. The poor creature burst into flames with a loud whomp. The Lizard let out a scream of pain as his flesh blackened before dissolving into energy, sliding across the frozen field to return to the Logical Phonoi.

Khione's lips peeled back as she focused on another one of their attackers. "I can feel you in the wind. You can't hide," she said as she twisted her right hand. A cry of shock came from her right. "You might have a trick for the cold, but let's see how you survive orbital diving, shall we?" Khione laughed as she threw both her hands above her head. She grunted with exertion as the surrounding winds picked up. She slowly sank to her knees as she forced her powers to lift the Annunaki. Her arms dropped limply to her sides as her nose bled from the exertion.

"I send thee to the depths of the earth," Gaia called out as the ground under their attacker opened. He let out a startled cry before the sudden slamming of the earth cut it off. Gaia shivered, "Ugh, he's nasty."

"Chronos will not be happy," gasped Khione as she ripped a rag from her ruined clothes to wipe the blood away from her face.

"No, he won't. We just killed his fixer," Aamira said as she took a moment to look over her changed body.

"He's still alive," Gaia pointed out as she encased her shoulder in stone, stopping the bleeding. "Maybe if he ever crawls out of his tomb, he'll be in a better frame of mind."

"Is there anyone else around?" asked Aamira.

Gaia placed her left hand on the ground, her purple eyes darting around but focusing on nothing. "Not that I can see."

While Gaia was looking, Khione wiggled her fingers, causing the wind to blow gently. "No, the expected wind currents are there. We are alone, again," she added with half-closed eyes.

"Great, what the fuck happened?" Aamira growled, light flames rippling through her hair.

Gaia opened her mouth to speak but was cut off by a flash of a body. It landed with a deafening thud in the middle of them. The trio leaped back, riding the small shock wave as the ground cracked. With a snarl, Khione formed ice daggers in her hands. "What the actual… Oh… I sent him a little high. What goes up must come down, I guess."

"Okay, now that we've been startled, did we leave anything else? No one else in the sky? Can we get to the splany thing now? Like how in the Gods' names am I an adult Humanaki? Who is Morimi? Why do I hear her laughing at me? How are the two of you adults? Why were we attacked? Was it some test?" Aamira snapped.

Gaia looked at her hand, shaking her head slightly. "I think the Great Mother agreed with our request and more. I can feel the ground."

"But who is Morimi? Why is she giggling and saying I'm a summer girl now?" Aamira asked.

Closing her eyes, Gaia let out a soft breath as she released the remaining power. Her eye color returned to its usual brown. "I think you and Khione were given the mantle of Summer and Winter. We need to get you into a safe space so that you can come to terms with your new powers. My father might know more. Come," she instructed, waving her hand at the pair. "He'll want to know about Phonoi's attack."

"Why don't the two of you need to worry about that?" Aamira

asked as she grabbed her pack.

"Oh, I assure you, Winter is demanding I listen to her," Khione reassured her, her bag swinging over her shoulders. "She understands you don't hover around your kill, so she's all like: let's go."

Gaia shook her head. "I grew up with my mantle. She doesn't need to merge with my essence. I can just hear her better now."

Aamira shook her head as she waved a hand at the fire that still was smoldering. The coals went dark, cooled from her will. "We don't want to start a fire after all," she explained as they left the holy ground.

Chapter 16:

The sun was just peeking over the horizon as the trio of goddesses neared the town. "Welcome, strangers," called a man, waving to Gaia and the other two women. He stood about two meters, with long brown hair that was greying and a full beard. He wore a simple tunic and pants that made pushing a cart full of leaf vegetables easier.

"Kalgar, you know us. We had dinner with you last week," Gaia said, shaking her head.

The man froze, his brow furrowing as he looked at the trio of women. "Gaia? Aamira? Khione? What happened?"

"We might have done some magic that did some things," Aamira answered with a shrug.

Kalgar shook his head. "You always said that you should understand what will happen before you cast the spell."

Aamira held up her hand. "The spell shouldn't have caused this. It was a simple adoption rite like we did for your daughter."

"Does this mean that you're a goddess now?" Kalgar asked.

"We think so," Gaia said as they entered the city. The early morning crowd milled about as they prepared their shops. The three giant women walking through the town gave many a pause until they noted their tattered clothes, recognizing the trio by them.

"While we were bigger than the human girls, we didn't stick out like this," grumbled Khione. They stopped at Kalgar's store front. "And we can't enter the shops anymore," she lamented.

"That means we can't enter the temple or the science center," Aamira groaned.

Gaia closed her eyes, her face going blank before she physically deflated like someone popped a bubble. She reduced her size by more than a third, making her stand at two meters versus the almost four she was before. She let out a few heavy breaths before she looked at the other two goddesses. "Ask your mantle they know how to blend in with the mortals."

"Wait, does this mean that we can shift into the Anunnaki?" asked Aamira.

Shrugging, Gaia said, "I honestly don't know. They are of this world, so probably."

Khione had shifted into a smaller form, standing at a little over a meter and a half. "Wait, they are? I thought that was something that your father liked to rub into Chronos' face. How our ancestors evolved into a flightless bird, that kind of thing."

"I recognize my planet's children," Gaia stated, while Aamira tried to shrink herself. She placed her hand on the fire goddess's forearm. "Relax, don't force it. Ask if you could use her power to serve," she said softly.

Aamira gave a few slow breaths, then she took her smaller form. She was returned to her human body. "Okay, wow, yeah, she doesn't like being contained."

"When you can sit down and merge with her, it will be easier. The sudden transfer can take some time to settle within you. The Sky Lords are said to spend three days and three nights before they come to terms," Gaia explained.

"She really would like to have that chat," Aamira softly said.

Gaia grabbed Aamira by the face and looked into her eyes. Her face blanched before looking away. "Khione, tell my father that we will be at the Femi's house. We don't have time to return to the nursery."

"On it," Khione answered as she hurried out.

"What can I do?" asked Kalgar.

"Have the packs taken to Aamira's hut or returned to my father," Gaia said as she led the newly created Humanaki away. They quickly headed down a few streets, thankfully devoid of most travelers. Aamira's hair sparked as she walked, her hands shaking slightly. Bits of flames appeared between her fingers. Gaia pushed her friend into her house.

"Go kneel in the fire pit, and meditate," Gaia instructed, walking a circle around the center of the room.

"But why not where I normally meditate before rituals?" Aamira asked as she knelt in the ashes of the cooking hearth. She took deep, slow breaths.

Gaia stepped inside the circle, and with a touch of her foot, caused it to light up, forming a dome around them of light purple sparks before fading. "Who came to you?" Gaia asked after kneeling in front of her friend.

"Morimi," Aamira said. Her voice was laced with power, almost as if there was a second voice speaking with her.

"Lady Morimi, I am Lady Gaia. I touched my true self and remembered my past. I remembered the eons that have passed. I remember the first fires, how the first ones feared you, how this fear turned into worship. Then, with enough energy given to you, the host you took."

"She was strong. She controlled me," Morimi whispered. "Then I was taken to where I didn't belong. They had their own Fire. I was rejected by my new people because of my old people."

"You are home now. Learn from Aamira just as she will learn from you. Speak to your new friend," Gaia whispered. The pair sat in silence for two hours. Gaia could hear movement outside the hut, but no one crossed the threshold.

Suddenly, Aamira rose slightly from the ground and burst into flames. Her body size restored itself to its larger form as the fire engulfed her. The tattered clothes were no match for the fire and, in seconds, burned away. Her lips lifted in a sneer. "We are the goddess of Fire. We are the summer. We are wonderful and beautiful while we are also your worst nightmare. Life and Death we hold in our hands. From us, new growth arises from the death of the old growth. We are Aamira and Morimi."

As Morimi spoke from Aamira's form, Gaia rose from the ground and returned to her full size. Her hair changed from long dreadlocks to tight cornrows. Each row was braided to the tip, cascading over her shoulder. Her eyes glowed purple as she hovered over the fire goddess. "Gaia welcomes you home. It has been far too long since the planet has been in true balance." Her voice was multi-layered, as was the fire goddess's own.

Morimi bowed her head, kneeling once more in the ashes. "As

my host has sworn blood sisters, I reaffirm my loyalty to Gaia."

Gaia bent down and kissed the top of Morimi's head. "I welcome my family home."

Morimi tilted her head and stood. "Thank you." The surrounding flames went out as Aamira shook her head. "Woah, that is odd. Is that what you've felt your whole life?"

"No, we spend decades, if not hundreds, of years to come to terms with our mantles. It is only a problem when a sudden transfer happens," Gaia said. She tilted her head to the door and smiled. "Time to explain this to my father."

"Do we have to?" Aamira asked.

Rolling her eyes, Gaia headed for the door. "Yes, we do. Come on, let's get this over with." As her body was a little large, she carefully opened the door. "Hello, father. Would you like to come inside? We need to talk."

Enki ducked inside and froze. He closed his eyes for a moment and looked again, "Alright, something happened. Who is your friend? Is she a sub-species of the Denisovans?"

"That is Aamira," Gaia said.

Enki did a double-take before he nodded. "Well, perhaps an explanation is in order?" Gaia grimaced as she sat cross-legged and explained what had happened the night before. He let out a sigh. "Gaia, I'm going to have to run some tests before the next cycle arrives."

"Oh lovely, this will be a fun year," Aamira groaned.

"We'll go on a long trip after," Gaia offered.

"Can we check out the north? I'd like to see some snow," Khione said.

Enki chuckled. "We do need to send explorers out. We can't spare any of our flying craft, but we can send you out with one of the new ocean-going vessels. First, however, tests and planning."

Gaia rolled her eyes. "More tests?"

Shaking his head, he pointed at Aamira. "That's new. Also, we do not know if a blood rite is required for full ascension. Or if it's time, or something between. She's turned into a goddess. Does this mean that they will become fully powered gods and goddesses if we complete the Annunaki Soul Famili rite? We have so many questions, and I need most of them answered before the next trip to Nibiru."

"Will we join you?" Khione asked weakly.

Enki turned to look at the light-skinned woman, who looked grey from her fear. "No, I don't think we will need to do that. Come, young ones, let's get you some rest. We'll worry about everything else another day."

Chapter 17:

Standing on an old watchtower, Enki looked over a dry dock. He placed his claws on the railing, noting that they were installing the rudder on the stern. "Hello, father," Gaia said from behind him.

Turning his head to look at his daughter, Enki nodded to her. "Hello, Gaia."

"Today's the day," Gaia stated softly.

"That, that it is."

"The day of days."

"Yep, the day arrived before we knew it."

"It won't be that bad of a day."

"But it's still the day."

"It will be at least thirty years before we have another day."

"Think about what you'll discover in the days between."

"But you'll spend your days in space. If we were meant to travel it, we would have been born out there."

"You're connected to this planet, little one. Of course, you don't want to leave it, even if it's just a day."

"It's time, milord," said Enki's guard.

Enki nuzzled his daughter before stepping back, looking over her. "Have fun exploring. I'll want to hear all about your adventures when I get back from speaking with the Sky Lord."

"That's going to be at least thirty years, more if you spend more than a month there," Gaia whispered as she flung herself at Enki, wrapping her arms around his neck.

"It will be alright, little one. You'll have plenty of adventures," Enki said as he returned the hug. "I love you, Gaia."

"I love you too, father," Gaia whispered back.

"See you soon," Enki said before walking away.

Gaia closed her eyes, tears sliding down her dark face. "Nope, not going to cry," she murmured. "Not at all." She let out a slow breath before watching her father walk over to the shuttle. She stared at the sky until she lost sight of his craft.

"Are you alright?" Khione asked from behind her.

"I will be," Gaia answered, wiping the tears away. "When will the ship be ready? They were hanging the rudder this morning."

"They are loading the supplies next week. We should be on time to leave in a month," Khione said.

"It hasn't even been launched, but they are planning on loading supplies?" Gaia snorted, shaking her head. "Push off the supplies until at least we know the ship will not sink. We have all the time in the world."

Khione shook her head. "Summer's coming."

"Summer comes every year," Gaia replied.

"No, my powers are waning, thanks to summer's arrival. If we head south, I'll feel strong again," Khione explained.

"What about Aamira? Has her power strengthened?" Gaia asked.

"Morimi gains strength," Khione said.

"No, what about Aamira?" Gaia repeated as the pair started walking away from the dry dock.

Khione sighed. "She is coping with the power. Having another life being shoved into her head in seconds threw her through a hard loop. She's lost where she ends, and Morimi begins. She's struggled with the constant threat of burning her house down at the slightest bit of frustration."

"Hopefully, we can help her with coping," Gaia said as she bent down and plucked a flower from the ground.

"She'll have to find her balance, but it is her nature. Rage is her greatest weapon and her greatest weakness," Khione replied. As she spoke, Gaia tucked the flower behind her ear and picked another.

"It is the cycle of life, but we will not abandon her. She is our sister." Gaia stepped in front of Khione and tucked the red flower behind the ear of her white-haired sister. "We will teach her on the trip."

As the pair started walking again, Khione snorted. "Someone who barely controls her fire on a wooden ship in the middle of the ocean is a great idea."

"That's why you're coming with us. You'll dump snow on the fire," Gaia giggled.

"Oh, so I have to suffer just so I can be your firefighter. Joy," Khione groaned.

"Oh, not only that, but you'll also provide the wind we'll need. However, don't worry, we'll visit colder places too. We have so much to explore," Gaia explained as she picked up a third flower. "Then Morimi will have to keep us from freezing," she said with a giggle and opened the door to her friend's place. "Aamira, darling," she called out.

"Gaia, are you here to torment the witch again?" hissed a female voice from the shadows.

"I'm here to see my sister, not shun her, Morimi. Now let Aamira out to play," Gaia commanded.

"But I'm here now. Do you not want to play with me?" Morimi demanded. "It's the fire, isn't it? It makes you fear me."

Rubbing her eyes, Gaia sighed. "And yet I control a molten core of iron, so hot that I don't even think you would survive a drop into. You don't cause me fear."

Khione snorted again. "While I can't make it rain, I can drop a blizzard to put out any fire. I'm not worried about you. Now come on, Gaia and I want to have lunch with you, and then we'll meditate together."

Morimi hissed, "I don't want to meditate."

"Thus, why we must meditate. Aamira must learn control or else everything burns," Gaia said as she gathered lunch.

"Aamira doesn't wanna come out anymore," Morimi laughed.

"Oh, too bad. She was invited to travel the world with us, but if she doesn't want to..." Gaia let her voice trail off.

"No, I want to go," Morimi half-yelled.

"Well, only if Aamira wants to go and will join us," Khione said as she cut a few roots.

The redhead stepped out of the shadows. She looked thin with slightly sunken cheeks. "Hey girls," Aamira said weakly.

"Oh, honey," Gaia gasped as she rushed over to hug her friend and sister. "Have you been eating?"

Aamira shook her head. "Don't wanna. She's always raging about everything. Makes cooking too hard since everything ends up as charcoal."

Gaia kissed Aamira's forehead before stepping back. "You could have asked us to help."

"Didn't wanna be weak," Aamira whispered.

"It is weaker not to ask for help. Everyone has their limits, after all. We are social creatures, even among the Annunaki," Gaia said as she sat Aamira at the table. "Yes, even the Titans are social despite their hate for anyone that's not a shade of grey. We are here to support you in whatever way you need us to."

Wiping tears from her face, Aamira nodded. "It's so hard to accept help. None of the mortals could understand, and you guys have been one with your powers since birth."

Khione dumped the roots into a pan and walked over to the hearth as she said, "That's because part of our education is to learn control. We go to great lengths to learn every aspect of ourselves, as we can't allow the corruption of our inner selves. A phrase comes to mind, with great power comes great responsibility. We've said it for generations, as has your line. Remember what your grandmother says about power? You have a responsibility to control the energy wielded, not for yourself, but for those who you could harm by lashing out. Gaia and I will be over every morning to meditate and talk. While traveling, we will work on control."

"I am not a baby," Aamira snapped.

"You are a baby. You were reborn as a Humanaki. The Annunaki had to work hard to gain control of their powers after arriving," Gaia said.

"Oh yes, the Solar God, the sun, was not happy at your father's calling of power," Aamira groaned, her eyes rolling.

"Perhaps he was just telling the world that we had arrived. He's been pretty quiet since the rest of the gods arrived," Gaia pointed out.

Aamira closed her eyes before giving a long sigh. She shook her head as if to clear it. "Okay, so where are we going?"

Gaia placed a puck down and a holographic map appeared. "We are here, in Athens," she said as a red dot appeared in the middle of the globe. "I thought we'd sail north to this boot-like peninsula and travel west from there. We can explore the coastlines before hitting the western continents. Then we can go on the east side of the middle mass, visit Athens before we visit the home of the Denisovans." As she spoke, a green line traced their perspective path.

"Oh, the ice wall. Can we see that?" Khione asked as she pointed at the ice cap that covered most of the northern hemisphere.

"Well, it looks like our plan is to sail south of the wall, so sure," Gaia said with a shrug.

"Do you know how cold that's going to be?" groaned Aamira, her forehead resting on her palm before her head shot up. "Wait, Morimi will be insufferable with water everywhere. We'll be on a wooden boat with someone who burns everything around her when she loses control. That's going to end very well for all of us."

Gaia placed her hand over Aamira's. "There will be a fireproof room for you to use. I have already overseen its installation and testing."

"Oh, that's good," Aamira said.

"We want you to come with us," Khione reassured her.

"I'm coming. Who else is?" Aamira asked.

"We'll have an Annunaki, Humans, and us. It will be a grand time," answered Khione.

"Will it? That Uranus guy is going to captain the ship. He's so annoying," Gaia lamented.

"You just think that the Human is cute. You've always had a thing for sailors," Khione said.

"I do not!" Gaia exclaimed. "I am not an ocean goddess, thank you."

Khione raised her eyebrow. "Sure, Gaia, sure."

Gaia playfully smacked Khione's shoulder. "I don't."

Aamira let out a hearty laugh. "Girl, you got the hots for Uranus."

Shaking her head as she stood, Gaia cleared the table. "What do you think we'll find first?"

"Arrows to the knee. Lots of arrows to the knee," Khione quipped as she poked at the hologram.

"So, we'll find more Humans?" Gaia asked.

Aamira snorted. "You represent the planet and you can't tell?"

"No, I can't," Gaia answered with a headshake.

"Well, that makes it exciting. Who knows what plants we could find for healing or what kind of food? The possibilities are endless," Aamira said.

"We'll find out in a few weeks," Gaia said, beaming at her friends.

Chapter 18:

"Why did we choose the water to travel on?" asked Aamira as she wiped her mouth from the sickness that she just finished expelling over the rail. The large ship bobbed along the waves, carving through several swells.

Khione giggled from the bow of the ship, the wind blowing her hair over her shoulder. "Because it's amazing. The smell of the ocean, the breeze passing through your hair, the creatures we've seen, it's all amazing."

"We'll be on land soon enough. Look over there, to port," Gaia said as she pointed to the emerging land.

"Gaia, dear, we call that direction left," Khione corrected.

"The sailors call it port and starboard," Gaia informed her with an eye roll.

"We are not sailors," quipped Aamira. "Oh no," she gasped before she leaned over the edge of the ship, vomiting again.

"We've been at sea for two weeks, and you're still vomiting as if it was day one," Khione said as she rubbed Aamira's back.

The sound of boots on the wooden deck approached the trio. "Ladies, we are approaching the Etruscan city of Tuscania. At least that is what the old records show," Uranus added. He stood two meters, with black hair, a thick eyebrow ridge, and olive-colored skin.

"Captain, I thought we were exploring? We've never contacted them," Gaia said.

Uranus smiled. "Just because you haven't contacted them doesn't mean we haven't had trade. There are cities all along the coasts."

"But we haven't sent that many boats out? Mostly fishing boats!" Gaia exclaimed.

"We've been meeting their caravans. Our hunting parties have continued to trade with them since we lost the old city," Aamira said, her hand moving to point off at the horizon. Her eyes rolled as she tried to stop herself from vomiting again. "Just because you," she burped, "didn't ask about our old charts, doesn't mean we didn't have a clue."

Gaia gave her friend a not-now look before turning to the captain. "Do we need anything from them then?"

"No, milady, we are stocked for three months out at sea," Uranus answered.

"Well, we should bypass the city, but I want to meet them. We are acting ambassadors, after all. Take us in," Gaia decided.

"Yes, milady," Uranus said with a click of his heels. He turned sharply and left the forecastle.

"That is so beautiful," Khione said right before Aamira tried to vomit again, but she only dry heaved. "Ok, so not that, but the view. The trees are different from our island."

"I hate you all so much right now," Aamira groaned as she slid down the bulkhead, holding her stomach.

"Haven't the sailors given you anything?" Gaia asked.

"They gave me a bag and wine," groaned Aamira. "Said to watch the waves, it would help. Fat load." She made an 'erp' sound and brought her hand to her mouth. "It's done."

"Oh wow, Aamira, you gotta see this. The crags that surround the beach are breathtaking to a snow girl like me," Khione said, awe coloring her voice.

Aamira groaned as she turned on her knees and pulled herself up. She gasped at the rich light blue water, the dolphins just under the waves Limestone cliffs lined the almost white sand, while brick houses lined the top of the cliffs. There was a zig-zagging staircase cut into the rock. In the distance, she could see several ships and docks. "You're right. That is amazing. You think we'll get to spend time on the beach?"

"It's a beach in the heat. It's the same thing as our beach," Khione said with disgust.

"But think about the party you could throw," Gaia pointed out.

The other two women gave Gaia a sideways glance. "You hate parties. It was the hardest part for you to learn," Aamira said.

Gaia laughed. "They are a place for everyone to mingle. They create families and they bond a community together. It also is a great cultural exchange. Our music and stories are different from theirs. Ours are blending the Annunaki and Human. How similar will tales be to our Human types?"

"That might be fun to learn. However, do we show our true selves, or do we mingle?" Aamira wondered.

"There are merits to both. However, discovering our larger forms will scare them more in the long term," Gaia commented.

"Yes, but they might assume we are Denisovans," Khione said.

"It's a risk we'll have to take," Gaia decided.

"What about Papsukkal?" Khione suddenly asked.

"What about him?" Aamira wondered.

"He's a talking lizard person. How will they react to him?" Khione shrugged her shoulders, her face showing concern.

Gaia hissed, her nose wrinkling. "They would probably try to kill him, like what happened when the Anunnaki landed. We'll introduce him after we can brace the locals for something not human looking."

"We could, but what about the King? Do you think he'll be alright with learning later that there is an Alien in his city?" Aamira asked before she swallowed hard, the back of her hand coming to her mouth.

Glancing to the shore, Gaia sighed. "Okay, ladies, it's time to dress to impress," she said as the boat was nearing the dock before leading the other women below deck.

They slid the gangplank across to the dock, the sound of seagulls and rope straining mixed with waves sloshing against hulls. Waiting on the pier were three men wearing light clothing with a blue sash and a small boat pinned on the right shoulder. Uranus walked down the ramp, wearing dark blue clothes and a cap that matched.

"Papers?" asked the lead person on the dock.

"Greetings. We are distant travelers looking for others to trade with," Uranus answered.

The man sighed and held out his hand. "Papers, please."

"It's hard to have papers for a place you've never been to. This is Gaia's Rest, and we are representatives of Olympus," Uranus explained.

"If you do not produce your papers, your entire crew will be arrested," said the man.

"Do you not listen?" snapped Uranus.

"If you had never visited our shores, then how do you speak our language? Since you do, you should know what to do," sniped the administrator.

"That is because of my magic," Gaia's voice boomed from the quarterdeck of the ship. Her hair was braided with gold and silver strands that complimented her purple top, showing her shoulders and midriff while complementing her skirt. Khione stood behind her left shoulder, wearing light blues and greys but in the same style, her skirt hemmed with silver. On Gaia's right, Aamira wore a matching red edged with silver. Standing behind them was someone dressed in armor that seemed to absorb the light but moved like a snake's skin.

"Are you to expect us to believe that a giant has magic and hasn't heard of us before? Your kind are always raiding across the sea," spat the administrator.

"That is up to you, but do you want to tell your King that you rejected gold and gemstones that we have brought to show our friendship?" Gaia asked as a sailor lifted a box with jewelry. "Come, Captain, I will spend my gold elsewhere. Perhaps these Denisovans they speak of would be more welcoming to Olympus."

"Perhaps I could look the other way," the administrator said as he extended his hand, palm up.

"I am perfectly willing to pay docking fees, but blatant bribes, no. Come, Captain, we are not welcome, and our gold is no good here," Gaia hissed.

"Now, wait a minute," the Administrator said.

Gaia raised her eyebrow. "Yes?"

"You said you represent Olympus?" the Administrator asked, writing something on his clipboard.

"Yes, and the ship's name is Gaia's Rest," Uranus answered.

"Got it." The Administrator wrote a few more notes. "Lukas, will you escort the ambassadors to King Acominatus?"

"It would be my pleasure," Lukas replied. He looked in his early twenties and stood just under two meters with dark hair that hung lightly around his face.

"Very well. Guards, attend us," Gaia said, holding her head aloft.

An Annunaki stepped out of the shadows. He was dressed in body armor from his head to his tail tip that glistened purple, black, and green like snakeskin. Embossed over the right side of his chest was his hunter's mark, identifying him as a hunt leader. His tail twitched slightly as he walked the gangplank, sniffing the air despite the apparent lack of nostrils on the suit. On his right hip was a long blade, while a pistol was on the left. The handle of the pistol glowed green with a white liquid floating in it.

The three men stepped back. "What in the Gods' name is that?" snarled the Administrator.

"That's the head of my retinue. He keeps us safe just in case you have any ideas about taking our wealth for yourself," Gaia hotly said as she followed the Annunaki.

"What is it?" asked the Administrator, his voice squeaking.

"A God," growled Papsukkal, the suit's microphone slightly distorting his voice. "Take us to your King now, human."

"Let's all go," the Administrator said in a shaky voice. "I'm Maximus Attaliates. This is Lukas Leppercian and Justinian Palaeglous."

"I am Princess Gaia Enkisdottir, This is Khione Boreasdottir, Aamira Kandottir, and my guard is my Sa-Tan, Papsukkal," introduced the goddess.

"It has a name?" asked Maximus, shock clear on his face.

"I have a name," growled Papsukkal, his nose almost touching Maximus' own.

"It's," Maximus swallowed hard, "he isn't a pet?"

"No, little man, I am a God. I am an apex predator. I could rip your spine out before you felt the pain. I help Lady Gaia because she's of my Sky Lord's line and because I choose to. Is that urine I smell?" asked Papsukkal in his gravelly voice.

"No," squeaked Maximus.

"Good, now take us to your King. I will not ask again," growled Papsukkal.

"Right this way," Lukas said, his hand gesturing down the dock. The group entered the town. The structures were made from mud and stone, with several buildings made from marble and had columns with grooves that ran from top to bottom.

"What is that thing?" came a shout. It was an older man, his salt and pepper hair almost like a crown around his temples. He held a golden staff and pointed it at Papsukkal.

"Pontiff Kurkuas, we are escorting royalty from abroad to King Acominatus," called out Lukas.

"Who dares claim to be of royal blood? Not that thing or the mindless giants, so who do you think you are taking to see the King?" spat Kurkuas.

"They have gold and gems," Maximus said.

"Pigs can find gemstones. It doesn't make them of royal blood. Who are you, and what is your lineage? Why should we accept a giant as equal to the royals like me? Much less one with a demon as a servitor," Kurkuas demanded.

"I am not a demon. I am a God," Papsukkal said.

"It talks," cried Kurkuas. "Blessed followers of the Aten, cast your eyes from the demon. Cover your ears so that you may not fall sway to its lies. There is only one God, and that is the Aten," he said in a loud voice.

"Can I eat him?" asked Papsukkal in a soft hiss.

"No, my friend," Gaia whispered as she stepped forward. "I am Princess Gaia, first daughter of Prince Enki, son of Deacon Enlil, son of Sky Lord Anu, son of Sky Mistress Belet-ṣeri, daughter of Sky Lord Uranus."

"Words, words, and more words. You are a giant who's learned the noble tongue. Why should we allow you to speak your lies to our King? Why should we allow demons near him?" Kurkuas demanded as he walked closer to the party. His staff tapped the stone with every other step, calling attention to him with each thud.

"Ice tomb?" whispered Khione.

"I do not know of this Aten you speak of, but a God that does not welcome others into his flock will soon lose his flock," Gaia called out. "We are from the Southern Islands, the Aegeans. My lineage returned to these lands after a long voyage among the stars. Long have we worked upon our new home. We merely wish to extend the hand of friendship to those around us. We bring gold and gemstones for a trade of spices and cloth. If you do not wish to engage in trade, we will depart. We simply ask to know what your territorial limits are, so we may avoid trespassing upon your lands."

"Demons often come bearing gifts," spat Kurkuas.

"Enough, Kurkuas, you are not King," a male voice echoed through the square.

Turning, the Pontiff dropped to a knee. "My liege."

A man wearing a golden circlet entered the area. He wore a purple cloak with golden thread woven along the hem, and a loose green and blue shirt that left his arms bare. Around his waist was a thick leather belt that held up a loose kilt made of yellow and green stripes. His feet had leather sandals that wrapped up to his knees. "It is not upon you to dictate who speaks with us. If the giants will speak rationally, then we will speak with them. Aten demands us to always open our arms to the peaceful."

The King turned to Gaia as he tilted his head to her. "We bid you welcome to our fine city. I am King Mirded Ptochoprodromus. Let us adjourn to the welcoming room and treat as two royals."

Gaia held her hand out, her eyes sweeping the scene. "My

entourage and I would welcome a moment of your time."

Mirded kissed the back of Gaia's hand with a smile. "Milady, what do I call you?"

"I am Princess Gaia," the large woman said as the pair walked down the street, heading deeper into the city. The group followed slightly behind the two, with the priest giving the large women an evil eye. "These are my sisters, Princesses Khione and Aamira. My Sa-Tan Papsukkal, he assists us with our needs and provides protection."

The King glanced back at Papsukkal, who kept half a step behind Gaia and the King. "Forgive me, Sa-Tan, but we have not seen your kind before. Where do you hail from?"

"The heavens," Papsukkal answered.

"We have much to discuss, and Papsukkal's origins will be part of that. It contains sensitive information that you might not want your subjects to know, King Ptochoprodromus," Gaia said with a slight head tilt.

"Please call me Mirded. May I call you Gaia?" asked Mirded.

"You may," Gaia replied.

"I look forward to hearing your story. It sounds like it will be fascinating," Mirded said.

"As your time is limited, could you give us a brief history of your lands?" Gaia asked.

Mirded gave a smile that lit up his face. "After the anger of Aten, the tribes of men came together as one people. We had many city-states, but that event transformed us into a unified nation. The

Giants come from Asia by sea, often pillaging a town, thus the fear you are seeing from my citizens."

"Thought that was the huge Lizard-man," Papsukkal grunted, causing the King to laugh.

"No, we do not have a good history with the Giants, but if you truly hail from the south, then we welcome a new nation of Denisovan's," Mirded said.

"We are not related to the giants you speak of," Gaia corrected him.

"You are not? But you consort with demons," snarled Kurkuas.

Papsukkal turned his head to look at Kurkuas. "Little man, do you want to antagonize someone who can remove your spine in a single move?"

"Please, Pontiff, let us hear their story before condemning them," Mirded ordered.

"Yes, milord," said Kurkuas, his head bowed.

The group entered a square full of vendor shops. The open expanse was lined with a street marking off a field. An open-air market was selling fruits and vegetables. The roads that led into the square had shops selling furniture, clothing, luggage, and many places serving food. The courtyard had two roads coming in on each side, with shops that lined those streets. A path through the crowd quickly opened, allowing the King and party to pass through.

As they passed a shop, several kinds of meat rotated next to a fire from a man turning a crank. "May I ask what that is?" wondered Gaia.

"We call this a shawarma. You have beef, lamb, and geese to choose as your meats," the shopkeeper explained with a smile. "My liege, may I offer you and your guests a selection from my shop?"

"We would not object to a chance to taste the local delights," Gaia said as she turned to look at Mirded. "However, we understand that the matters of State that we must discuss require immediate attention."

"Shopkeeper, please send a meal to the royal palace. We shall discuss our matters over lunch," Mirded said as he dropped a bag of money on the counter.

"Milord, we couldn't possibly charge you for-" the shopkeeper said but was interrupted by Mirded's raised hand.

"Nonsense. We are placing a rather large order for delivery. I will let the guards know to expect delivery from," Mirded stepped back to read the sign, "Mango's Shawarma Shack. Are you Mango?"

"Yes, milord. No one can resist the Mango,," he said with a wide smile.

"What's a mango?" whispered Khione to Aamira, who shrugged.

"Very well. I shall expect a feast in an hour," Mirded said before anyone else could speak. He sharply turned and walked away. He entered a roadway that had more upscale homes while the group followed. "This is among the original settlements from when our roaming tribes settled here. We are celebrating our five hundredth anniversary in a few weeks."

"Five hundred years united. That is something few cultures can say," Gaia commented as they walked by a fountain that had four spouts with a center one that lifted well above the others.

"When did your people unite?" Mirded asked as they turned to the path to the palace.

"The Annunaki and Humans united around the time of the last storm of the Gods," Gaia answered.

"That long? Your people are indeed old," Mirded said as a guard opened the side gate for them. "Welcome to the Palace."

"Magnificent," Gaia commented. The structure stood thirty meters, with half a dozen columns supporting a red clay tile roof. Recessed within was a two-story complex with red siding. The side wings were about seventy-five meters long and twenty meters tall. The stairs leading to the front were on a light slope that was lined with nerium and bougainvillea. There was a stream that went through the left side before falling into a pond that held fish.

"What stone are the white columns made of? Kulla would love to work with it," said Khione.

"That's called marble. We must import it from the northern mountains several days' ride away," explained Mirded. "It is the finest in Europe and Asia. Where do you hail from?"

"We call our lands Olympus. If we could see one of your maps, I would gladly show you," Gaia answered. "Regardless, we traveled from the southeast, between the islands. We didn't see any settlements to visit, but we might have missed them."

"You are in the sea of the Kraken then," Mirded said.

"What is this Kraken?" asked Gaia.

"It is a squid thrice the size of our largest ships. The creature often takes a ship in one attack from below, its long tentacles wrapping around and pulling it under the waves. It has long kept our ships from venturing that far from the shores of Asia," explained Mirded as they climbed the steps.

"My people have stories of such creatures, but they have not been seen within living memory," Aamira said.

"You speak as if you are separate from one another," Mirded commented.

"We each reside with our subjects, mingling with several tribes from the islands and the coast of Asia. We all live in harmony around Mount Olympus," Gaia said.

"I look forward to learning more. If you wait within the dining hall, I have some arrangements to make," Mirded said with a slight bow.

"Of course, we understand the needs of the State," Gaia answered as the party entered a large room with a long table that could seat at least forty. The marble columns lining the walls had golden creatures carved into them, while the flooring was polished wood.

A servant moved to pull a chair out from the table, causing the King to pause. "I'm sorry, but I don't have something your size. Let me have a rug delivered for you to sit upon."

Gaia tilted her head as she spoke. "Mirded, I would not worry about that," she said before shifting suddenly. Her form deflated with every step until she was the same size as the King. The other two Humanaki, shrank with Gaia as they moved to take their seats.

The King blinked a few times before turning to the Pontiff. "Kurkuas, figure out what magic that was. Be nice about it. I have letters to write," he harshly whispered before rushing out of the room.

Pontiff Kurkuas gave a wicked smile behind his King's back. "By your command."

Chapter 19:

The moment the King was out of earshot, Pontiff Kurkuas snapped his fingers. "Guards, ensure no one interrupts us. We shall not allow their heathen ways to worm into our lives." He walked over to a stand that held several decanters. He poured wine for five before hesitating for a moment. He gritted his teeth and placed the pewter drinkware on the table.

Gaia flashed the Pontiff a smile before sampling the wine. "Is this a mulberry wine? From sixty-seven?" She sipped the wine again. "No, it's from sixty-six. Aged twenty-six years, cut with water from a lead decanter."

"It is from four-fifty, which was twenty-six years ago," Kurkuas said, shock crossing his face. "What witchcraft allowed you to know that?" he spat.

"The flavor? We produce wine. Those two summers left a distinct taste that every wine we've made has, thus providing a timeline," Gaia explained as the other two women sipped their own wine. At the same time, Papsukkal watched from the corner of the room.

Setting down his goblet, Kurkuas narrowed his eyes. "Regardless of your taste in wine, why should I not have you three dragged out of the palace for the crime of witchcraft? We could overlook the demon as it has done nothing but the blatant usurpation of the Aten's power. No, that is something that demands the inquisition."

"We, however, follow the Great Mother, Tiamat. We are welcome as healers, educators, explorers, and part of every walk of life by our laws. Your liege did not seem bothered by the display. If it is offensive, we will refrain from using our powers," Gaia offered.

"The word of the Aten says that there is but one God, and that is him," Kurkuas said as he picked up a scroll. "The scroll of Kath describes the truth of our Lord," he explained before handing the item to Gaia. "Will you read his word?"

"I will read. I make no other promise," Gaia replied as she sat the scroll in front of her. "Are you aware that lead causes insanity and reduced intelligence?"

"Nonsense, lead is the Aten's gift to man. It can be used in so many things. The scroll of Simon details all the uses," Kurkuas said, his chest puffing up.

Gaia glanced at Aamira, who was rubbing her eyes in frustration. "I would love a copy of your religious texts."

"Oh, only the priests can read them," Kurkuas said.

Picking up the scroll, Gaia gestured with it at the Pontiff. "So, you expect me to read this, how?"

"Oh, I'm sending a priest to convert your lands with you, so he'll read you the will of Aten," Kurkuas said in a tone that offered no challenge.

"What? Why would we allow your citizens in our lands?" Khione asked with a snort.

"All belongs to the great Aten. We've spread his word all up and down the lands, to the mountains. Aten has protected us from the Giants and from the Neanderthals. The fact you are here is a sign from him he is extending his rule," explained Kurkuas.

Aamira gave Khione a look that screamed 'take a load of the arrogance'. "What if we are happy with our faiths?" she asked.

"Then the cleansing fire of the Aten shall remove all as he struck the ground and drove our very civilization together. It has been many years since the third crusade. The fourth shall commence, if necessary," Kurkuas said as he held his goblet in both hands, his elbows on the table. "God willing, of course."

"Of course," Khione agreed with an eye-roll.

"Why have you not gone beyond the mountains?" asked Aamira.

Kurkuas sat his goblet down. "We haven't, because we had to divert the third crusade into Asia. We pillaged many lands, removed many Giants and their filth from the lands."

"Your King implied your people didn't have a foothold in Asia," Gaia said.

"That is true," Kurkuas shrugged.

"That means the third crusade was not as successful as you suggest," Gaia pointed out.

"We did what we set out to do. The beasts shall not mess with the Kingdom of Etrusica," spat Kurkuas.

The trio glanced at each other before Aamira leaned forward. "Who did you lose to them?"

"My son," Kurkuas said harshly. "Do not worry about his soul. The will of Aten shall guide my hand. The word of Aten shall wash over the four corners of the Kiskia."

"Can you tell us what the Kiskia is?" Khione asked.

Kurkuas grabbed another scroll and unrolled it over the table.

"The Aten resides in the solar disc in the dome of the heavens. The lights at night are how Aten watches over everyone, reforming into the light of God every morning. Eventually, the ice wall surrounds us, keeping us from falling off the edge."

"Wait, do you think the planet is flat?" Khione snorted.

"What is a planet?" the Pontiff asked.

Aamira sighed as she picked up the scroll that was given to Gaia. She opened it, scanning through it. Gaia smiled at Kurkuas. "A planet is an enormous sphere that is in the void of space. You might have observed several in the night sky."

"The eyes of Aten, constantly moving and watching all of us, so says the scroll of Mantota," Kurkuas explained. "It is forbidden to look at the eyes of our god."

"Right. The eyes of Aten are planets in orbit around the sun," Gaia explained.

"Blasphemy!" shouted Kurkuas. "Heresy shall not be permitted within these walls," he snarled.

"The truth shall set you free," Aamira said. "So says the scroll of Simon, does it not?"

Kurkuas reared up, shock on his face. "You said you were not aware of the word of Aten. How do you quote it to me?"

"It says it right here," Aamira answered, running her finger along a line. She looked at Gaia. "It's the same language passed down as the words of Femi and of the council of Chiefs."

"Then you should already know that we are the rightful faith and Lords of your lands," Kurkuas said with a wicked grin.

Aamira snorted loudly. "I'm sorry, what? Gaia, look at this." She glanced at the angry look of Kurkuas. "No, not whatever you said but this line. It says that lead shall never be used with products that are drunk or eaten," she recited as she slid the scroll over to Gaia.

"She's right. How can we trust your word when you can't translate your God's sacred texts correctly?" Gaia asked with a pointed look at Kurkuas.

"Lies, all lies. Only the priests of Aten can read his writings. Women are not worthy of understanding his great tongue," Kurkuas spat.

"Apparently not. I can read it as well," Khione said with a smirk.

Kurkuas slammed his hands onto the table, leaning forward as his face reddened with his rage. "You know nothing about Aten. You are nothing. I am your better in every way by the fact I am a man. You are women, worth nothing more than growing our tiny babies within you. You do not belong anywhere but in the house. Women simply can't understand anything more than cooking or making our clothes. Why your men allowed you to leave, only Aten knows. Why he would allow it to happen will forever escape me."

"You want to calm down," Papsukkal growled, the edge of his blade under Kurkuas' throat. "They are Princesses of Olympus. You will respect them as they are your better in every way possible."

"And you are a filthy demon, born to subvert man. Perhaps these unnatural women are also demons, as Giants cannot change their shapes. Kill me, and my people will rise and remove your filth from the presence of Aten. Remove your blade, beast. You have no power here," Kurkuas snarled.

"Then calm yourself," repeated Papsukkal.

"You first," Kurkuas spat.

"If I was angry, your head would be on the table," Papsukkal growled.

"Enough," said the King in a loud voice. "Pontiff Kurkuas, you are no longer required to attend us. Depart, now."

"My Lord," Kurkuas said, leaning back from the table as Papsukkal put his sword away, "they are blasphemous and require the cleansing fires."

"They are guests in my house. Aten demands that we respect our guests. You will do well to remember that. Now leave. We will speak before the festival," Mirded commanded. With a huff, the Pontiff stormed out of the room. "Please, do not think ill of all of us. He means well and has passion."

Gaia bowed her head slightly. "Think nothing of it. There was no harm done."

"Thank you. Our mid-day meal has arrived with many of the city leaders. If you are feeling up to it, shall we break bread together?" Mirded asked.

"That would be acceptable," Gaia answered with a smile.

"Thank you, my King, for allowing the Mango to serve you," said the shawarma shopkeeper as he carved meat for the party.

Chapter 20:

Gaia looked at her plate, doubt crossing her face as she glanced around for a knife and fork. "Pardon me, Mr. Mango, but how do you eat this?" she asked as she leaned over to the man placing a plate in front of Khione.

"Why, you pick it up and bite it," said the royal food taster, who stood next to the King's chair as he picked up his liege's plate and took a large bite. He chewed slowly before placing the plate in front of his King.

The King mouthed 'thank you' to Gaia as other plates were given to the rest of the guests. Once everyone was served their food and drinks, the King tentatively took a bite of his shawarma. He nodded before swallowing. "Mango, please make arrangements with my cooking staff to have this delivered at least monthly," he instructed as he stood. "I welcome my guests to partake of the provided feast. We hope we can have Etruscan and the Olympian Kingdoms form an alliance, or at the very least trade. I invite everyone to eat and converse," he said with his arms spreading wide before sitting back down.

"Milord, where are the Giants?" asked an older man with a full head of white hair sitting to the king's left. He was wearing a red sash over his tunic.

"Lord Shen, the three women across from you are they. It turns out that they can reduce their sizes," the King explained.

"That's not possible," gasped a younger man with dark hair and a short beard sitting next to Khione. He wore a green sash over his tunic.

"Basil, I witnessed it with my own eyes. After the meal, perhaps our visitors will show us again," suggested Mirded.

"Yes, but what about what the word of Aten and what says about magic?" asked a man. He wore an eyepatch and sat to the right of the King.

"That is a good question, Paola, but these women can read the old texts better than our own Pontiff. Perhaps the Aten sent them to us to show us how we've gone astray. I, for one, look forward to learning more about their history and opening up trade with them," Mirded said.

"Do you worship Aten as well?" asked Basil.

Gaia placed her shawarma on her plate before speaking. "We do not worship deities, but we acknowledge those who live on another plane of existence that we visit between our mortal lives."

"Are they not your God then?" asked Paola.

"I guess one could consider the Great Mother and Father Gods. However, they are more like front-line managers with the Grandfather and Grandmother as middle management," Gaia explained.

"Front-line? Middle management? What is this management you speak of?" asked Shen.

"The person in charge and then the person in charge of that person," Gaia said as she fought an eye roll.

"You worship them, then?" asked Basil.

"No, they are more the caretakers of the energy of our souls. We return to their dimensions, where we meet with the Great Mother and Father. Once we've reached a level of development, we are allowed to ascend to the next dimensional plane. This is a very diluted view of our afterlife," Gaia explained.

"So, you ascend to heaven after a time in purgatory?" asked the King.

"That is one way to view it," Khione said.

"If your God does not exist, then who gives you the power to change shapes? The Great Mother?" asked Mirded before he took another bite of his meal.

"The Annunaki," Gaia started, with a nod to Papsukkal. He had yet to eat or expose his face. "They use a staff to assist an organ that can access the background radiation. This allows them limited actions. The Humanaki," Gaia gestured to her friends, "were created by my father. He enhanced the organ's connection to this background energy, allowing us many abilities."

"But you said you didn't have a God. How were you created then, if not by a God?" asked Basil.

"Those among the Annunaki understand the very building blocks of life and can manipulate them. One such person is my father, Sa-Tan Enki. He adjusted those blocks and created the Humanaki," Gaia explained.

"Then your father is a God, as only a God can create life," said Shen as he leaned back in his chair from shock.

Gaia shot him a look of disbelief. "Did he though? Did he? He worked from your form and," she paused as a thought crossed her face. "Oh, do you know that if you build a bunch of magnifying glasses, you can look at the parts that make you, you, right?"

"What?" snapped Basil. "What do you mean that if you, oh, stack the glass and it gets bigger and bigger, you can see really small things."

"Does that mean that she's telling the truth?" asked Shen.

"Oh yes, she probably is. Now that she's explained how we could do it, it makes sense. I'll have to run some tests. Perhaps we could exchange something for this tech?" Basil asked.

Khione nodded. "I am sure we could come to an agreement in a later meeting."

"I will hold you to that," Basil said with a grin.

"I can see why the Pontiff was so angry at the Olympians. So much of what they represent is an antithesis of the Aten," Shen said.

Mirded closed his eyes, shaking his head slightly while pinching the bridge of his nose. "Our citizens will have issues with learning this. Oh, for the love of," he shook his head before sighing. "Jenkins, bring the Pontiff to my secondary chambers. We will need to have a conversation. Not my brightest idea to send him out to make up wild theories."

"Right away, milord," he replied with a nod before leaving.

Basil sipped his wine. "We've had a lot of shocks today. I think you can be forgiven."

"It is not our intention to cause dissonance within your lands," Gaia said.

The King waved the comment away. "Change brings unease among the traditionalists. We must continually grow, or else we will fall to invaders."

"The Pontiff seemed shocked that we could read the sacred texts," Aamira pointed out after wiping her mouth, her meal finished.

Basil dropped his wine goblet to the table, causing red wine to spill over his shawarma. Paolo blinked a few times in shock, looking for someone to say just kidding, while Shen lifted his goblet to Aamira with a wicked grin. "It seems that we have much to barter for," Shen said.

"Hang on. How do you construct all of this without writing?" asked Khione.

"Oh, we have written. We have only forgotten how to read the Aten's language," Mirded answered.

"Seems like it might be important to learn," Khione quipped.

"It was lost in the sacking of Hyelassus, our original capital, some three hundred years ago. Since then, only the Priesthood could learn it by decree of King Georgios Lecapenas," Mirded explained.

"Did he not teach his children how to read it?" Aamira scoffed.

"He was seven at the time of the decree. His uncle had been King. The Giants killed that entire branch of my family. It led to the first crusade," Mirded grimly replied.

"I would like to offer lessons to you, Mirded, as a gift between our two nations. Education should always be freely given," Gaia said with a smile.

"Thank you for that offer. I will accept your tutorship," Mirded said, tipping his head at Gaia.

Mango rushed back into the room, pushing a cart. "Hope everyone left room for dessert," he half sang with a wide grin. He placed a plate in front of Gaia. "I call this mafrukeh. It's a sweet and nutty dish."

Gaia took a small bite before she grinned at Mango. "It is very flaky. It almost melts in your mouth."

"Wonderful," Mango said with a clap of his hands. He quickly placed the dish in front of the others. "Thank you, my King, for the honor of serving our guests today."

Mirded raised his glass as he stood. "Thank you, Mango, for your delicious food. To Mango!" he yelled.

"To Mango!" the table shouted, lifting their drinks to the shopkeeper. His face flushed as he bowed several times and then fled the room.

"To new friends," Mirded said, lifting his glass to Gaia.

"To new friends!" the table called out. Servants came in, bringing bowls of warm water to wash their hands before the two groups mingled.

Mirded went up to Gaia with a smile. "My Lady, would you care to explore the palace garden?" he asked with a slight bow.

"Why, yes, yes I would," Gaia answered, smiling back at the King.

"Alert me when the Pontiff returns," the King instructed as they walked past the guards.

Chapter 21:

"Oh, wow," Gaia gasped as Mirded led her into the back of the palace. She could see a garden that covered multiple acres with water flowing through the center from various streams. Seeking sanctuary within were multiple animals, such as beavers, songbirds, several cats, deer, and others.

"This has been long considered the prize of our Kingdom, the Hanging Gardens of Tuscania. This is the centerpiece, where the gardens flow into. Beyond the rear wall of the palace has terraces," Mirded explained from one of the grand entrances.

Gaia slipped her sandals off before stepping onto lush grass. "We could make gardens like this, but we are so focused upon saving our way of life, no one stops to smell the flowers."

"I wish to show you something," Mirded said, waving Gaia deeper into the garden.

"Oh my, but we hardly know each other. Don't you think that's a little soon?"

"What? Oh. That's later. But for now, I'd like to know more about where you're from," Mirded explained as he led Gaia down a path.

The Lady of the Earth stopped to smell a red rose. "Exquisite. It was more than time to explore and experience what she offers," Gaia mumbled.

"Who offers?" Mirded asked.

"The planet we reside upon," Gaia said as she straightened.

Pointing to a mosaic, Mirded frowned. "I was going to ask you where you are from. That is the known disc. The Aten teaches us that we float upon a plate. He lives in the sky, just above the blankets of Aten's blindness."

Shaking her head, Gaia walked around the tilemap. "The Annunaki come from beyond the skies. Father landed beyond this point." She pointed beyond the largest island in the southwest. "From there, we contacted your race. The idiot hunters tried to kill the humans for food."

"Hunters? Like your walking Lizard?" Mirded asked.

"Yes, but no. He is my assistant and guard. He is a dear friend and confidant. After a touch-and-go first contact and my father's discovery of, well, for the lack of a better term, magic." Gaia held her hand up to stop the coming comment. "It's the same reason I can change my size to blend in. The flaw of the Annunaki is that they no longer can access the system's power easily, save for a few. My father is one of them, as he caused a solar storm when we arrived."

Mirded gasped. "That is the last time Aten's wrath struck. Are you saying your father caused that? Is it not proof that the Aten is the one true God?"

Taking Mirded's hand, Gaia smiled at the man. "We can trace the actions to the storm. Enki worked with our Femi's to learn control. This led to my father expanding his experiments, and that led to my birth."

"But he's a Lizard-person, right? He's your adopted father then?" Mired asked as he sank to a marble bench.

"The way you'd understand it, we are of blood. Our knowledge of the universe allows that. All the Olympians have the same blue blood as the Annunaki. This gives strange compatibility, making us effectively the same species if you consider that as a definition of a species," Gaia said as she sat next to the King.

"Oh, kinda like a mule," Mirded suggested.

"What is a mule?"

"A mule is the offspring of a male donkey and a female horse."

"How odd," Gaia commented as she stood, moving to look at a deer eating the grass. "What do you call that creature?"

"That is a red-tailed deer," Mirded said as he stepped next to her. "Do you not have deer?"

Gaia let out a soft giggle. "No, we do more fishing, but we do hunt these large grey creatures, elephants, that are about four meters tall."

Mirded's face scrunched up. "What is a meter?"

"About this far," Gaia said, holding her hands apart. "Four meters is roughly the same height as I was."

"They seem rather big. How do you hunt them?"

"Sometimes when the herds grow too large for the island to support, we hunt them. We only take what we need. We have fields, but we do a lot of our growing within growing chambers underground. Still, those are failing," Gaia explained as she sat on a water bank, letting her bare feet dip into the water.

"How do you grow underground?"

"You provide special lights. However, we can't fix them, so when they break, they are gone forever."

"Why can't you fix them? If you made them, you should know how to repair them."

Gaia let out a sigh, her hair cascading down as she bowed her head. "We still have to teach the Humans how to make the electronics."

"Teach the what?" Mirded looked confused.

"Things beyond this world," Gaia shrugged.

Mirded shook his head. "So much that we don't know."

"We are always learning. I don't know how to repair the devices, but my father does. He has a few classes planned when he gets back from the Nibiru."

"Where is this Nibiru?"

"Far away. It will take him fifteen years to get there and at least the same to return."

"He will be an old man, if not dead, by the time he returns," Mirded said as he took Gaia's hand.

"We age far slower. The whole trip for him would be like a week to you," Gaia corrected him with a slight smile as a fish investigated her legs.

"How old are you?" Mirded asked, his face confused and his head tilted.

"I am fifty-seven. I am still a child to the Annunaki and shouldn't be a full-grown adult, but my sisters and I played with something we didn't understand and grew up. My father thinks the Olympians will remain as children for about eighty to a hundred years."

Mirded blinked a few times before shaking his head to clear it. "You are twenty years my senior, but look like you're twenty years my junior," he said as he stood and started pacing. "What is the magic that slows your aging like this?"

"The same building blocks of life I talked about over the noon meal. There is a lot to it, but it basically means that my body repairs itself better than your body. I can die from decapitation, blood loss, or any number of physical wounds. Still, old age is something that I don't have to worry about for a very long time," Gaia answered as she tucked her hair behind her ear.

"How old is your father, and do they live as long as you?"

"My father is about three thousand years old. Lord Enlil is ten thousand, while the Sky-Lord is nearing nineteen thousand. His younger brother, Chronos, is about twelve thousand," Gaia explained as she lightly splashed the water with her feet.

"How long is a year?" gasped Mirded from shock.

"A year is three-hundred and sixty-five days. A day is twenty-four hours. The same as your day and year."

Mirded tried to speak a few times, blinked a few more, then let out a slow breath. "All alright, I can't fathom life spans like that. Do you expect the same life-times?"

"Probably, but my father expects me to live to at least thirty-thousand."

"The things you'll see in that time," Mirded said in awe. "Why are you wasting time with me? You have all the time in the world. Does time even matter to the Olympians?"

"Time can blend for us, but it matters. We are also not afraid of a task that might take a few years to complete."

"I could see that. To live that long would be a blessing."

"The children I grew up with are old men and women now. Only Khione and Aamira have aged with me, and even that's not the same."

"What do you mean?"

"That's not important, just different."

Mirded shook his head. "Yeah, wow. So much to process here, just wow."

"Cultural exchanges work both ways. How long have you ruled?"

"Five years. My father passed away in his sleep."

"Well, you said the kingdom has been around for five-hundred years. Surely something happened in that time frame."

"The first crusade was two hundred and thirty-five years ago. We captured the peninsula in that war. Aten was very much with us." Mirded shook his head. "Well, apparently, he isn't real, so he wasn't."

Gaia took the King's hands. "The warrior spirit can take strength from a cause they believe in. You could say he was with you."

"I guess. The second and third crusades, we attempted to bring Aten to the barbarians to the east. Aten was not with us in those days, no matter what the Cult of Aten claims. We won the early battles, took several strongholds and cities, but we could not hold against the Giants. Just to take down one of their warriors, twenty men died. We just didn't have the numbers to fight them." Mirded sighed as he dipped a goblet into the stream, handing Gaia some water before drinking his own.

The King ran his fingers through his hair. "The Pontiff, however, preaches a revised history where we walked in and laid waste to their lands. That we left of our own free will because the Aten now lives in the Giant's hearts or something. The faith has been trying to draw up for a fourth crusade. The commoners have been donating a lot of their wages."

"Sounds like they are scamming the followers of Aten. We will translate the texts during our voyages. We plan on sailing around the world."

"You can't sai-," Mirded snapped his jaw closed and shook his head. "No, you can do that."

"Perhaps for local spices, we could provide an accurate map of the world?"

"That would be more than acceptable. What about other things, such as education?"

"I will have to speak to the Sky Lord as to what he willfully allows. Maps and goods exchange, not a problem. More than that." Gaia shrugged. "I'll need permission. We were not expecting to find such cities as they didn't exist when we mapped the planet. The locals we met lived in mud huts with a wooden wall and a cave to hide in."

Mirded chuckled. "Why would they hide in a cave?"

"That event that you called Aten's wrath, they feared it and worshiped the sky figures. They later would become part of Olympus, merging with the Adama to become one," Gaia explained.

They heard heavy footsteps coming closer to the pair.

"My Lord," called out the Paige between heavy pants, "The Pontiff has riled the city up and has taken Khione and Aamira hostage. We tried to stop them from entering the palace, but some guards betrayed us and took the women."

Gaia snorted. "Welp, I hope that your Pontiff likes fire and ice because he's playing with both."

Chapter 22:

"Where are the Giants?" someone screamed. Khione and Aamira knelt on the ground at the top of the Palace steps, their arms bound behind their back. They remained in their smaller forms.

"These are two of the Giants. We have sent a runner to collect the third," said a guard.

"A runner? What good would he do?" asked someone from the crowd.

"The King is with her, so having them come of their free will is easier. No matter, we will burn the witches anyway," the Pontiff explained to great cheers from the crowd. At the back of the citizens, a portion of them had a pyre and poles being set up.

"Oh, no!" Aamira screamed. "Not the fire, anything but fire. Our gods demand our bodies be intact," she sobbed.

Khione gave her friend a sideways glance before she cried out, "Without our bodies, our souls can't find their way to the afterlife! Please, anything but the fire."

"Burn the witches!" the crowd chanted.

The Pontiff had a smug look on his face as he bent down and whispered in Aamira's ear. "In what world did you think a woman and a Giant could outwit a man?"

"Clearly, not your tiny world," grunted Aamira.

"What is this?" demanded the King from the door. "They are our guests, envoys from another land. The Aten demands we offer our hospitality."

The Pontiff turned, smiling at the King. "The Aten demands non-believers to be stricken from the very ground we walk on. The holy writ demands that witches perish. What did you think was going to happen? Do you really think you are the one the people follow? We learned long ago that we got all the benefits of being King with none of the downsides. You get to take the blame for everything we do. It really is too bad that you are without a direct heir, but alas, the next King I select will be better for Aten." He pointed to a guard. "Bind both of them." Six men drew their blades and lifted them to Gaia and Mirded. Another used rope to tie their hands behind their backs.

Gaia shook her head. "You do not understand what you're messing with."

Kurkuas let out a belly laugh. "What? Three women who can shape-shift. Even if you had Giant strength, there is more than enough of us to slit your throats. Bring them," he ordered as he turned and headed for the poles. There were four stakes with wood piled around them. Someone was dumping pitch over the wood. They tied the four of them to the poles.

"Any last words, my traitor of a King?" Kurkuas asked.

"There is nothing to say to you," Mirded spat.

"Then I cast you to the Aten. May he have mercy upon your soul," Kurkuas replied. "Time to die," he said as he took a torch and tossed it onto the pitch.

Aamira laughed as the fire wrapped around them. "You really did it. You actually tossed us into the fire." She snapped her fingers, causing the fire to twist into a snake before wrapping around her bonds. The rope burned away before the snake ate the ropes of the others.

"Guards, kill them!" bellowed Kurkuas. Several guards strung bows as others looked at each other.

"Are you sure you want to attack someone who can control fire?" Aamira asked.

"Draw!" yelled a guard. "Aim and fire."

Gaia leaped over the fire, her foot slamming into the ground. A wall of stone shot around them, blocking the arrows and cutting them off from their attackers. Khione helped the King down. "Are you alright?" Gaia asked.

"Yes, just shook up," Mirded answered. "You all have actual powers. That wasn't a lie."

"Nope, not at all," Gaia said as she put her hands on the wall. The stone shifted to angle the top to prevent arrows from going over. Khione waved her hand, that created an ice lattice to help protect them.

"Kill them all," snarled the Pontiff, his voice dimmed by the thick wall.

"Now what?" Mirded asked.

"Well, where is Papsukkal?" Gaia responded.

"He had stepped out for a bathroom before the attack," Khione said.

"We wait for him then," Gaia said as she sat cross-legged on the ground, her wrists resting on her knees. The sound of ice cracking came from above them from arrow impacts.

"Did we not tell them I control fire?" asked Aamira.

Khione giggled. "yes we did, but apparently they don't remember."

"What are your powers?" asked Mirded.

"I am summer and fire," Aamira answered with her hands doing a 'ta-da' gesture.

"Winter and ice," Khione said as she pointed up.

"I am the planet. I can feel the core burning, the shifting of the continents, metals within the dirt. I can control stone. I can feel the weight of the three hundred and seventy-seven humans on the other side of the wall. Papsukkal is coming around the back of the building," Gaia explained as she pointed her finger at the back wall and opened a doorway.

"My Lady, you are unharmed?" Papsukkal asked as he poked his head through the new door.

"We are fine. Let's get back to the ship," Gaia said as she pulled out a communicator. "Captain, prepare for departure. We have outstayed our welcome."

"Aye aye," came the response.

"Papsukkal, plan Theta-seven," Gaia ordered as stone flew to her wrist and formed a large shield. The moment Khione noticed, she grew her own ice shield.

"I don't have the ammo for Theta-seven. Kappa-Nine would work better," Papsukkal said as he drew his blade.

"What about Gaia making a tunnel for us and walking under the city?" asked Mirded.

"My body can't channel power for that long, at least not at a flow that doesn't cause a Coronal Mass Ejection, or known as the Wrath of Ra," Gaia explained. "The planet has amazing stores of energy, but tapping into them takes preparation and time that we don't have. Quick power is drawn from the Heavens, which causes the sun to refill the void left." She closed the door after Mirded stepped through.

"So where does that leave us?" asked Mirded as he led them out of the palace.

"Fire and ice," Khione and Aamira said together.

"I'll provide the defense while they push forward," Papsukkal said.

"What about Gaia?" asked Mirded. "Hang on, let me put on at least a chest plate and a blade." He stepped into one of the palace armories and moments later walked out as he slid a chest plate over his head. A short sword rested upon a new belt. "Come on, this way," he instructed as he turned down a narrow hall. "This is to the servant's quarters. There are several exits that way that few know about."

"We'll follow your lead," Papsukkal said.

They took a set of stairs, wrapping around before entering the kitchen. "Milord!" several shouted as they knelt.

"There is no time for pleasantries. The Pontiff has overthrown me and we must escape. Can I count on you not to betray me as he did?" Mirded asked.

"We would never," said the head chef. "My family has kept the royal line fed for generations."

"My friend, we are blessed to have you, but I must escape. I also am asking you to stay behind for your family's sake," the King replied with sorrow in his voice.

"Of course, milord."

"Sleep," Gaia whispered, causing the servants to drop into a deep sleep.

"What happened?" demanded Mirded as he spun to Gaia.

"It's better for them if they appear unconnected with the escape," Gaia explained as she took pots off the fire.

"Shall I put them out?" asked Aamira.

"No, they will awake within the hour. Mirded, lead us to the street. We must make haste; they have taken hammers to the wall I made," Gaia said, her hand gesturing at the door.

"Come," the former king commanded before taking the group down several staircases before they found themselves on the streets. The palace was several blocks away. "Harbor is that way," he said as he pointed. The sun had started to set. The group headed that way, with Papsukkal taking point with Aamira and Khione half a step behind him.

"They have broken through the wall. No doubt that they have discovered our escape," Gaia informed the others.

"We are almost to the harbor," Mirded said. "Maybe ten minutes."

"My Lord?" asked a voice in front of them.

"Oh, Mango," Mirded replied. "The Pontiff has betrayed me. You never saw us, understood."

Mango nodded. "Of course." He stepped into a doorway for a moment before popping his head back out. "Don't worry, the city won't see you either," he said before giving three sharp whistles. "Go."

Mirded clasped his hand on Mango's shoulder. "You are a good man. May Aten bless you," he said and then rushed away. Shouts could be heard in the distance, causing the group to hurry. "The dock is around the corner," he panted as they ran.

"They are getting away. Shoot them!" bellowed the Pontiff from behind them.

"Go," Papsukkal snarled as he turned to face the threat.

"We are not leaving anyone behind," Gaia said.

"Do you really think that their steel will penetrate titanium nanofiber?" asked Papsukkal.

"No, but their blows could still break bones," Khione argued as she blew a cold wind down the street, freezing the ground and leaving strips of black ice. "That will only hold them for a few minutes."

The group tore down the street and arrived at the docks. They slowed down to keep from slipping on the wood. Suddenly, Gaia restored to her full size, spinning as she did. Arrows bounced off the rock shield that had grown with her. "Go," she snarled as she slowly walked backward. The others ran down the dock to Gaia's Rest.

"Captain, go!" Gaia shouted as she stepped on board.

"I need wind! Now!" snapped the captain. Khione spun her fingers, the wind catching the sails, allowing them to pull away from the dock. The gangplank fell into the water with a loud splash. The ship turned to leave the harbor as the crowd dashed onto the docks. Arrows fell short as the ship gained distance.

Chapter 23:

"Well, that happened," Gaia panted as she sank to the deck, letting her stone shield break back down into its base parts.

"Less than a day away from the ship, and already we've started something," Khione sighed. "Perhaps next time we shouldn't show up as Giants?"

Aamira grimaced. "She makes a good point."

"Now what?" asked Mirded.

"I am sorry that you lost your whole world," Gaia said.

"I should have seen it coming. Thinking back, I can see all the signs that the Pontiff was angling to do something like this." Mirded sighed. "I guess I'm about to learn how most of my citizens live," he added and rubbed his left forearm.

"There is no use crying about the past. You can't change it, not even a God of time," Gaia replied.

"Wait, you have a God of time? I thought you had no Gods?" asked Mirded.

"We are above humans as if we were Gods. We call ourselves a Pantheon of Gods. The Annunaki are becoming the Olympians. Some of our kind crave to be worshiped. Others are content to help or be in the shadows. It's all very involved, and you'll need a lot of red twine to trace it all out. This doesn't even cover the Titans and their sect."

"The Titans? Oh, boy. I'm going to have a lot to learn," Mirded said.

"Excuse me," Aamira groaned as she rushed over to the rail and vomited.

Mirded got up and walked over to the fire goddess. He broke a brown-skinned root before handing her a piece. "Chew on that. It will help your stomach. We found that out during the last crusade. We call it ginger, and a lot of sailors swear by it."

Aamira's face grimaced as she chewed on the root. "Strong flavor," she gasped.

"They often make drinks out of the root, but this is all I could grab. However, it's enough to start a new grow," Mirded explained.

"You know, I feel less queasy already," Aamira said.

"Great, in the morning, we should stop to pick up some soil. Get this guy growing for you," Mirded replied.

"Captain, do you have a spare bunk for Mirded?" Gaia asked.

"Only if he wants to bunk with the men. We could add another hammock," Captain Uranus suggested.

"Khione and I will share a room," Aamira offered.

"I didn't want to impose on you two," Gaia started.

"It's not a big deal. We'll adapt," Khione said with a sly smile.

Mirded placed his hands on the rail, watching his city darken as the sun dropped below the horizon. He wiped a tear away as Gaia placed her hand on his shoulder. "I get the feeling I'm never going to set foot again on Etruscan soil," he said.

"Perhaps, but we do plan on returning in a few years after we meet other cultures. Hopefully, they will be more open to strangers," Gaia replied.

"The Aten I believe- no, believed in, would have been appalled at the Pontiff's actions today," Mirded said.

"It is rare that one's core values are shaken to where you have to find new ones. Perhaps, one day, your people will have accepted their error and welcome you home," Gaia murmured as she tucked the former King under her arm. He closed his eyes and leaned his head into her side.

"Perhaps," Mirded whispered, "just perhaps." The pair stared at the shrinking city long after the sky had darkened completely, allowing the stars to come out. "So beautiful, and to think, you've traveled among the jewels of the sky." His voice sounded like someone who'd had a hard cry.

Gaia gave a soft laugh. "My sisters and I have never left the ground. My father and the Annunaki are the ones who travel among the stars."

"Does that not bother you?" Mirded asked as he leaned over the rails again.

"I have no desire to travel in the sky. I could have taken a shuttle. That's a boat that travels in the sky like a bird, but this allows me to experience things from the same perspective as everyone else," Gaia explained.

"It's an experience alright," Mirded spat.

"We do what we can, accept the past, and move forward," Gaia said as she leaned on the rail as well.

"All he had to do was just listen for an hour, but no, he had to use this as the excuse to toss me out. I thought we were friends. I trusted him as my primary adviser," Mirded snapped as he slammed his fist into the top of the rail.

"The ones we care for the most are the ones who can cause the most hurt," Gaia murmured.

"Doesn't matter anymore. Where am I sleeping? It's been a long day. I'd like to lie down," Mirded replied.

"This way," Gaia said as she led him away from the rail, her form shrinking to allow them below decks. "This is the galley, then if you go aft, you'll find stores and the crewman's bunks. We have several decks that hold them. If you go to the bow, you'll find your berthing. The first room on your left is Aamira's, as it's fireproof and connected to the kitchen to make hot meals for us. The door on the right used to be Khione's room, but it's now yours. My room is the door across."

Mirded bowed his head. "Thank you for your hospitality, milady. It's not expected after the lack of the same from me."

"You did nothing wrong, but perhaps after resting, you'll feel different," Gaia answered. She watched the former king gently close the door.

"That has to be rough," Khione said behind Gaia. "To lose everything like that. It has to weigh on the soul."

"That is true," Gaia agreed with a sigh.

"How would you know? You've lost nothing," Aamira demanded.

Gaia turned and looked at her friend. "The planet has lost everything more than once. The latest one was when she lost the Annunaki. She mourned them for a millennium. Just because she isn't the same as us doesn't make her less alive."

"Forgive me. Morimi reminded me of such past loss after I said it," Aamira said with a slight head bow.

"I often forget that you did not grow up with your powers and connection to your mantle of power," Gaia replied as she leaned against the bulkhead.

"We've had a long day," Khione intervened as she wrapped her fingers around Aamira's. "Perhaps a night's rest will bring clarity."

"Perhaps. Jiala, can you tell the captain that we should make for the west? I wish to check out the western side of Europe," Gaia instructed the sailor working in the galley.

"Europe, ma'am?" Jiala asked.

"Oh. Right. The same landmass as the boot, just on the western side," Gaia explained.

"Right away," Jiala agreed before heading to the wheelhouse.

"Good night and both of you try to rest," Gaia said to which the other two just giggled and entered Aamira's room.

After entering her room, Gaia moved to the front of her cabin, where the two sides came together. She knelt before an open window and closed her eyes. Drawing the remains of the stone shield from where it dropped to her cabin via the open portholes. She let out slow breaths as she manipulated the rocks, turning them into usable soil for the ginger root. She grabbed a box and put the dirt within.

Gaia looked up when someone knocked on her door. "Come in."

The door opened to Captain Uranus. "I hope there is no one

wounded? Your Sa-Tan gave us a brief rundown and expressed lament that he didn't get to 'nom noms'. His words."

"Nom noms?" Gaia snorted. "Okay then, well yes, we are fine. The man we brought used to be the king of that land. Sadly, he's been replaced by a religious figurehead. The same religious figurehead that chased us out of town. Had some great food, that's about it."

Uranus pursed his lips. "I hope that next time won't be busy."

"We can only hope. Will you help Mirded learn what he needs? Catch him up to the rest of us," Gaia requested.

"Of course, milady," Uranus replied. "Jiala said you named the landmass Europe?"

"The locals call it Europe and the other Asia," Gaia explained.

"I will make a note of it. Do we have any idea what we are sailing into when we arrive in a few weeks?"

"No, we are sailing into the unknown. I wonder if this is how my father felt when they left Alpha Centauri Proxima for this system."

"At least we have a better idea of where we are going. They just knew that there were planets here, while we know we'll find habitable lands."

Gaia stifled a yawn. "Thank you, captain. We will speak later about our exploration plans. For now, it's time for bed."

"Good night, milady," Uranus said before departing.

Chapter 24:

It took three weeks to sail across the waters between islands to reach the western edge of Europe. They had sailed into the bay that almost looked like a claw reaching down to the gun-shaped landmass to the south. The ship moored in a shelter a few hundred meters out from the coast.

"Lady Gaia, we have lowered the boat and are ready for you to explore," Jiala said with a slight bow in Gaia's cabin.

"Thank you, sailor. Let the captain know that we'll depart within the hour," Gaia instructed as she tied the laces of a boot that came to mid-thigh.

"By your command," Jiala replied with a clap of his heels before he left.

Mirded slipped in as the other man left. Gone were the trappings of state, and what replaced him was a plain man with a few weeks-old beard. He still wore his royal armor, but the emblems that marked him as King had been removed, with a brown cloak attached to the shoulders. Around his neck was a chain that held his signet ring. His legs had long laced sandals that wrapped up to his knee and he wore a plated kilt. "Leather looks good on you," he commented.

Gaia stood, smiling at her friend. "Thank you. Are you ready to explore the unknown?"

"Let's go," Mirded said. The pair headed above deck, only to find Khione and Aamira waiting for them. They both wore leathers like

Gaia, but the goddess of winter used an umbrella to keep the sun off.

"Is there something we should know?" asked Aamira suggestively while Khione closed her sunshade.

"No," Gaia and Mirded said at the same time.

"Rigggggghhhhtt," Khione drawled as she swung over the edge of the ship to climb down the rope ladder.

"Perhaps the love birds would like to go next? Maybe Gaia so she could catch Mirded?" Aamira giggled.

"Oh, shush you," Gaia snapped as she climbed down. The rest of the landing party followed.

As the boat rowed away, Mirded had a confused look. "Gaia, I saw you work with stone at the palace. Why haven't you raised the stone so we could walk to the shore?"

"While I can shift the earth under the waves, that mantle of power belongs to another, my father. It is far easier to have control over the ground while on dry land. Once we land, I'll create a causeway," Gaia explained.

"That makes sense. I think," Mirded said as he rested his chin on two fingers, his brow furrowed in thought.

It was not long before they came to a stop on the beach. Gaia slung her legs over the edge of the boat, her foot sinking into the golden sand. She scooped a handful up as her dark eyes scanned the forest.

"What do you see?" asked Mirded as he came up behind Gaia.

"They remind me of elephants, but with a ton of fur," Gaia replied.

"They sound like Mammoths. We've come across them on the other side of our," Mirded grimaced. "Of the Etruscan Kingdom."

"Mammoths look awesome," Gaia said.

"Where are they?" asked Khione.

"You don't see them?" Gaia questioned.

"No," said Aamira, Khione, and Mirded.

"Oh, well, they are that way, down the field," Gaia stated as she pointed past the edge of the forest. Heading north from the border was a massive field that mainly had brown grass, a few hills. "What are those?" she asked, pointing to a flock of large birds.

"I have no idea," Mirded said. "They look like you could ride them, however. Can we tame them?"

"Khione, do we have time?" Gaia asked.

The goddess of winter closed her eyes before shaking her head. "We would have to head further south. Winter is coming."

"Let's make a note for later, for when we can set up a full lab," Gaia said.

"Do you want us to set up camp?" asked Uranus.

"Set up over there. Let Papsukkal hunt to his heart's content. Khione, can you get samples from the beach? Aamira, let's get a few samples of wood after I take care of our ship," Gaia instructed. She turned to face her ship and closed her eyes. She moved her hands slowly, as if raising something. A few moments later, the ground rose from the shore half a meter. The limestone slowly reached out to the ship. After half an hour, there was a three-meter-wide causeway. Gaia reached out as the chef shoved a large cup of ambrosia towards her. "Thank you," she said after a long gulp.

"Of course, milady," the chef replied before he headed off to find wood for cooking.

Gaia finished her drink and started walking. "Come on, you two, we have things to do." Mirded and the goddess of fire started following.

"Why did we all take the small boat if you were going to make a dock?" asked Mirded, his eyes scanning for threats.

"What? You want your first steps in a new land made by Gaia?" asked Aamira.

"I guess not," Mirded said.

"It also allows us to take the risk for the crew if there are hostiles around," Gaia explained as she led the group along the tree line.

"Do we know if there are other humans around?" asked Mirded.

"Nope, but isn't that exciting to find out if they are?" replied Aamira.

"I guess," Mirded said.

"What is that? Is that poop?" groaned Aamira. She pointed at a pile the size of Mirded.

"Afraid of a little poop?" teased Gaia.

"I am not getting a sample of that," Aamira snapped.

"Mirded, would you take a sample? It will help us understand the diet of those mammoths," Gaia said.

"How do you know it's not from the birds?" asked Mirded as he took the sample kit from Aamira.

"Size. It's half of the bird's chest. No way it came from the birds," Gaia explained.

The trio spent the rest of the day taking samples from the trees, fallen trees, dirt, grass, leaves, and anything else that caught their eye. The sun was setting as Gaia sat on a log by the beach. There was a campfire a few meters away, with a few other logs around it. The chef was slow-roasting a bird using a rotisserie that he was hand cranking. Gaia took a long drink. "Ah, fermented water."

"It's beer. We've always called it beer," Aamira corrected.

"Oh, that's what we called it too." Mirded grinned before sampling his own. "This is honestly better than I expected."

Aamira sat on the beach in her full form. She reached out and pulled a bit of fire away from the campfire and molded it like it was made from clay. Khione sat next to Gaia. "Find anything good?"

"Just that your woman is afraid of poop," Gaia replied.

"Did you see the size of that thing? It was taller than me in human form," Aamira snapped. The group laughed together.

"We had a few felines run away from us. They had light brown fur, unlike the tigers around our island," Gaia said. The chef came over with plates for everyone. Gaia sampled the white meat. "Very juicy, busting with flavor. What are these white discs?"

"I found a few roots, and after testing them, thought why not? I am calling them carrots," the chef replied. "I think they would go well in a stew. Enjoy," he said before departing. He went back to his fire, turning something within.

Mirded ripped a slice of bread. "What is the plan for tomorrow?" he asked before taking a bite.

"We are going for a long walk tomorrow in our large forms. We can cover a lot of ground in a short time," Gaia explained. "We are going to walk towards the sun until it gets overhead and then come home."

"I see. Then I'll explore along the coast. Perhaps take the boat north and see what's there," Mirded said.

"Take Papsukkal with you," Gaia ordered.

"Yes, milady," Mirded agreed with a wide grin. Suddenly, he leaped over the log as he snapped to Aamira, "What in the Aten's name is that?"

"What? You've never seen a cat before?" Aamira asked.

"Yes, but they are not normally on fire," Mirded replied.

Between the group, a ball of fire was shaped like a large house cat. "Meow," the fire kitty said as it stretched out its forelegs and pranced back to Aamira.

"He will not burn you," Aamira reassured him as she petted the kitty.

"We're not Fire Goddesses, and I am pretty sure fire will melt me," Khione retorted with a glare.

Gaia placed her head in her hand, shaking it slowly. "Aamira, we live on a wooden boat. Do you know how hard it was to make your room fireproof? If you want a cat, we'll find you a real cat, but please, no fire kitty."

Aamira pushed out her lower lip. "But he's cute."

"Fire on a wooden boat," Gaia reminded her a bit forcefully.

"Alright, fine," Aamira sighed as she waved her hand, sending the flames back to the fire. "I'm going to hold you to that."

"We are not getting the large ones, the ones with the super long teeth," Khione interjected.

"But they are so cute," Aamira replied.

"They will eat you. House cat, and that's it," Khione said.

"Fine," Aamira pouted.

Chuckling, Mirded grabbed his dropped cup before heading to the beer keg. "Refills anyone?"

"I'll have another," Gaia said.

"Do you want a keg or a cup?" the chef asked.

"We might as well relax, break out the kegs for the three of us," Gaia replied.

"It will be several weeks before I can refill them," the chef informed her.

Gaia waved him off. "We've been out to sea for months. We can let our hair down and relax. Oh, and ask Papsukkal if he wished to join us."

"By your command," the chef agreed before stepping away and speaking to his sous-chef.

The fire was casting long shadows as the sun only gave a narrow strip of light on the horizon. Gaia stood, grabbing a tambourine from behind her. She let her form grow to her normal size, making the musical instrument grow with her. Tapping her palm against it, the zills jingling.

"Yazzz," Khione drawled, grabbing her own tambourine, different from Gaia's as hers had a drumhead.

"Now it's a party," Aamira said, her form flashing to human-sized and darting over to the boxes by the cooking area. She withdrew a lute before returning. As she walked, her size went back to giant, the lute growing with her. Flopping to the ground, she let out a groan of exhaustion. "Okay, I shouldn't have changed shape so rapidly."

Gaia jingled her tambourine as she danced around the fire. Khione let her hips move as she found the rhythm, her hand tapping the drum. Aamira strummed the lute, her body swaying with the music. After a few moments, she sang a song about finding love. Mirded smiled as he joined in the dance around the fire. Several crew members joined them. Several songs later, the chef delivered the beer kegs, lining them up behind a log.

"Before the Anunnaki taught us how to purify water, this was really the best way to ensure clean liquids," Aamira said as she stood and walked over to the kegs.

"Really? When was this?" Khione asked.

"Back before Enki accidentally knocked over the original city, a few centuries before I was born," Aamira explained as she opened a keg with one hand while the other grabbed it. Tossing the wooden plank aside, she took a long gulp. The keg looked like a slightly large mug in her hand. "The oak casks really enhance the flavor."

Gaia had followed her friend and drank her own keg. "This is a good brew. My compliments, chef. Mirded, get a mug and drink up."

Mirded raised a mug. "I'm already there."

They danced and sang around the fire long into the night. Thirty kegs laid discarded as the fires grew low, sailors passed out all over the beach. Khione was swaying as she stood on the shore, waves crashing over her giant feet, ice cubes flowing in the wake. "Yeahhhh, I'm singing now. It's a party on the beach, Ooooh yeeaaah," she drunkenly sang.

"She's pretty good," hiccupped Mirded as he sat on the ground, leaning against Gaia's leg.

"That she is," Gaia agreed. The pair were standing near the pile of empty kegs as Gaia was finishing her drink. "You're pretty good too."

"I don't sing," Mirded corrected her, his voice slurring slightly.

"Not like that," Gaia said, her free hand moving Mirded aside as she sat the keg down. She shrank to her human size, kneeling next to her friend. She poked him in the chest. "That's pretty good too."

"Oh, thank you, I guess," Mirded replied as he lifted his mug.

Gaia smiled at Mirded as she stopped him from drinking, "I like you, like a lot. You're all kinds of sexy," she said before she kissed Mirded. He dropped the mug into the sand, stunned for a moment, before kissing back. Their passion built over the next few minutes before Gaia removed Mirded's shirt.

"We should go somewhere, more alone," Mirded gasped.

"Let's," Gaia agreed as she stood, taking Mirded's hand. The pair went deeper into the darkness.

Chapter 25:

As Enki walked through the Nibiru, he turned to his assistant. "I never noticed how noisy the Nibiru is. It's even noisier than the grav-cylinders."

"It's always been like this. You've just been planet side for over five hundred years. You are not used to it," said Ninurta.

"I am sure that's true. Did you run the tests?" Enki asked.

"Yes, and it is as you feared. Here are the results from five years of testing and decades of research," Ninurta replied as he handed over the report.

Enki glanced at it, stopped, and then took a few minutes to read the report. "Well, damn. That is a rather large problem."

"Yes, it is. I don't see any way to fix it without major consequences," Ninurta said.

Enki stopped outside a golden door. "Noted, that will be all, Tan. I will report to the Sky Lord." He quickly entered the petition chambers of the Sky Lord.

"The interstellar wind has penetrated through the southern hemisphere. From our scans, the crust has cracked a few hundred kilometers and ten kilometers deep in places. It was probably from the impact a few thousand years ago," reported Ninurta.

"Can you repair it?" asked Chronos.

"We will need to fill the trench, which would require visual inspection," said Ninurta.

"Thank you. We will advise you later about what we are doing," replied Anu. The engineer bowed his head before leaving.

"Lords of the Annunaki, I present Lord Enki returned from Olympus," introduced the Harold.

Enki walked to the center of the room, bowing his head to the Lords. "Thank you for this in-person audience. As everyone remembers, the Great Mother has blessed us with returning to our home of Olympus. The natives have a few that can touch the Spirit Molecule, and as per Lord Anu, I've tinkered with their DNA.

"The natives have access to the Spirit Molecule, among other advantages. This led me down a path that allowed me to refine their form to become even more suited for their environment. I've raised their intelligence levels and made a few tweaks. We have flying humanoids," Enki flashed a human with white wings before changing the image to a creature with one eye. "These are the cyclops. They are master blacksmiths and have a mind for engineering. There are other creations, but the one that brought me here is the Humanaki. They are a blend of Anunnaki DNA and the natives."

"Why would you create such an abomination? I get the flying and the smiths, but why would you dare blend our kind with their kind?" Chronos snarled.

"We will never learn if we do not explore. I believe that the Great Mother had a hand in my design. Regardless, the Humanaki are far stronger than any of the natives or Annunaki. They have the best of both worlds, while none of our negatives," Enki explained.

"Can they work on the Nibiru? Any of the natives or your Humanaki?" asked Anu.

"Any of them can handle viewing the vastness of space, unlike our psychology. However, the natives lack the knowledge to repair the ship. We could use the Humanaki, but right now, fewer than twenty exist."

"You've been gone for a thousand years. Are they not educated enough?" asked Enlil.

"It takes time to build the knowledge base. They were in the early Bronze Age when we arrived. They are now in the middle of an Iron Age. Our trade with the natives has caused a flash of learning in them, but the industrial base isn't there yet. My daughter explores the planet and contacts the native tribes, but they are still in the Bronze Age. Our local humans still have a thousand years before we can uplift them to the Space Age, but that leads us to the problem of the system's primary," Enki explained as he activated a hologram, showing the solar system. Bursts of plasma erupted from the star, dispersing in every direction.

"When we arrived, I sent monitoring satellites to look at it. Even after a thousand years, it is still highly active. The natives say that it hasn't been this angry in an eon. We suspect that since it hasn't calmed down, it might be why they are reporting more mages than ever. So far, the few Humanaki who have been born have access.

"This brings us to Gaia, Khione, and Aamira. These three created a blood binding that put them in touch with their mantles. Aamira, however, was a native until Morimi found her and took her as a host. Her body evolved into a Humanaki form. She also remembers our departure from here and how lost she felt upon An," Enki explained.

"Are you saying that the lost mantles can return?" Chronos asked.

"That is something we'll have to explore, but the evidence suggests this," Enki replied as he brought up an image of a dozen children. "On my orders, I had the following Humanaki birthed. We can infer which gods they are likely to become. Some of the lost are returning, such as Hades and his connection to the underworld. I would hazard that he will have a foot in both worlds. We also had the goddess of fire return to us, taking the body of a mortal."

"Impossible," spat Chronos.

"Clearly, it's not impossible," said Enki.

Lord Anu lifted his aged hand. "We will need more details."

"My daughter Gaia and her friend, Khione, have spent the prior fifteen years learning from the local tribe's shaman. Gaia has been teaching me their rites. These three women thought it would be a great idea to become blood sisters. For mortals it would give them a sense of when the others are at risk, but with the Humanaki, they become literal sisters," Enki explained as an image of the trio spun slowly. "Their DNA shows familiar connections, where there were none before."

"How is this possible?" demanded Enlil.

Enki gave a soft sigh of someone mentally facepalming. "As I reported to you from when we first arrived, we've been investigating our connections. Tan Ninurta handed me the genome analysis on the way in. What he found is startling." He changed the image to show strands of DNA. "Our DNA shows the chickens are our devolved descendants. Something happened after we left that forced them into that to survive. However, that is not the problem. Our own DNA is being damaged by the interstellar winds. The outer hull has fractured, allowing neutrinos to penetrate our last habitat cylinder. We could survive with the transport ships, but we would have to dock them inside. I am afraid that this means that we have to abandon the Nibiru."

Anu tilted his head, cutting Chronos off before he could speak. "We knew the day would come. The Great Mother blessed us with our return to our ancestral home. Start moving everyone and everything we can."

"Do we stop the cyclers?" asked Enlil.

"They will stop at their next destinations. One at Olympus and the other here. In fifteen years, we will all move to our new home," Anu replied while glaring at Chronos.

"It will take a few years to unload everything," Enki said.

"You will also research how to shield against the star's coronal mass ejections. I am sure Chronos would love to get his hands on one of the other planets," Anu explained.

"The fifth planet calls to us," Chronos confirmed.

"If the other planets are habitable, then why didn't we just settle there instead of traveling the stars? Our myths say we fled Grandfather's wrath as he destroyed Olympus," Enlil wondered.

"Perhaps there was a reason, maybe we already were getting ready to explore. Maybe we were being invaded, and we lost, the other planets could have a reason why we couldn't live there, or a myriad of other reasons," Enki suggested.

"Right now, we are too few to worry about spreading across the stars. We will rebuild Olympus, and then we will take the other planets. We also wish to test your creations, as we know Lord Chronos' view that we are the superior species," Anu said.

"The holy writ says that the Great Mother herself gave us these bodies. Of course, we are superior," Chronos replied.

"It also said that those who wield her power are of her flesh and blood. The Du-Ku Cuneiform doesn't directly call out our species," Enlil snapped.

"Therefore we will test who is stronger. The Grey Titans are the warrior caste. They will fight four of your creations. Enlil will select the four after we return to Olympus," Anu said, ending the discussion. He tapped the staff three times on the deck. "So concludes the Session of Elders."

Chapter 26:

A hacking cough came from the bed. Once it stopped, Gaia laid a warm cloth across an old man's forehead. The bed was made from bundles of straw, wrapped in a thick blanket. The bedroom was in a stone house, allowing the place to stay cool in the summer. Gaia's other hand took a liver-spotted hand, smiling sweetly at her husband. The Goddess of Earth remained looking like she was in her early twenties.

"Still as beautiful as the day we met," Mirded rasped, his voice weak with age. He weakly lifted his free hand to Gaia's cheek, brushing a tear away. "The last forty years have been nothing but breathtaking."

"I could turn you into a God," Gaia whispered, her eyes closing as she tilted her head from the torment in her heart.

Mirded smiled sweetly at Gaia. "That is your pat-" a cough cut him off. "It's your path, not mine. That path belongs to Rhea. I will return to the Great Mother a happy man thanks to what I leave behind. We built Bahía, turned it into a thriving city, and traded with Tuscania and Olympus. I am proud of that."

"You're just happy that dumbass was assassinated, and your nephew is king now," Gaia pointed out as she poured a glass of water.

"Kurkuas, not dumbass," Mirded corrected her as Gaia helped him sit up and take a sip. "Do I long for the days of strength? Yes. Do I accept that all things have an end? Yes. Even you will die."

"Papa?" asked a young voice from the door.

"Rhea," Mirded greeted warmly, his beard shifting as he smiled. "Come, give me a hug."

The young teen rushed over to the two, wrapping her arms around the old man. The girl had olive skin, long dark hair, one blue eye, and one brown eye. She wore a simple dress with a floral print. "School was long today. I was worried that," her voice hitched, "that I wouldn't get to say goodbye."

"Hop up, little one," Mirded warmly said. Gaia helped him sit up, resting on a few pillows. "I will be right here," he murmured as he tapped Rhea's chest over her heart. "Always."

"But I want you here, not in my heart," Rhea sobbed.

Mirded reached out and took his daughter's hand. "I know you would, but it's time to let me go. Perhaps in the next life, I'll be one of the Olympians. Or you'll come across me in town as another human, but remember I will always love you, little one."

"But that wouldn't be you. I want you to be here. Mama, can't we adopt him like you did, Aamira?" Rhea asked.

Mirded started to laugh, it quickly turned into a hacking cough. Gaia smiled at her daughter, tears in her eyes. "Rhea, I've offered, but your father knows his time is over. The Great Mother calls for him to return home."

"It's not fair," whined Rhea.

"Life is often not," Mirded replied. He closed his eyes in thought for a few moments.

Rhea shook her father's side. "Papa?"

"I'm still here," Mirded said as he lifted the chain from his neck. A golden ring hung from it. Gaia helped him sit up and place it over Rhea's neck. "If you ever return to the Etruscan Kingdom, show them that. They should welcome you as royalty. I love you both," he murmured as he relaxed into the bed, his eyes closing for the final time as the breath left his body.

"Papa? Papa!" Rhea screamed. "Come back, no Papa, you can't leave yet."

Gaia bowed her head as she took Mirded's lifeless hand. "He's gone now." Rhea let out a wail of pain. Gaia moved around the bed and scooped her daughter up in her arms. She sat back down as Rhea wrapped her arms and legs around her mother. "You have me still, Rhea," she whispered as she slowly rocked her child.

"Papa," Rhea sobbed into her mother's shoulder.

"I'm going to miss him too," Gaia said with a lump in her throat. The pair sat there a long time, rocking and crying. "Come, you need to eat," Gaia stated as she stood.

"I don't wanna. Papa's gone," Rhea sobbed.

"You have to try, even if it's just to drink some tea," Gaia urged as she put Rhea down for her to sit at the table. "Anything?"

"No," Rhea replied. Gaia nodded before she prepared water for tea. Twenty minutes later, the pair had dark tea. They sipped in silence for a long time. Rhea's mug was almost empty before she spoke again, "I want to see where father's from. I want to understand his culture. We have a trade with them. It shouldn't be that bad."

Gaia nodded. "We'll make plans. When you're sixty or seventy, you'll be old enough, I think. When you come into your powers, that's when you can go exploring. You'll need something to protect you. As good as Papsukkal is, having powers around saved us."

"Yeah, you and Pa-Papa told me the story of how you met enough times. It will give me time to plan out the trip. Even design the ship." Rhea swallowed hard and shook her head in anguish. "Ma-Maybe I'll use Papa's last design."

"I have his drawings stored away. They are yours," Gaia said as she took her daughter's hands.

"Yes, please," Rhea replied before finishing her tea. Gaia left the table, heading for the bedroom. While her mother was trying to find the drawings, Rhea lit a few candles. Gaia returned a few moments later with a stack of paper.

"This is what Mirded was working on for the last five years, the flagship of our merchant fleet. He named it the Hercules class ship,"

"Who is Hercules?" Rhea asked as she laid the paper out to put together like a puzzle.

"Mirded always had a strange grin when I asked, but he'd never tell me. Maybe you'll get to find out," Gaia commented as she refilled their teas. "We've been here for forty years. It's time to explore more. I'll take Gaia's Rest, and you'll take a new ship."

"Where would you go?" Rhea asked.

Gaia shrugged. "Well, we know that there are Giants in Asia. We haven't come across any humans on this side of the isthmus of Eros."

"I'm going to see my cousin. Yes, that's where I'm going. I'll go south and around that continent. Come up the east side and then visit the Etruscans." Rhea said.

Gaia smiled at her daughter. "Good. Let's plan our trips. When you have the plans figured out, we'll get the ship built."

"It's going to take like ten years to build them. I do not know how you had built your ship in a year," Rhea commented as she bent over the diagrams.

"Power tools. Really, that's it. Not having to do everything by hand really speeds up woodcutting," Gaia said.

"You've told me about electricity. It's like lightning but contained," Rhea commented.

Gaia sat her tea down, nodding. "It requires metals like copper."

"And? You can move metal around and shift the stone. Why is that a problem? We use copper for our mugs after all," Rhea pointed out as she followed a line on the paper with her finger.

"While true, I know how to make the spiny thing that creates power," Gaia shook her head as she spoke. "I was always told that we haven't built the machines that make the machines that make the machines to power things, so I didn't need to learn maths yet."

"Okay," Rhea replied, distracted by the drawing. "Oh, this ship should be swift. Do you see here, Mama? These channels will move the water around the hull easier."

"Can we adapt it to the Gaia's Rest?" Gaia asked as she leaned over the prints.

"Yes, but I'll have to replace the hull below the waterline completely. We'll have to put it in dry dock to change it," Rhea explained. "We only have two docks right now, and both are working on the replacements for the Chimera and Devastator."

"Well, we should let them finish before we take the docks. Those two were part of the Olympian Fleet," Gaia noted.

"So, we have plenty of time," Rhea said before tears returned to her eyes. "Time without Papa," she choked.

Gaia rubbed her daughter back. "I'm going to miss him too."

Chapter 27:

Standing at the bow of her ship, an adult Rhea looked over the waves, letting the wind wrap around her giant form. Her long dark hair blew around her from the wind. Closing her eyes, she inhaled the smell of the sea air. The hint of salt carried, among other scents, as a dolphin pod jumped out of the water near the ship.

"In about an hour, make for the coast. We are nearing another settlement," Rhea instructed a sailor next to her.

"By your command," the sailor said before leaving.

Rhea watched the dolphins play around the front of the ship before they had enough and swam away from the boat as they tacked across the water, looking for a shelter for the boat. The sun was setting as they slowly pulled into a lagoon and dropped an anchor.

"Milady, it's near dusk. We should wait for the morning before going ashore," the ship's captain said from behind the goddess.

"Of course, a well-rested crew is always best," Rhea agreed. "I wish to go ashore as soon as possible past first light."

"Aye, we'll have a shore party ready for you," the captain replied.

"See you in the morning, captain," Rhea said, her form shrinking as she left to go below deck. She stopped by her guard's quarters. "Papsukkal, we're going to head off the ship in the morning. There are natives a few hours' walk away."

Papsukkal snorted. "I hope it goes better than our last two first contacts."

"What? Just because there has been combat doesn't mean it's been bad," Rhea chuckled.

"If you say so, but I was there, you were not," Papsukkal reminded her as he moved to his armor stand and inspected his equipment.

"I guess we'll find out. Rest up. We are leaving at first light," Rhea said.

Papsukkal bowed his head slightly. "I'll be ready."

"See you in the morning," Rhea replied before leaving and entering her quarters. She quickly undressed and went to bed. Early in the morning, she stood at the edge of the ship, the sun barely providing enough light to see the waterline.

"Little more on the aft," ordered a sailor, watching the rowboat being lowered into the water. The two sailors on the rope let out a little more. "Good, now evenly lower." A few minutes later, the boat was resting in the water, still attached to the ship. It was not long before the shore party had arrived on the beach, the sun fully up. A thick forest blocked the view a few kilometers to the north, while a savanna-like climate was to the west and south. They could barely see animals in the distance.

Papsukkal was in his full body armor as he sniffed the air. "Megafauna, to the east. Probably elephants. There is another group to the north. They smell feline. There are a few other creatures in the forest, but nothing to worry about right now."

"That's fine. We are heading south," Rhea replied as she stepped off the boat. She was wearing light leather armor that grew with her giant form.

"I thought you were going to go as a Human," Papsukkal growled as he stepped in front of his goddess.

"We are far enough from the land of Giants. We should be fine," Rhea said.

The Annunaki Sa-Tan snapped his head to look at Rhea. "Why did you say that? Now we're going to get attacked by a pride or a herd. By Fortūna's saggy left tit, you've cursed us."

Rhea laughed as she watched the rest of the landing party unload their equipment. "Fortūna, I've never heard of her."

"She's the Goddess of Luck, good or bad. Tempt her at your peril," Papsukkal growled as he scanned for threats.

"Right, I thought we were the Gods?" Rhea asked.

"Just because we are higher beings doesn't mean we are not free from the powers of others, as if they were Gods," Papsukkal said as he crouched and felt the ground.

"Stop being paranoid. Nothing's going to happen," Rhea snapped.

A young man came up to Rhea. "Lady Rhea, we are ready. Which direction are we walking?"

"Thank you, Percy. The village is about three hours south. See where the land comes out like a bulge? They have a second one about ten kilometers south. They use that to shelter from the sky when it gets mad," Rhea explained.

"Couldn't we have parked next to that one? It would have saved a lot of risk," Papsukkal pointed out.

"The water is calmer here than down there," Percy explained.

"Papsukkal, what do you think? Walk along the savannah or across the beach?" Rhea asked.

Rhea's guard scanned the horizon once more. "We will walk on the grass, but close to the shore."

"I'm not a Water Goddess," Rhea commented. "There is a reason we also have to follow the natural wind."

Percy snorted, getting a look from Rhea as Papsukkal responded, "You are the same as your mother, an Earth Goddess. You can shunt any attacker into the water. I thought that would be clear."

"Am I a warrior? I don't have to think about tactics," Rhea said as the group started walking along the grassy sand. They walked through the morning without taking a rest, drinking from waterskins when needed. The sun had reached the zenith as the group neared rounded earthen bulges.

"Something smells dead," growled Papsukkal.

Rhea coughed, "You think?" Percy and several other sailors made gagging sounds as the wind blew a putrid smell from the waves. "Go check it out," Rhea gasped as she covered her mouth with her shirt. The Sa-Tan darted forward, his feet leaving four-toed prints on the ground. As he rounded the corner, he skidded to a stop. He immediately turned around and darted back towards the group, looking like he was pushing himself as hard as he could. Several spears landed where he had stopped.

"That means it's time to go. Humans, start running," Rhea commanded.

"My Lady-" Percy started.

"You are slower than Papsukkal and I. Just go, I will cover our escape," Rhea interrupted as she knelt on one knee, pushing her palm onto the ground. She looked up and saw a dozen men running after her assistant.

"Run!" roared Papsukkal.

Rhea closed her eyes as she whispered the words of power her mother had taught her. The ground erupted between Papsukkal and the chasing tribe. She lost sight of them as a ten-meter wall appeared. She fell to her hands and knees, head bowed as she gasped from moving so much stone so fast. She felt claws on her shoulders, shaking her. She looked up into the face of Papsukkal.

"Rhea, we need to go. Come on!" Papsukkal snapped.

Nodding, Rhea stumbled to her feet. "I put too much into it."

"They always do their first time under real stress. I am sure they are trying to understand what happened, but let's not chance Fortūna anymore," Papsukkal snapped. Rhea jogged away, a speed that the average human ran at. The Annunaki guard easily kept pace with her. They ran for about ten minutes before catching up with Percy's group. They slowed down to keep pace with them.

"I think we are far enough away, but let's not let our guard down," Papsukkal said, causing the group to slow down to a walk. "That's now three for three. Next time let's just attack first," he groaned.

"Now, what fun would that be? We'll play nice. They all can't want to kill us, after all. Speaking of death, what did you see, Papsukkal?" Rhea asked.

"They had a dozen men hanging by their genitals and four women hanging by their breasts. I am glad you didn't have to see that sight. Two were still alive as they hung there. It wasn't pretty," Papsukkal explained.

"What kind of warning to others was it?" asked Rhea.

"Don't mess with us and we won't kill you in horrible ways?" suggested Percy.

"Perhaps," Papsukkal said. The sun had reached the mid-afternoon point as they climbed back into the rowboat to head back to their ship, departing for safer shores.

Chapter 28:

Walking through the Temple of the Gods for the first time in years, Enki noted that two Humanaki experiments were waiting for him. One had hair that reminded him of rust and stood over three meters. Her skin was the lightest beige with pink undertones. The second woman's hair hung over her shoulders, dark brown with hints of blond streaked through it. She stood at about two and a half meters, with skin that looked golden tan with hints of yellow undertones. Their skulls were elongated, showing their increased cranial capacity. It made them look like they had large hair.

"Amphitrite and Aphrodite, are you two ready to prove Lord Anu correct?" Enki asked, having recognized them from his Tan's reports.

Amphitrite smiled at Enki. "Yes, I can access old memories. We can remember An and life before the rebellion. Our powers are so much stronger here than what we ever had in the second world." She tucked her dark brown hair behind her ear.

Aphrodite's smile flashed across her face, lighting up alluringly as her eyes changed to an enticing grey. "As the Goddess of Love on An, I had to work to encourage the breeding parties. Here?" Aphrodite let out a cute snort. "I haven't had to do much more than to flash a smile and bat my eyes to drive people crazy enough to drop what they are doing and screw the closest person." The redheaded Goddess spoke in a sultry tone, her back arching ever so slightly.

"Well, first, tone it down. There is no need to start a threesome right here in the hall. Second, save it for the coming battle," Enki instructed as they entered a lift to the Lord's floor. There were two more waiting for them outside Anu's chamber.

Enki nodded to the pair. One was male, standing about three meters. His hair was jet black, hanging down to his waist. His complexion was a vibrant olive color. Around his neck were golden rings made from gold, titanium, and platinum. The Elite's clothes had a fluid look about them, clearly for movement. The man obviously had body armor under the blue fabric. His cold grey eyes gave an appearance that one didn't want to have him judge them. It felt like he could see someone's very soul.

Next to him stood a woman with long chestnut-colored hair. She had it done in a tight French braid that had golden threads woven within as highlights. She had a lighter olive color than the male next to her. The guard was wearing leather body armor that was custom made for her. While one could tell she had breasts, they were ostentatious. On the right side of her chest was a golden symbol that declared her the leader of the Amazonian Guard.

In her left hand was a spear made from titanium. At least the tip had been. The shaft had been formed from a carbon fiber-like substance that they had brought with them from An. The fibers made it almost indestructible, requiring a weapon also made from An to shatter the long rod. Clipped on the guard's right side was her shield that, like her spear, was made from titanium and painted a base red color. The emblem showed three women shield blocking with their blades held in a Roman fashion, resting on the top of their shield. Drawn behind the defenders were four women that had bows.

"Athena. Hades. I trust you are well?" Enki's head bowed slightly to the large humans.

Hades bowed his head ever so slightly. "Sa-Tan Enki. We are quite well."

The Goddess of Wisdom also bowed her head slightly. "My Lord," came her loud voice. Her eyes darted around the hall, looking for any threats. "Our Lord and Master are expecting us," she said with a slight bow of her head towards the door.

Enki's hand lifted with his tongue flicking out. "Please, Lady Athena, open the doors."

The female Elite gave a wicked grin before opening the door and stepping through it. They followed Athena into a throne room that was decadent and extravagant. Gold-wrapped columns with gemstones set in them lined the room. Statues of An, Anu, and even a sculpture of the Great Mother stood behind the throne. Her presence was the only Goddess that was above all others. Her location reminded them that even the Sky Lord was beholden to her will.

Athena stopped in front of the aging Sky Lord. She dropped to one knee, her head bowed to him. "Sky Lord, my God, I have brought Sa-Tan Enki and the experiments as ordered." Her tone became one of devotion, showing the respect she held for her God.

The Sky Lord snorted, his head shaking ever so slightly. His eyes darted around the room before focusing upon the woman that knelt before him.

"Of course, Lady Athena. Has the complaint arrived?" Sky Lord grumbled, his voice sounding tired.

From a door to their right, a voice called out. "We have, My Lord. We look forward to destroying the imposters trying to be Gods," growled a male with a snarl as he stepped out of the shadows.

The newcomer had pale grey skin, as did most of the group behind him except for two and another that was red. Chronos wore the stole that identified him as the Keeper of Time, the head of the Ohrmazd line, and the current leader of the Grey Titans. In his left hand was a spear like Athena's. Standing on either side, just half a step back, were his guards with blades on their hips.

"Ahura Chronos. As the objector to the experiments and creations, you have demanded a trial by combat to prove or disprove their worth. We have noted your objections regarding these forms and their connection to the Mother Goddess. We directed our Sa-Tan's to create forms for testing. We will allow discourse to commence before the Trial of Combat to assist us in this decision." Anu, the Sky Lord, had a regal tone in his voice, sounding less tired than he had moments before.

Enki stepped forward, his hand moving over one of the holographic displays. "A hundred and thirty solar cycles ago, with the Sky Lord's approval, we performed the Rite of rebirth from the Great Mother. My daughter, Gaia, was born from this rite, as were these Elites," he lectured. "Over their lifetime, they learned how to harness their powers. They learned how to communicate with Tiamat. After ensuring that they held the maturity needed, we completed the restored rite that gave them their memories of their past lives. Over the last thirty cycles, we have verified that they genuinely have the souls of the Anunnaki Elite. They display knowledge of An's lost home in such detail that proved satisfactory to the Sky Lord.

"The powers that they demonstrate show far greater access and control than our lore claims ever to have. For example, Hades can commune directly with the Spirit Moth -" Enki barely could finish speaking before the screaming started.

"Hearsay!" "Blasphemy!" "Traitors!" "Abominations!" came the cries from the Greys.

"Amazing," "Praise be Tiamat," "By her will," muttered most of the green-skinned Annunaki.

Chronos slammed the base of his spear into the floor, cracking the marble under him as the sound thundered through the chamber. His eyes were alit in his rage. "Sky Lord, you cannot believe this blasphemy!" he snarled. "If the Spirit Mother wished for us to have these powers and access to her, she would have given them to us before now."

"She created us in her image," The Keeper of Time continued, his anger clear in his voice. He hit the spear's base into the ground again, but he didn't crack the marble this time. "If she wished for us to speak directly to her, we would have done so long before now," he leaned the spear closer to Hades as he spoke. "What does that abomination think? That he will control our very souls? That is reserved for the Mother Spirit alone!" Chronos snarled, spittle flying from his frothing mouth. "You! You claim you control the very water on this planet," he growled as he turned to address Amphitrite. "You claim what is not yours. You claim the realm of Oceanus as your own, stealing his due."

Amphitrite tilted her head to the side, smiling at him, but she did not speak as per tradition. She clearly found the whole speech laughable.

Chronos turned to face Enki. "And you! Don't forget the crimes you have committed. You created these nightmares. You turned away from the will of the Mother and Father. The Great Spirits shall forever reject you."

Anu raised his hand. "Ahura, you forget your place. It is not your position to make a promotion of dismissal. We reserve such condemnation for the Spirit Mother, and through me, she speaks," came the soft rebuke.

Lord Chronos looked like he wanted nothing more than to run his spear through the Sky Lord's chest. Instead, he bowed slightly. The jerky movement was insulting. "Forgive me, My Lord. I meant no disrespect," he muttered, sarcasm slipping into his tone.

"Forgiven, Ahura Chronos. I trust you have brought examiners?" The Sky Lord asked.

"I have. I demand the Trial to begin forthwith!" Chronos demanded in a regal tone. "We shall end these abominations and their blasphemy here and now."

The Sky Lord slowly rose to his feet. "The Trial of Combat has been requested. Sa-Tan Enki, prepare your creations. As per our laws, the two squads shall face-off," Anu ordered as he slid his golden staff into a slot next to his throne.

There was a grinding noise, then the square floor in front of the elder God lowered. Once the cracks appeared, the four Human Elites stepped onto the east side while ten grey-skinned Annunaki moved onto the west side.

As the two groups mentally prepared themselves, they rode the lift down ten meters to the lower level. While the marble floor turned into a cage, Enki glanced over to Deacon Enlil. He looked quite interested in how it would turn out. If the younger Lord didn't know better, he'd suspect he would rather side with the greys, but he had much more pride than that. He often agreed with the Ahura's feelings regarding the new form of Elite, but he took the Sky Lord's will above all.

Anu stepped up to the newly formed ledge, his right hand lifting over the expanse. He lifted his snout to the sky before he let out a breath. His breath turned into a jet of flame that scorched the marble on the ceiling, fifteen meters above him. "Ahura Chronos has challenged Sa-Tan Enki's creation and assertion that if we wish to survive on this planet, we must adapt. The Sa-Tan presents these four as proof of this claim," Anu stated, his right hand motioning to Enki.

"The honorable Keeper of Time has demanded that the Great Mother offer her great wisdom in this affair. He has brought ten of his greatest warriors and followers to defend his claim," the Sky Lord Anu said as his right hand gestured to Chronos.

"As we are bound to Tiamat's will, we feel that this is an acceptable challenge. As per tradition, only one-quarter of the accused party may have weapons. The challenger may only be half armed with blades or other weapons." Both hands of the Sky Lord came together in a thunderclap.

In the middle of the arena appeared several weapon racks and a shield stand. There was a line of flames wrapped around the items. The fire reached over three meters, often reaching another four or five meters. Everything about the event tilted the win to the challenger, often resulting in a brutal slaughter.

Anu pulled his hands apart, holding them parallel to the floor. The fighters readied themselves for the moment the Sky Lord lowered his arms. The leader of the Annunaki Elite looked over both sides, suddenly dropping his hands.

Enlil focused his attention on Enki's creations, using power to enhance his hearing as lead-Grey threw his blade across the open space for Hades. The metal became a silver blur before the watchers gasped as Hades deflected the blade with ease.

Hades bowed to the leader, his blade snapping up and twisting to the side. He then spun it next to him to test the balance. He shrugged before glancing at Athena. She was at a full run across the floor, her shield pulled from her side. As she neared the flames, she jumped into the air, her body flipping and holding the shield between her and the fire. Most of the heat was diverted, allowing almost nothing to reach her body.

Hades snorted before following her at a slower pace. He glanced back at Amphitrite and Aphrodite. The first woman had her face furrowed in concentration, her hands twisting in front of her. She snapped both arms forward, but nothing appeared to happen.

With each deliberate step, Aphrodite fell in time with Hades. "I assume Athena will acquire our weapons?"

Hades laughed, a rich baritone that was out of place for the field of battle. "My dear, that is Amphitrite's duty."

"Then why did-" Aphrodite's voice faded out as a column of water spun through the window and over the flames. The moment the tube of liquid touched the blue flames, a flash of steam formed. Amphitrite's left hand twisted in a loop, causing a gust of wind to push the hot vapor into two of the armored warriors, instantly cooking them alive.

"FOUL!" Screamed Chronos. "That abomination used an item that was not in the arena!" he snarled at the Sky Lord.

The Sky Lord held up his right hand. "You claimed that they were weak and that they lacked the proper will of Tiamat and the Great Mother. This proves otherwise." Anu paused, thinking for a moment. "There are no rules that they have to only use the items inside the area. It merely is that no one held such power prior to this. We will permit this." Anu turned to the pit, his foot pressing on the amplifier. "We demand that they display all powers in this demonstration," came his order to the pit, much to Chronos's ire.

Upon hearing this command, Athena and Hades smiled broadly, knowing now they didn't have to hold anything back from the display of their power. The glory of the Spirit Mother would be theirs and theirs alone that day.

Chronos gnashed his teeth, his lips peeling away from his

fangs. His eyes tracked Athena, who was in the middle of the arena, throwing a second blade to Hades, who caught it in his left hand. A feral grin formed on Hades' face as he ran his tongue across the edge of the new blade.

As the blades touched, a burst of blue flames ran across both blades' spines and through the hilts. The outside of his arms glowed blue, a streak that reached his shoulders. Both lines of blue reached across his back to his spine.

As the light reached his waist, white flames wrapped around his stomach. The white light formed into a tree. Many of the watchers gasped in shock. The crowd took the image to equate the Tree of Life, representing the gifts of the Great Mother. The onlookers took the markings as a sign of Tiamat herself, approving of his existence.

The man that would later become the God of the Underworld felt his hair burst into a bright blue flame as he slipped into his power, accepting the will of his Goddess within his flesh. He turned to look at Chronos, a sneer forming on his face.

"You dare question the will of the Mother?" Hades bellowed as he lifted his right blade to point at the lead warrior. "She demands these warriors' life force! She has seen into their hearts and found them wanting. Mother Tiamat warns thee to let go of the hate within you or face eternal damnation!" Enki winced at the volume of his voice—the downside of his hearing focus.

As Hades yanked his blade down, purple energy was stolen from the lead warrior. The creature's body fell to the ground, lifeless. The Annunaki's soul floated where his body stood moments before.

Aphrodite tilted her head down slightly, her left hand reaching out to the exposed soul. Gasping, her eyes wide, she let out a snarl. "You are full of fear, hate, and loathing! I cannot find love or compassion within your spirit. The Great Mother demands that you wander the lands until you learn your lesson of kindness to others," the Goddess of Love called. "Begone!" Aphrodite shouted.

The Goddess of Love twisted her hands for a moment before thrusting both arms forward. The spirit let out a scream of horror before he was yanked out of the arena and out of sight.

On the edge of the arena, Chronos snarled as his rage reached apoplectic proportions. "This proves that they stole from the Mother her greatest powers! They take her will for themselves! They are unnatural! Slaughtering as if we are nothing. Blasphemers! Heathens!"

Anu snarled, his left hand snapping out. His fingers wrapped around Chronos' throat and lifted him from the ground. The grey-skinned creature clawed at the arm, raising him as the old man showed the strength that made him the Sky Lord.

"It is clear what her will is! She wants us to evolve and become more than this weak flesh," Anu snarled as he turned to hold Chronos over the pit. "The Great Mother gave them their powers! She is speaking through them," he growled.

Chronos let out a quick scream as Anu let go, letting him fall into the pit with a hard crack. His legs broke as bones ripped through the flesh in his thighs and calves. The Sky Lord leaned over to spit on the broken Grey Elite.

The Annunaki Greys seemed to freeze, watching their master fall to the ground. Their inaction lasted long enough for the body to hit the ground, spurring them into action. Several tried to jump to the side, while another lifted a blade as he stepped closer to Athena.

"I banish you and your clan from the Annunaki. Thy Grey Titans are nothing but a heretic sect! Forevermore, thy clan recants the will of the Great Mother. This makes them unfit to remain within the greater faith," came the Sky Lord's decree.

"If my people wish to be stronger, with Tiamat's blessing, they shall be. Thou shall not hold us back," Anu commanded.

Anu looked down at Hades. "Leave only Chronos alive, as it is the Great Mother who holds his life, not us. If he dies from his wounds, then he dies. Kill the rest of the apostates. Aphrodite may banish their souls if the Great Mother agrees."

There was a sound of a sword bouncing on the ground. Blue blood pooled under the two halves of the Annunaki that Athena split from the right shoulder to the left hip. She lifted the bloody blade to her Sky Lord. Blood ran down the metal and over her hand before dripping from her elbow to the ground.

"By thy will, it shall be done!" Athena exclaimed with relish, her eyes alight with joy.

Amphitrite's grin widened as she spun her right hand over her left, which she twisted up, her thumb slowly moving to touch the tips of her fingers. She tried to take the wall of water and wrap it around the remaining six.

As the wall of water moved across the floor, one Grey cocked an arrow, took careful aim, and let it fly. It soared true and struck the Ocean Goddess in the thigh. She let out a cry of pain as her left leg gave way. The wall of water fell as she lost her focus.

The flood of water no longer under the control of Amphitrite washed across the ground, taking the Greys off their feet. It had the unfortunate side effect of taking Athena from her feet.

Amphitrite lifted her right hand and made a fist as she lifted her head. Enough water to encase one of the Greys bodies was summoned and lifted him from the ground. His hands moved around as he tried to leave the bubble of water.

Aphrodite calmly walked over to Athena to take a bow and several arrows from her. She also slipped a sword belt over her hips in just such a way to cause arousal. Athena shook her head in frustration.

"Must you always do everything with your extra sexy style?" Athena demanded as she used her shield to block an arrow.

The Goddess of Love shrugged. "Not doing so would go against my nature," she said before drawing her bow. "If I must fight, then I shall distract our foes."

Athena blocked another arrow a moment before Aphrodite let loose one of her own. The Grey tried to dive out of the way, but the projectile went through his right foot and pinned him to the ground.

Another Grey jumped forward to knock his friend free that was drowning in the glob of water. Amphitrite just shook her head as she lifted her left hand, causing the bubble to grow, sucking water from the ground. All the attacker managed was to join his friend as the bubble drifted from the remaining group. Sweat beaded on her forehead from the strain of the added mass.

Hades used the distraction to take a step to the left, both his blades striking forward. One was blocked by a shield that the now leader of the Greys used. Hades was quicker than his opponent. The Grey was not fast enough to prevent the second strike from the other blade with his sword.

The shield slipped from the Grey's hand, narrowly missing Hades' right foot. The near-miss caused the God of Death to snarl as he pushed his sword deeper into his opponent's stomach. The free blade snapped around and decapitated the man.

Enki glanced over from the fight to his father, Enlil. There was a longing in his eyes for the power he was witnessing. Drool dripped from the side of his mouth as he shifted to observe the fight better. He would demand rights to inhabit the first Human Elite form after the Sky Lord approved.

Snapping her hand out to the left, the Goddess of Love snapped another projectile off, trying to force the Grey to sidestep right into Athena's rush. He noticed too late and took an arrow to the knee. He let out a scream of pain as he dropped.

The Goddess of Wisdom and War rushed up to the falling Annunaki and propelled herself into the air. Athena used her shield in her left hand to collapse one Annunaki's head, while the blade in her right hand decapitated the other that was trying to rush them. The head rolled into Chronos' side.

Dropping the bubble of water, Amphitrite felt her powers give way. She had held on for nearly too long. The rush of water pushed Chronos onto his side, causing him to scream in pain once more. The two Greys that were within the bubble had drowned.

When Chronos fell, his legs snapped from the hard impact, making him unable to move from the side of the arena. He screamed as the water rushed towards him, he waved his arms to try to keep the water from his mouth before he choked. Athena stormed over to the fallen God, picking him up by the throat. She slammed him quickly into the wall. She repeated the move several more times, causing all the water to be expelled from him.

Athena lifted the God of Time and then head-butted him. "Pathetic," she grumbled as she dropped the unconscious Grey Titan. The four Human Elites stepped into the center of the arena and lifted their weapons.

"My Lord, we have emerged victorious," cried Athena before slamming the spine of her blade into her shield.

Anu looked over the four, his tongue flicking out, savoring the taste of blood in the air. "Considered to be some of our best fighters, yet they have been dispatched with such ease." He turned to look at Enlil.

"Deacon, what are your thoughts?" Anu inquired as he lifted the golden staff, triggering the combat arena to rise.

Enlil shook his head slightly. Enki could tell the bloodlust within him desired those powers. The advisor looked pensive for a few moments, pondering what he just observed. His tongue flicked out as he nodded slightly to himself.

"We assumed that the Spirit Mother forsake us on An after the peasants removed us. However, it was a test of our faith in her. While it is true, some will protest the new bodies, the flesh has always been less important than the connection to Tiamat," Enlil said thoughtfully.

Anu nodded in agreement. "That, my old friend, echoes my thoughts. Speak with Lord Hades, he has some control over the soul. Perhaps he knows a method that will allow us to call one's essence directly. If that is possible, as my most trusted and the heir, then it is time for you to assume the role of Sky Lord, but in these Human Elite forms."

"My Lord?" Enlil sounded shocked.

"I fear that Chronos and his clan will wage war on us in anger. I have aged my child, I am no longer the pillar of strength that I once was," Anu said as he took a deep breath and placed his hand on Enlil's shoulder.

"I suspect that this will be my last body. I have no desire to learn anything else. I am content with what I can offer the Great Mother and wish to return to her eternal embrace." Anu's voice was soft.

The Sky Lord turned to Enki and tilted his head in respect. "Sa-Tan Enki, the Spirit Mother gave you to us for this blessing. You too shall inquire about rebirth into proper Godhood. You shall become the Deacon of the Annunaki Elite once your father assumes the Mantle of Sky Lord."

Enki bowed deeply in gratitude. "By thy will, Sky Lord." He glanced at the bodies of the Grey Titans. Such a waste of life. "May the Great Mother guide you," he started the Last Rites of their faith for mass casualties.

Shockingly, the former Keeper of Time's left hand moved as he let out a low groan of pain. The Sky Lord's mouth twisted in disappointment. He pointed at the ranking Grey. "Take your Lord from here. If he lives, then he has the Great Mother's blessing. Until then, be gone!" he snarled.

That got the Greys moving, one carefully picking up Chronos while six others formed a guard around him. They marched from the room. Flicking his tongue out, Enki could taste their anger at the events that had almost killed their Lord and still might.

Hades stepped forward, the three women behind him. They knelt in unison to the Sky Lord. "My Lord," he said softly, his head bowed.

"You have proved the Great Mother stands with us. Tell us, who were you on An?" Anu inquired.

"Sky Lord, I was Salavaic, the shaman," Hades informed his Lord.

"You were the Shaman before Enki. We declare thee Lord of the Underworld," Anu said before tapping Hades with the golden rod, first on the right shoulder then the left. It reminded Enki of a knighting ceremony.

The Sky Lord banged the staff into the floor three times. "Rise Lord Hades, take your place among the Pantheon of Gods," The Sky Lord of the Annunaki commanded, his right hand extending slightly behind him.

Anu turned to face the three Goddesses. He pointed at the redheaded one. "Lady Aphrodite, tell us who you were on An."

The Goddess of Love and Fertility bowed slightly. "My Lord, I had been known as Urania, Patron Saint of Seafarers. While this incarnation has some control over the sea, I have a stronger affinity for emotions. I see the bonds of love in both the Annunaki and our creations."

Anu tilted his head in acknowledgment before stepping forward to tap the rod on each of the Goddess's shoulders. "Rise and become one with us, Goddess Aphrodite, we name thee the Goddess of Fertility, take your place among us," he said as he motioned with his left hand for her to take a position on the left of the throne.

"Tell us, Athena, your opinion of this day's events," Anu ordered.

"My Lord, I feel that those who lost their lives stole from the Great Mother. They lost what knowledge they could have learned. They failed this life, ultimately leaving Lady Tiamat wanting." Athena pondered a moment. "However, the biggest issue was their poor tactics. They failed to work together and come to a proper formation. That allowed us to smite them easily."

Anu tapped Athena's shoulders with his long rod. "Rise, Goddess of War. Take your place among the Gods."

The Sky Lord turned to the last Elite. "A Goddess of the Sea, I presume?"

Amphitrite tilted her head down slightly. "Yes, my Lord. I have some control over air, but water manipulation is my primary power."

Once more, the Sky Lord tapped with the rod in his hands, once on each shoulder. "Rise and take your place among us as an Ocean Goddess."

Chapter 29:

Gaia leaned over the map that the captain of the Gaia's Rest traced their course on. "This is Tuscania, and here is Athens. Lady Rhea has spent some time exploring this landmass," the captain said as he tapped the dart-like mass south of Asia. "She's currently heading to Tuscania. She then plans on exploring the coasts between Europe and Asia."

"She also explored the southern tip of the big continent. From her geological survey, there are some resources we'd like down there. She also tells us that the humans there differ from the Denisovans and Neanderthals we know about. They have a lot more body hair. From the description, they are probably one of the early forms of man," Gaia said with pride in her voice.

"Right, we are sailing past Athens, about a hundred kilometers north of us," the captain explained.

"We could go visit," suggested Khione.

Gaia waved her friend's suggestion away. "We'll visit on the way back. When we have established relations with the Giants."

"You're the boss," Khione said. "Just seems like we should drop by and see your father. The winds don't feel right."

"It will only be another year. We have all the time in the world," Gaia replied.

"Have we figured out where the Titans went? I saw a report that suggests that the dart island or the other quarantine island. What if they bashed some Giants' heads in?" Aamira pointed out.

The captain shook his head. "We have had no reports about them heading that way. But we don't have-- what was the term–ah, eyes in the sky anymore."

"I don't think we have anything to worry about," Gaia said as she traced the southeastern shore of Asia with a finger. "It looks like we could sail between these islands and explore this large bay. The islands would protect the mainland from most major storms and it seems like a great spot to build a city."

"It's also far enough that the Etruscan Crusaders would have left it alone," Khione pointed out.

"I am concerned about the depth of the ocean here," the captain said and pointed between two islands where Gaia wanted to travel through. "Lady Gaia could clear any rocks in our way, but she won't know about them until we run aground."

"It would slow us down, but I could put a layer of ice over the hull to take the impact," Khione offered.

Gaia shook her head. "The warmth of the water would take too much out of you."

"If we go slow, we should be alright. We just must be careful not to hit anything. We'll need lookouts and hope," the captain said.

"It will still be a week before we get there. We'll figure something out," Gaia replied. A week later, she found herself standing on the bow of the ship, watching for rocks in the crystal-clear water. She could see fish and sharks swimming below them.

"Well, if we were worried about finding the Giants," Khione trailed off as she pointed off to the port side. Several men stood over five meters, while the women that stood next to them were only three and a half meters tall. They were shirtless but had something covering their waists. Several children were building sand sculptures as their parents watched the ship. Behind them was a thick tropical forest. As they sailed past, the shore jutted away from them, giving them more space.

"Do you think we have anything to worry about?" asked Khione.

"Probably not, but you should see the captain and see if he wants more wind," Gaia suggested. Khione flashed a smile before heading to the wheelhouse. Two days later, the ship found itself anchored off the coast. There weren't any docks, but a wall ten meters thick and thirty meters tall wrapped around a city, the ocean side open.

"Captain, just the three of us will visit. Humans might upset them. As we learned from the Etruscans, they hated the Giants," Gaia said.

"Enki would hang me by my entrails if anything happened to you," the captain noted.

"Then I better make sure nothing happens. Have the boat lowered. We will head out shortly," Gaia ordered.

"Yes, ma'am," the captain said through gritted teeth. The three Olympians went below deck, and when they came back up, they were dressed like royals. Gaia had gold woven into her dreadlocks, a purple dress that had a wide golden belt. Aamira was dressed in a fiery orange dress with a matching belt. Khione was dressed in light grey and had her own golden belt. They sat regally as they were rowed to shore.

"Return to the Rest. We'll alert you to come to get us," Gaia commanded.

"The captain was quite clear. I was to wait here for you," the rower said.

Gaia shook her head. "Just stay safe. Come on, girls," she instructed as she turned, her form enlarging. There was a worn path that wasn't far from the beach. They could see a large gate in the distance that they started walking towards. It didn't take long before they arrived, discovering that the gate was a stone wheel that the giants moved to block the entrance. Two guards stepped in front of them, long blades pointed at the women.

"Halt. We do not recognize your clothing. What is your tribe?" asked a Giant. He stood at four and a half meters, had a black beard that was easily half his size, his skin a light brown with almond-shaped eyes.

"We are from lands beyond the waves," Gaia said with a slight bow.

"Not possible. Boats are too small for us. Where are you from?" the guard demanded.

"I am Gaia Enkisdottir. I am the princess of Olympus, and I've come to speak to your King," she introduced herself, drawing herself up to her full three meters.

"Haven't heard of them. Only the tribes may enter the sacred lands of Shangri La. Be gone," the guard said.

"What would it take to enter?" Gaia asked.

"Belong to one of the twelve tribes. You wear none of their

markings, do not know what the requirements are. Be gone before I take your head," spat the guard.

Gaia held her hands up. "Is there a city we could enter?"

"There is a town to the north where the Longi trade with us, but otherwise, no. Now leave," the guard said as he took a step towards them.

"One more thing. If I move your stone gate without touching it, does that prove my worthiness?" Gaia asked.

The guard gave a belly laugh. "No woman could move the great gate. It takes six men to move it."

Gaia rolled her eyes as she waved her hand in front of her face. The gate moved and fell into its closed state with a thud. Both guards watched with their jaws dropping before they spun, their blades moving to strike.

"Witch," spat the guard.

"For the love of Anu, was your tribe the only one that used magic?" Gaia asked Aamira as she took a few steps back.

"Apparently," Aamira mumbled before looking at the guard. "Guard, if we are witches, do you really think you have a chance?"

"Turn me into a toad, I care not. Witches consort with the evil walkers. They will take our souls, damming us to eternal hellfire," the guard growled.

"Next time, we are just staying home. Can we do that? Stop this exploring thing?" Aamira asked Gaia.

"Look, we mean you no harm. We are exploring the world and just wanted to introduce ourselves to a new nation. We are from west of here, on the islands," Gaia tried once more.

The guard lifted his lip in a sneer as he attempted to swing his blade at Gaia. Rock flew from the ground, wrapping her left forearm in stone as she lifted it to block the strike. Sparks flew as the metal impacted. Gaia grabbed the blade, twisted her hand as she smashed her right foot into the ground. A cylinder of rock slammed into the Giant's groin, causing him to fall to his knees.

"Do you want some, too?" Gaia demanded of the second guard. He shook his head. "Good, we will leave for now. Where is this trading city?"

"Four days' walk along the coast," the second guard said, his blade shaking in his hand.

"Thank you," Gaia replied before sharply turning and walking away, her head held high.

Chapter 30:

"My Lord, scouts have spotted a small craft heading this way. It is a small, one- or two-person kind of sailboat," Nabu said as he opened Enki's door to his office. "From the distance, it looks like one of Rhea's lifeboat designs."

"We haven't received a distress beacon, so it can't be one of ours. How far away is it?" Enki asked as he turned from his writing.

"About an hour," Nabu said.

"It is confirmed that the craft is heading this way?" Enki wondered.

"There isn't any other reason to head between the islands but to come here," Nabu answered.

"Well then, shall we go meet our visitor?" Enki asked.

"Thought you might," Nabu replied before the pair left the complex, heading for the docks. When they arrived, someone was tossing a line to the small craft. A lone occupant stood within, a giant woman that clearly was pregnant.

"Giantess, I am Enki. How can we help you?"

"Grandfather," Rhea said, relief in her voice.

"Grandfather?" Enki wondered with a slight head tilt. He sniffed the air as his eyes narrowed. "Are you little Rhea?"

"Not so little," Rhea corrected him as she climbed on the dock. Her face had a healing bruise along with several cuts on her arms.

"Where is your ship? Gaia said you had a masterpiece built," Enki said.

"I did until I visited Tuscania," Rhea replied, shaking her head. She glanced around, taking note of the walls. "Why are the walls sloped like that? They don't seem effective at keeping invaders out."

Enki waved Rhea's comment away. "Minerva designed them to protect the city from plasma shock waves."

Rhea raised an eyebrow as she half turned to Enki. "If someone like Chronos attacks, he'll walk right in."

"I'm not worried. Chronos knows Anu would decimate any attackers. Who is the father?" Enki asked, trying to change the subject.

"Chronos," Rhea replied. That caused Enki to stop in his tracks.

"He doesn't have the tech to grow embryos. As it stands, we have very few growing chambers left, so how did he impregnate you?" Enki asked as they resumed their walk, heading for the science building.

"He completed the birth ritual, ensuring one of his line," Rhea explained, her voice cracking, her eyes growing distant from remembering.

"Oh. Come, let's get you into the nursery," Enki said as he led her downstairs and into the underground chambers.

"Mama never told me about these tunnels," Rhea replied, noting the delicate stonework.

"We created the shelters just in case the walls failed to protect us from the solar storms," Enki said as they entered an exam room. "Would you allow me to examine you and make sure the baby is healthy?"

"Please, Grandfather," Rhea agreed as she sat on the exam table. A few hours later, Enki had shown her to the resting area in the nursery.

The Annunaki Lord talked to his father as they watched the sunset from near the beach. "Lady Rhea arrived this morning. She's about to give birth to Chronos' heir any day now."

"That's not possible," Enlil growled. "He's a Lizard. She's a Humanaki."

"Well, I did sort of make the Humanaki's DNA compatible," Enki explained sheepishly, dragging a toe across the dirt.

Enlil closed his eyes, shaking his head. "I don't want to know how that would even work. Do you think Chronos will come for her?"

"No, why would he? He despises the Humanaki," Enki reminded him.

"She still carries his only heir," Enlil commented as the sun left a streak of light on the water between the two islands.

"How would you know?" Enki demanded of his father.

Enlil turned and looked at his son. "Reasons you don't need to know right now. Maybe once it comes to fruition, but the how isn't important right now. Where did Rhea come from? Did she come from the Dart?"

"I don't know, but she spoke of her nephew's Kingdom of Tuscania, several thousand kilometers away from the Dart," Enki said, the sun slipping under the horizon.

"Perhaps they have expanded, but I would have expected them to go west, not into Europe."

"Maybe Rhea was on her way to Bahía, stopped in Tuscania, and was attacked by the locals."

"We could ask her."

"She's had a rough month. She was dehydrated, beaten, and cut up. Rhea hadn't eaten in a week, but overall, she is healthy. I don't think there will be any issues with her giving birth."

"Something doesn't sit right with me, son. Father is aging rapidly, but it doesn't feel right. I just can't put my claw on it, and Rhea's arrival really has me concerned about Chronos."

Enki let out a barking laugh. "He ran from us with his tail between his legs after we kicked his tail in the Arena."

"That embarrassment for him probably is a driving force for revenge."

"Father, you worry too much."

"You didn't grow up with him as your elder brother. He's always been a little eye for an eye."

"We are the Olympians. What could go wrong?"

Enlil closed his eyes, head tilting as if to say what is wrong with you. "Do not tempt Fortūna, you know that."

"We make our own lives, luck has nothing to do with it."

"We still must not tempt her. You know there are beings greater than us, and we should not tempt them to interfere with this plane."

"Is she an Old God?"

"No, but she might as well be. Even they bow to her whims."

"Should we prepare for an invasion?"

Enlil waved the question away. "I don't think so."

Enki's communicator beeped. "Enki here."

"Rhea's gone into labor, milord. Do you wish to be here to assist?" the voice asked.

"I trust your skills, Tan. Let us know when she gives birth," Enki replied before ending the call. "I have this feeling of dread that she is a harbinger of our doom. Family squabbles are always the worst."

The sun had slipped below the horizon as Enlil looked at his son. "Then we learn the hard lesson of betrayal before our return to the Great Mother. However, Chronos will not attack the city. Not as long as Anu lives, Chronos is afraid of his father."

"And what happens when Anu dies? Will he be afraid of you?"

Enlil looked at his son, his eye ridges narrowing. "Of course he is. What a silly question. I'm the next Sky Lord, after all."

"You tell me not to poke Fortūna, but you do the same thing."

"I only state a fact."

Enki chuckled. "Alright, father. Will you join us on the hunt tomorrow?"

"No, I have a meeting with Nabu over your wormhole ideas."

"Ah, that's his project, but I support it."

"Good to know. See you tomorrow afternoon, my son."

Chapter 31:

"My Lord," said Nabu. His skin had greyed slightly, the ridges over his eyes becoming more pronounced. "We have completed the design for the Great Protector."

"What is the Great Protector?" rasped Anu. The Sky Lord of the Annunaki looked ancient. The moment he crossed the Heliosphere, his body visibly started to age. Once he landed to pass judgment on the new forms, it accelerated. The few feathers that remained on his head were white from age, while the rest had fallen off. His hands barely moved from the staff, as arthritis in his hands made it almost impossible to move the claws. Standing on his right was Enlil and to the left was Enki.

Nabu activated the hologram, showing the solar system. "We can have the Humans install monoliths on the inner planets to alter the frequencies in the solar system. This should change the resonance to diffuse the plasma away from the solar plane. The side effect of this is that anything beyond the magnetic shields of planets, our ships will short out. They will eventually absorb the heat and turn into slag.

"To solve connecting the habitable planets, we can ground the loose energy into Olympus itself. I have spoken to Lady Gaia. She has shifted the correct mixture for a battery under the central landmass. From there, we finally will be able to power wormholes," Nabu finished with a flourish.

"Wormholes are two hundred years away. They are always two

hundred years away," Enlil said.

"That was, until we arrived here. The energy requirements were just too high for us to produce. Apollo just vomits it out, and we can tap that. While we haven't had a direct hit since our arrival, the star is still highly active. We haven't had plasma bursts since landing here. Still, the Human Femis say that Lord Anyanwu is having nightmares in his eternal rest," Nabu said. He changed the hologram to show the coronal mass ejections filling the solar system with highly energetic particles.

"What does this mean?" Anu gasped each word.

"With some tuning to find the right power waveform, we can use the stored power to connect each gate. We think we can fully power two gates, one for each direction, per event, like the one Enki caused upon our return to Olympus," Nabu explained.

"I simply drew directly from Apollo, the star, not the kid. I had no focus and grabbed a live wire twice. I'm lucky I didn't turn into a deep-fried God. We've learned how to draw from the locals. Worst case, I can grab the wire again, but this time direct it into the battery and capacitors," Enki suggested.

Anu nodded. "Only you have," he paused for several breaths, "the power to do this."

"Lady Gaia has the power, as does Hades," Enki corrected him.

"Approv- Approved," Anu gasped.

"My Lord, let us bring you to Damu," Enki offered.

"There is nothing he can do," panted Anu.

Enlil stepped next to Anu. "Father, you are not well. We can do this tomorrow."

"It's bet-" Anu's eyes rolled back in his head, his body crumpling.

"Father!" "My Lord!" came the shouts from around the room.

Enki snapped his healed but scared hand out to grab Damu's attention. A burst of light flew from him, phasing through the stone. He then grunted a few words, trying to find the life force of the Sky Lord. "Father, he's awaiting the ferryman on the River Styx."

"No, he's still here!" exclaimed Enlil. "The power of the Sky reside-" A flash of purple and blue light burst from Anu. Enlil rocked back as his body absorbed most of the light. It brushed over Enki and Nabu, giving them a feeling of love before it faded into the walls.

Enlil gently closed his father's eyes before letting out a slow breath. His hand snapped out, the Sky Lord's staff flying into his claw. Heads bowed to the new leader as he stepped back to the platform.

Damu entered, checking the prior Lord of the Sky. "We will prepare the shell for the great journey."

Enlil tapped the staff on the floor three times. "May the Great Mother accept your soul," he whispered. "By her will, I ascend to the throne of Lord of the Sky."

"Lord Anu is dead, long live Lord Enlil," the few in the room chanted. Sky Lord Enlil's eyes glowed yellow for a moment as they darted around, focusing on things only he could see. Taking power within him seemed to age the Deacon as his body adjusted to the Sky Lord's power.

"The Sky Lord will be unavailable for the next few days as he processes all the knowledge," Enki announced.

"As per Anu's command, I shall start preparing the Grea-" Nabu was cut off by a wailing alarm tearing through the stone.

"Report," snarled Enki as he ripped his communicator out. There was only silence for the response. Enki tried a few more buttons, but there was still nothing. He started for the door, heading for the Amazon Guardroom.

"My Lord, the guard shall escort the Lord to the secondary chambers," Damu stated.

"That is something you can't do. The mantle has accepted this as a safe space. He will remain here for three days and nights. We must defend him and our home," Enki ordered.

"That is not how tradition dictates," Damu argued.

"Tradition is from our past lives. We are no longer those nomads, nor are we on the planet of An. Clearly, the Great Mother demands that he accept the new mantle at this very moment. We simply do not have a say in her will. Now, I am going to save the Mortals," Enki snapped as he left the room.

Nabu hurried behind Enki. "Perhaps the alarm is for the new Lord?"

"This alarm is to muster my Amazon Guards. That is one of two things, a natural disaster or one of the other tribes thinks it is a good idea to attack us."

"Could it be Chronos?" asked Nabu.

"There is no way that the weakling would stand a chance. It can't be him," Enki said as he entered the command center at the base of the pyramid. The off-duty Amazonians were rushing to gear up.

Athena stepped up to Enki. "A large group of Denisovans are throwing boulders at the city. They are targeting your pyramid."

"Has there been any damage?" asked Enki.

"There has been no damage yet," Athena replied as she grabbed a note from one of her guards. "Do it. We need the Guards on the eastern side," she told the guard, who nodded and left.

"We haven't heard from the northern runner yet. She should have returned by now," another guard said.

"This looks like we are being pressed from all sides. We need to get a runner to Amphitrite, she needs to guard the western harbor," snapped Athena.

"We will protect the Northern side," Enki stated.

"At least let us know what in Anu's name is going on," Athena requested.

Enki gave Athena a stern look. "About him, Lord Anu died less than an hour ago."

Athena threw up her hands in frustration. "By Hades' realm. This is awful timing on their part."

"Or, he was murdered, as the attack sign," Nabu suggested.

"We don't have time to debate this. We don't even have the spare forces to inspect the Palace right now. I need to get to the south and take out those Giants," Athena said. Enki waved a clawed hand, dismissing the Goddess of War. She pointed to one of her guards as she moved deeper into her command center. "I trust Minerva has a battle plan ready?"

"Yes, milady. She's at the South Gate," the guard reported.

"Come on, Nabu, let's find out what's going on with the north side," Enki said, heading for the Lord's Armory. The pair quickly assisted each other in getting their armor on. It was last worn for combat on An. Enki paused as he reached for his spear.

"That weapon is for someone of lower caste, milord," Nabu interjected as he adjusted his facial armor. "You will wish to bear the blade of Marduk."

"I am not a sword-Lizard. I trained on the spear, not the blade," Enki said as he grabbed the staff. He let out a cry of pain as the spear shocked him in rejection, causing it to fall. "Well, maybe I should take the blade after all."

"Wise choice, milord," Nabu chuckled.

"Time to get the crash course in blade play," Enki muttered as he finished strapping the hilt to his hip.

"Alright, let's go," Nabu said.

The pair left the armory, heading for the north wall. A loud crash ripped through the city as a stone impacted the center stone building. A quarter of the way from the top, the southern side's casing stones exploded out, causing the granite to rain on the worker village next to the structure.

"They have found their range," Enki observed.

"Bigger problem, the Denisovan's are the diversion. The real attack is here," Nabu said as he came to a stop. They were near the North Gate. The stone fell from the crushed wall, landing with a thud. Blue and red blood could be seen flowing from the now useless gate. Climbing on the top of the wall were the Greys. Their hands alight with fireballs, ready to assist the Neanderthals crawling into the city.

Chapter 32:

"Zu-ka!" bellowed Enki as he thrust the Sword of Marduk at the damaged wall. It glowed red as the stone melted into a solid structure once more. Screams echoed from the wall as it turned flesh into stone, trapping a dozen within the wall. Two were trapped by their weapon arms inside the wall. The Titans that stood on the wall screamed in pain as their feet liquified from the heat. They fell backward, landing with a crunch of breaking bones.

"Now, how do we counterattack if the wall is solid?" asked Nabu.

"The important thing here is that they are no longer entering the city," said Enki as he looked around.

"While true, we can't go to them either," Nabu pointed out with narrowed eyes. He threw his spear, catching a Titan before he landed on the wall. With a flick of his tail, the weapon shot back to his hand. "Then again, the only option they have is to go over the wall."

Enki flicked his charred claws toward Athena, a ball of light shooting across the town. "We only need to delay until reinforcements arrive. Athena should make quick work of the Giants."

"What about the waterfront? Lady Amphitrite should be free to suppo-" Nabu snapped his mouth shut as the wind picked up, coming together in several waterspouts heading out of the harbor. "Well, I guess that answers that. How in Hades did the Titans get a force this large?"

"Oh, I don't know. Maybe they gathered the rest of the natives. Gaia is on her way to check out the landmasses to the east," Enki offered between bursts of wind from his hand that knocked climbers from the wall.

"How's that working for us? Maybe we should have sent her sooner?" suggested Nabu. He threw the spear once more, taking a Denisovan in the face. "Can you ask Amphitrite to flood the area outside the gates?"

"I already did. She's a little busy. We have to hold the line until she's done with the Harbor," Enki said.

"Hold the line. Got it. With the two of us versus thousands. Yeah, that's going to work out well," Nabu lamented.

"Well, they might help," Enki stated, his tail flicking towards the Adama running along the streets, heading for them. Several arrows soared over the wall.

"My Lord," said the Femi as she stepped next to Enki. She was a much younger woman, fresh to her role. "We wish to defend our homes from the Titans. Can you give us a way to defend the wall? Set it about a meter and a half down from the top as well as access to it?"

Enki glanced at the stone before nodding. "Zu-ka," he said again, this time a lot softer. A walkway formed along with several stairways. The Adama ran up the walls, taking over the defense. The Annunaki Lord stumbled, shaking his head to stay awake.

"Are you alright, milord?" asked the Femi.

"I've used too much energy. I risk tapping directly into Apollo.

I'd rather not cause him to have gas," Enki replied before taking a drink of water from a trough. He shook his head, obviously trying to clear a headache. "Okay, Hunter, what do you smell?"

"The city is under attack by tens of thousands, and you want me to pick out individual scents? Even with the Great Mother's blessing, I'm not that good," Nabu said.

"Femi, what do you see?" Enki yelled.

The old woman hurried back down the stairs and over to the two Lizards. "Milord, they have ruined the north harvest with the twenty thousand camped there. Their front lines are a mix of Denisovans and Neanderthals. They even have found a few Erthós."

"What are the Erthós?" Enki wondered.

"Oh, they have fur, but are Human. We haven't heard about them for many generations, from before you found us years ago," the Fermi explained.

"I need you to send runners to the other walls to get their status. Also, send one to the Guard to alert them," Enki ordered.

"Thy will be done," Fermi said. She put two fingers into her mouth and let out three short, sharp whistles. Six women appeared in front of her. After being told of the request, they took off in a sprint. "We should have information within the hour, milord."

"Enki, we do not have the manpower to fight back. At best, we have two thousand Anunnaki in the city right now. Then we have five thousand Amazonians within the city by the luck of having a senior training seminar this month. That leaves us outnumbered three to one," Nabu explained.

"There are an additional six thousand Humans that are moving to defend their homes. One simply does not forget the anger of someone defending their homes," Femi pointed out.

"Evens the odds greatly, only slightly outnumbered now. We just need a sound battle plan," Nabu said, right before a hoot sounded. He lifted his arm for the owl to land, then read the note tied to its leg. "Athena reports that they have five thousand Denisovan Giants beating the south wall. The eastern wall is being seiged by ten thousand Neanderthals and Erthós. She asks what forces are on the north wall. Our runner hasn't arrived yet. The Giants count as two Humans taking us back to three to one. Not the best odds, but not the worst."

"Why attack now?" the Femi asked with the shake of her head.

"They expected seven to one odds. Even with the Gods, that is hard. We don't know which Titans they are bringing to the field, if not all of them. It's smart on their part. We exhaust ourselves by stopping their hordes, allowing Chronos to walk right in," Nabu said.

Another owl landed on Enki's shoulder, pecking at him. Nabu took the note. "Minerva requests help on the South. We hold the wall."

"Send runners every half hour," Enki ordered as he turned to leave.

"If we can, milord," Nabu replied.

Enki nodded before leaving in a hard run. The sound of battle got louder as he approached the south wall. Smoke rose from damaged buildings as a boulder slammed into the few non-sloped parts of the wall, exploding shrapnel from both sides of it. Blue bits joined the exploding stone next to the gates as an Annunaki was obliterated. They had killed multiple Humans, while wounding another dozen.

Athena used her shield to deflect most of the debris. She wore a leather skirt with armored folds and a tank top made from the same material. It allowed her full range of motion. A few smaller bits of rock ripped her thigh, leaving a thick line of blue appearing. She winced at the damaged flesh. "Theta squad, fill that hole!"

The rock had barely settled when several Giants gripped the opening to rip it apart. Arrows shot through the air, including several that were on fire. One Giant dropped from taking an arrow in the throat before catching fire. Another let out a terrifying roar as he took several arrows to the knee. A dozen women in leather armor charged the giants, blades reflecting in the dying sunlight.

"Drag the Giant into the hole," ordered a blonde woman with short hair covering her long skull. Her body was fully covered in leather armor with metal bands around her wrists, her waist had two sais strapped to it. They looked like small tridents with the center point longer than the outer two. They had been forged from the fires upon An, using metals they could no longer create.

"You heard Minerva!" yelled Athena. She pointed at several of the Guards. "You there, back up Theta company." She turned to Enki. "Milord, can you give us a walkway along the wall?"

"I can't control it. I used too much power patching and doing the same on the north wall. The shifting of mantles from Anu's death has left me unsettled," Enki explained.

"She was right. We should have done better than the deflection wall. Minerva is always right," grumbled Athena. "What good are you to me if you can't magic up a solution to our problems?"

"Tell that to the Annunaki that poisoned Grandfather," Enki spat. "If he were still alive, the three of us would have cleared the field. Father is absorbing the Sky Lord's responsibilities, and I must deal with the Deacon's power. I can feel it under my skin, shifting around like a trapped panther. I will have to hold it at bay until we expel Chronos from our lands. Until we move against him, save your vitriol for Chronos."

"Yes, milord," Athena said softly.

"Where is Girra?" Minerva asked.

"With Gaia, they are heading to explore the continent in the middle of the ocean to the east, " Enki replied.

"Well, fuck," cursed Minerva. Another rock slammed into the wall, rolling over the top of the wall before slamming into the ground, cracking into several pieces. "Whose bright idea was it to make the walls sloped like that? Oh, right, it was my stupid idea, unless we can-" She shook her head, a grin crossing her face. "Enki, we need to draw the Giants closer. A retreat might work. We carved out the shelter with the sonic diggers."

"Yes, but what good would it be to go there?" Enki asked with a hint of anger.

"We fall back to the shelter and seal it. From there, we can send the younglings away, even if we have to dig more," Minerva said.

"But why would we want the Giants closer?" Enki spat.

"Because they are standing on the air vents. We set a trap on this side of the wall to trap them here. Then the Guard pops up through the shafts, killing them from behind. Even the other forces," Minerva explained as she pointed to the other walls.

"Get me a battalion of your Amazons, Athena. I am going to lead a charge here while you escort everyone underground," Enki ordered.

"We will need to push the other two walls at the same time to reduce reinforcements," Athena said.

"No, that would tip that we have more Guard here than they expected. We should only have a battalion here," Minerva interjected.

"My place is leading the charge. It would also tell them something's wrong if I was to leave. If we split the column up, we could split them better," Athena suggested.

"I want them to see me. Their Lords will want my death or capture. I created the abominations after all," Enki hissed.

"For the love of Anu, it's been over a thousand years since I kicked their asses. Are they still tail broke over that?" groaned Athena.

"So, we shall lead the charge as they will want both of us. Minerva, start pulling everyone back. Do make sure you swing by the maternity ward under my labs. Lady Rhea just gave birth to Hestia a few weeks ago. I would prefer Chronos not to get his claws on her," commanded Enki.

"Wait, she was pregnant? We are talking about Rhea Gaiasdottir, right?" asked Minerva.

"Yes, her. It's not my place to speak of it, but just be happy for her. Get ready. We charge at sunset," Enki said.

Chapter 33:

As he stretched his scarred hand out, Enki said a word of power. Lifting rocks was a lot easier than melting stone in an instant. He started walking through the gate; the debris floating around him. He punched his good hand out, sending a large chunk into the face of the Denisovan in front of him.

Athena let out a bellow before darting forward. Behind her, seven hundred Guards followed her. Arrows soared over the battle lines, but it was like bee stings to the Denisovans. The women split and Athena led half of them to the left and into a dozen Giants. Enki led the other half to the right, flinging the massive rocks to clear the path for his forces.

The Goddess of War leaped for the back of a Giant, a blade in each hand. She let out a bellow of triumph as she slid down the large Human's back, leaving two long cuts that severed tendons from the arms. With a loud thud, he fell to the ground. Athena stood on his corpse, lifting a bloody blade to the nearest target. "I'm going to mount your head on my wall," she snarled.

"You, big girl. Chief would love to see if you could kick his ass. You could be one of us. Why you fight for the evil ones?" questioned the Giant.

"Would you fight your family?" asked Athena as she slightly crouched, ready to dodge.

"Only the strong matter. If family stronger, then they are in charge. It's simple," the Giant answered.

Athena did a backflip, her feet slamming into the Denisovan's jaw, knocking him back. He stumbled but didn't fall, at least until an Amazonian ran behind him, her blade slicing his hamstrings. As the Giant fell, a blade sliced an ear off him before stabbing the sword through the wound. The War Goddess nodded to the Guard before moving to find another.

"Brother!" bellowed someone behind Athena. She glanced behind her, a four-meter-tall Giant was breaking into a run, a rock in his hand as he prepared to throw it. His face was contorted into one of mindless rage. Athena sidestepped the poorly thrown rock, barely noting the scream of pain from a bystander who had his back to it. She had little time to get her hands in front of her to catch the club with a loud impact, followed by the sound of wood cracking.

"Rascyra, now!" Athena yelled. The Guard moved behind the Giant, who tried to kick at the much smaller attacker. Two quick movements of cutting hamstrings followed by shoving the blade into the Denisovan's spine in three locations took it down.

"May your travel to the Great Mother be free of stones," said Athena as she closed the Giant's eyes.

"Look out!" yelled Rascyra.

Athena tried to drop to the ground, but a tree trunk of an arm scooped her up. The Goddess thrashed as she tried to break free, but the Giant wrapped both arms around her, locking his six-fingered hands around her waist. She slammed her head back into the Denisovan's face, shattering the big man's nose. He reflexively dropped his target as he clutched his nose. A swift backflip slammed the top of her feet between the man's legs. Rascyra drove her blade from behind through the left side of his back, the sword emerging from his chest.

"That wasn't too hard," Athena said, her breath heavy.

"If three isn't hard, remember, there's a few thousand more to go," reminded Rascyra.

"Right. Who's next?" demanded Athena as she gripped her blade with both hands, looking for a target. She broke into a run, leaping for another Giant.

Across the field of battle, horns blared. From behind them, the sound of rocks impacting stone tore through the air. Several heart-pounding seconds later, the sound repeated but suppressed as something fell in the city. It caused one giant to turn slightly, Athena landing on her backside as she missed him.

The Giant slammed his club down, Athena rolling away just in time for it to slam into the ground where her head had been. A Guard moved to distract the Giant, only to get caught by another's club from the side. Bones crunched as the impact of the club turned her hips to powder. The landing was worse as she landed on her side eight meters away. "Bugs to smash!" bellowed the Giant as he smashed his foot into the ground as one would an ant. He caught another Guard in the legs, ripping her calves from her knees.

With a leg flip, Athena was back on her feet. She turned only to have a pair of hands grab her and start pulling as she was lifted. The Giant let out a bellow and started tugging. Athena let out a scream of pain as she felt something pop within her back. The Giant let go, his hands moving to catch himself as his legs gave out. Rascyra moved swiftly behind another Denisovan with two quick moves, dropping another.

"We need a Harpy over here!" came a yell nearby.

"Danger close, no landing zone. Clear a place for us to land," came a response from above them. Athena looked up, and a dozen women were hovering over the battlefield. They wore a white outfit with a rod with two red snakes wrapped around it on their backs. Their wings were white, nimble enough to allow them to dodge the Giants that swiped at them.

"Clear your own damn zone!" bellowed the Guard.

"What do you think we've been doing?" The flight leader snapped back. Athena laughed as she realized that they were raining arrows from above.

"You heard her, clear a landing area. Stack the bodies of the Giants if you have to," Athena ordered. Ducking under a Giant's legs, she slammed her blade into the man's knee, his tendons coming apart, dropping him to the ground as he screamed in pain. A quick flick of the wrist ended the Denisovan's pain.

Enki stormed forward from the gate; chunks of stone were flung into the Denisovans' face before zipping back to the Annunaki Lord. The blood of Giants dripped around the large Lizard. It caused the attackers near him to slow their assault on the town. The bodies of the fallen littered the ground as he walked forward.

Amazon Guards moved behind him, slicing the throats of the Giants felled by Enki. Half a squad would also move to intercept a

Denisovan while the other half would try to slip around to cut the hamstrings. While others were trying to draw enemies away from the wall by trying to annoy the creatures.

"Lizard-man, you look like Master Chronos," said a Giant as he ducked a block flung at him. "Why you fight your Lo-" the Denisovan was cut off as the stone came back and took off the back of his head.

"That's why you pay attention," said Division Commander Krousses.

"Indeed," agreed a rich voice.

"Atlas, you still follow the blind," Enki commented.

"I follow my family. I do not blame you for doing the same, but you can see we are the stronger ones," Atlas replied, his clawed hands moving out to point at the forces. The Titan stood at three meters, primarily upright, a long snout with sharp teeth and a tail counterbalanced him. He held a massive stone on his shoulder.

"Might does not make right," Enki said.

"Yet, you lord over the natives in the same way," Atlas countered.

"Our Lords do not throw our lives away. They care about us," snarled Krousses.

"Child, you are but a stepping stone for their power. Even now, they are stealing your forms for this. Rhea explained all of this before she, unfortunately, was stolen from her husband," Atlas said.

"Lady Rhea hasn't been seen in Athens for two hundred years," Enki replied with an eye roll.

"That was before your Master stole her from us," Atlas spat.

"We've done no such thing. Rhea is indeed inside the city, but we rescued her off the shores," Enki said with narrowing eyes.

"Lies, it's all lies. Master Chronos showed us the body of one of your toys," Atlas protested.

"Atlas, listen to me. I do not know where your home is."

"Liar."

"I oversee research, this includes trade maps. We have maps of northern Africa and eastern Europe and their cities. They only have Neanderthals, Humans, and Anunnaki within. There are no Titans or Denisovans that reside there," explained Enki.

"All lies. My Master would never lie to the Titans!" screamed Atlas.

Enki let the stones fall with a soft thud. "Listen to yourself, you know I speak the trut-" He was cut off as Atlas lunged forward, throwing the rock at Enki. In his rage, the boulder went wide. It impacted one of the half squads, obliterating six in seconds.

Spinning, Enki slammed the middle of his tail into Atlas's face, knocking him to the ground. This gave Enki time to draw his blade. Glaring at his attacker, he spun the sword to bring it into the other god's neck. Atlas pulled back just in time so the blade struck stone, sparks flying. As the Titan stood, he ripped a stone ball out of the ground and threw it at the God of Magic.

Enki snarled a word of power to grab the blood-soaked boulder, flinging it in the path of Atlas's rock. The impact shattered both boulders, dust and shrapnel flying in all directions. Krousses threw herself between her Lord and the coming death. She had one advantage: a shield of the Legions of An. Stone impacted the shields of the Amazons, damaging the paint but left no physical damage as she landed on the ground with a thud.

"You have your Adama die for you?" Atlas roared.

"They have free will, which is more than can be said for you and your Adama," Enki spat back. He grabbed the ground and shook it like someone would a rug. The stone rippled in the same method, causing Atlas to stumble. The Annunaki Lord folded his hands, causing the rock to roll over and slam into the Titan's legs. He let out a bellow of pain as bones shattered, leaving stumps behind.

Enki breathed hard as he looked around. Athena held her left arm close to her waist, using her blade to block club attacks. She was down to about a hundred defenders, unbeknownst to the Goddess of War, who were slowly pulling back and out of battle with their Lady. He glanced at his own forces. They hadn't fared much better.

"Retreat!" Enki shouted, using his powers to magnify his voice. A dozen Giants broke into a run, their size allowing them to block the gate quickly. Another group moved to cut Enki off from Athena, but he flicked his hand to roll round pebbles under their feet, causing them to fall. The sound of tree trunks breaking ripped through the night air, then Enki realized it was the bones of Denisovans breaking.

"Enemies everywhere," gasped Krousses, her face bloodied from the fighting.

"Right where we want them," Athena replied as she ducked a club swing.

"Looks pretty bad from here," Rascyra said.

"Well, it could be worse," Athena reminded her.

"Stop all fighting!" came a bellow from the field. The Giants instantly stopped their tracks as they turned to look at the speaker.

"Lord Chronos, is there a reason for your rather aggressive visit to your brother?" Enki asked, the sounds of battle slowing.

"Why yes, the acceptance of your new Sky Lord. Me," Chronos said

Chapter 34:

A chuckle started that slowly climbed into full-on laughter, but it came out as soft hissing that turned into loud short bursts of a kak-k-k-k sound from Enki's throat. Athena joined in, and that caused her Guard to join in as well. It infected the Giants, turning the whole field into a roar of sound.

"Enough!" Chronos bellowed, ending the sound.

"Oh, my, thank you, Uncle. I haven't laughed that hard in a millennium," Enki said as he wiped a tear from his eye.

"Am I a joke to you?" spat Chronos, his staff slamming into the ground. Ripples of power rolled out, causing a wave through the dirt.

Enki looks Chronos dead in the eye. "Yes. Yes, you are. Look, I have better things than dealing with your tantrum. Either fight or shut up and let your nose drip."

"My nose does not drip. I am not a Setesh Guard," Chronos said, slamming his tail into the ground. "We are not discussing my nose, but your surrender to me."

"Who has the power of the Sky Lord then, you?" asked Athena.

"I am here, am I not?" Chronos said as he gestured widely.

"That does not make you the Sky Lord. You will need more than that to prove it," Enki replied.

"Well, where is Anu? He should defend his cattle, should he not? What about Enlil? Why is he not acting like the pitiful shepherd he is?" mocked Chronos.

Enki glanced at Athena, his eyes narrowing slightly. "I do not know where they are. I have sent runners to look for them, but they can't find either," Athena said in a half-truth.

"If they were alive, their presence would resonate within the Tiamat. We could feel them from here. Ergo, I am the Sky Lord as the eldest living member of the house of Anu," Chronos proclaimed.

"My Lady, is this true?" asked Krousses.

Athena shot her a look, but stepped next to Enki. "Until we see the bodies, we shall have to assume that they are still with us on this plane."

"Why do you insist upon your death? I am offering you all a chance to complete your tasks in your current cycle. What good would it be to have to repeat this one because you failed to learn what you needed?" asked Chronos, moving closer to Enki and Athena. After a few steps, he paused and tilted his head.

"You forget that perhaps this is what we need to learn. Perhaps the selfless nature of giving your mortal shell so that your family could live is what they are here to learn," replied Enki, his voice raised slightly.

"All that matters, young one, is power. The Great Mother understands this and commands us to project our power," Chronos said, his attention snapping back to Enki.

"But she also says that there is no greater love than laying your life down for your family. Power must be used wisely. Besides, we both know that anything physical cannot be brought with us into the next," Enki reminded him.

"That was from when we were trapped on Nibiru. On Olympus, we've returned many things to the Great Mother. The River Styx is a conduit for this," Chronos argued.

"The River Styx. The River Styx? The one to the Underworld?" Athena asked, her voice incredulous. "You've found the physical manifestation of the great river?"

"Yes," snapped Chronos.

"Come now, Athena. Chronos expects us to swallow every lie as truth. That's why he's the God of Time. He wastes it with his manure spreading. We can only access the great river through death and soul magic. Everyone knows this," Enki said.

"I will smite both of you where you stand," spat Chronos. "You will respect me."

"Well, why don't you try to make me, NOW!" Enki yelled the last word. When he did, Minerva leaped over the hill, her sword pointed at Chronos. Behind her, thousands of warriors charged over the hills.

"Defend me!" bellowed Chronos.

Enki knelt on the ground, one hand sending a ball of light out to the harbor area before he gripped the ground with both hands. The Lord of Magic ripped two spheres of limestone out of the dirt, tossing them into the air, repeating the action until he had eight orbs floating around him. Taking a deep breath, his hand snapped out. The spheres flew one right after another into Chronos' face.

At least that's what he tried to do. Chronos twisted his staff, causing the air in front of him to turn into a gel-like substance.

The first sphere entered and stopped. The second also entered and stopped. The third slammed into the first two and exploded, sending shattered rock everywhere but into the gel. Each rock hit into the prior one. The Titan stopped spinning his rod, the gel fading to nothing. The stones fell to the ground with thuds.

"Enki, give it up. I am the greater power here," Chronos proclaimed.

"Are you?" Enki asked, his voice sly.

Chronos let out a cry of pain as two more rocks slammed into his side. The sound of his ribs breaking was audible, causing the Lord of Time to drop to a knee. He gasped a word before his fall reversed and the stones pulled away from the impact sites. Stepping back, the balls slammed into each other in front of the Titan.

"Cute, Enki. You should have gone for the head. It is a hard lesson that every hero must learn," Chronos taunted.

"Well, only you could come back from having their chest crushed," Enki said. He dropped his hand and Chronos flung himself to the side, another rock slamming into the ground. As the Lord of Time got up, Minerva tackled him. She lifted her blade with both hands, pointed at her target's head. Her head turned as she heard a couple of thuds, a long sword appearing through her chest, blue blood dripping as it lifted her from the ground from the force.

"MINERVA!" Athena screamed, her voice breaking as she watched her wife's death. Enki slammed a rock into the back of the Giant, causing the Goddess of Wisdom's body to be tossed away. The War Goddess had flung herself a few hundred meters, her blade arcing as it sliced the Denisovan's arm off. She brought it down on the other arm before she faced Chronos, her face wild with anger. "Time to die, old man," she spat.

Chronos dodged the telegraphed moves. "Oh, did that hurt? I didn't know that abominations could feel," he taunted.

"You never learn," Athena growled as she elbowed Chronos in the jaw.

Chronos spat blood before slamming his tail into Athena's stomach. "Learn? We are the First Anunnaki. We are the Greys. We are the Titans. The rest of you should have always served us," Chronoa spat.

"The Great Mother sees everyone as equal. Our job is to be the shepherd of the young," Enki said as he stepped up to attack Chronos. A Giant picked up the blade of the one Athena killed, causing the God of Magic to defend himself from the new attacker.

"We are the ultimate being. All shall worship us. Every living thing on the planet of our ancestors belongs to us. Nay, everything on this planet belongs to the Titans," Chronos stated.

"You learned nothing from An. That is why the old Adama removed all the Gods from their planet. It's why the Greens took power; it was your punishment for your failures. It is why your grandfather relinquished the Sky Lord into Anu," Enki replied, his breath heavy from fighting.

"If Anu hadn't helped the Adama, they wouldn't have won. It is his fault we were stuck in space," Chronos said.

"Uncle, it was Belet-lil that helped the Adama. Your grandmother and wife of Uranus, the Cruel," Enki corrected him as he blocked the Giant's blade. He let go of the bottom of the hilt and whispered a word. His unburnt hand flashed white before the Giant was flung several hundred meters. The sounds of trees snapping ripped through the battle.

"Lies!" bellowed Chronos, using his staff to block Athena's relentless assault. "It was Anu."

"Okay, Titan," Athena quipped, her voice condescending. "Maybe you should have Damu check for brain worms. Anu wasn't born when we left An, forty thousand years ago."

"Does it really matter?" Chronos asked.

"You can't even remember how old your own father is. You need to have that checked," Enki pointed out.

From Chronos, a device started beeping. He leaped back, clearing space away from his attackers, pressing a button on his wrist. "We have found Rhea," a voice reported.

Chapter 35:

Chronos' face split into a grin. "Take Rhea back to Mount Othrys. Just make sure all her body parts are intact. Did you find the child?"

"We found her in child-care. Congratulations, milord, you have a daughter. It's not a real Titan however, it's one of those disgusting Elites," the voice said.

Chronos dropped his wrist as he made a ruck-ruck sound. "You have failed, Enki. I have my concubine back and my child."

"All that trash you vomited, and yet you claim a Human Form as your child?" Enki asked.

"She will be useful in keeping the Adama under control," Chronos replied with a shrug.

"My Lord," the voice spoke again fearfully. "We also found Sky Lord Enlil."

"I am your Sky Lord!" Chronos snapped.

"When we found him, he was bathed in orange light. We could not even enter the room, and nothing could pass the threshold," the wrist communicator reported.

"Kill him now, Crius. Or your life will be forfeit," Chronos commanded, panic coloring his order.

"We can't.".

"Then blow up the building! Do something," spat Chronos.

"We've tried," Crius replied. Whatever else he was going to say was cut short as Athena sliced Chronos' hand off through the communicator.

"Dumb conversation. Now you die for attempting to take power that isn't yours," Athena said, her face savage.

Chronos hurled himself back, trying to get out of the way of the angry Goddess. He dodged right and left. Athena was slower than usual. "Athena, Giant, left side!" Enki yelled.

Thanks to someone manipulating space around her, the War Goddess lunged to the right, but she was too slow. The Giant wrapped his arms around the woman's chest. A second Denisovan moved over and quickly had her hands and feet bound to a pole. One slung her over his shoulder, breaking into a run to catch up to his Lord, who was almost a hundred meters away, retreating. Horns blared from beyond the hills, causing the attacking forces to fall back.

Enki knelt over Minerva, whispering as he pressed his hands into her left side. She was gasping for air, trying to hold still. Her lung glowed for a few moments, allowing Enki to see where the wound was. The worst part for her was the collapsed lung.

"Krousses, if I am to give her a chance, I need more life force than I can tap into," Enki said.

"Anything for her," Krousses replied as she knelt next to Enki and placed her hand on his shoulder. Another placed her hand on his other shoulder, while another half dozen Guards lined up with their hand on the shoulder in front of them. A glow started from the end, slowly growing brighter. As the light enveloped the next, they glowed.

"Lady Tiamat, the Great Mother, hear our plea. Take our own

life force to heal this woman's mortal shell. If we have pleased you, grant us this boon to keep this soul among us, as we still have much to learn," Enki whispered. He released the gathered energy and pushed it into her.

Purple light gathered around Minerva's lung before soaking into the wound. She let out a gasp as her lung expanded and knitted itself back together. The damage slowly stopped bleeding before Enki let the spell go. The women touching him fell, their eyes closed with the slow breathing of sleep. Enki caught himself from falling, as did Krousses.

"She will live for now. Her other wounds, while threatening, won't kill her tonight. Where are the Harpies?" Enki asked.

"They were by the gate, trying to triage the wounded," Krousses said, her chest heaving.

"Have everyone fall back. We are going to be under siege for a long time. Gather the wounded, and we shall allow our attackers to do the same," Enki instructed.

"Yes, My Lord," Krousses said as she dragged herself to her feet, stumbling slightly. She blew her horn several times, her hand shaking from sheer exhaustion. After taking several long drinks from her waterskin, she moved to check on the fallen.

"Where is one of the Eves? Did Rascyra survive the attack?" Enki asked as he checked a body.

"I last saw her being carried away by a pair of Harpies. I am the ranking Eve with Athena and her down," Krousses explained as she lit a small light, setting it on a Guard who was still breathing.

Enki knelt over an Amazonian Guard, her hip crushed. He placed his hand on her forehead. "Sleep, little one," he whispered. The woman stopped tossing her head back and forth. The Lord of Magic took deep breaths to stabilize himself. He clipped a red light on her before standing, with only a slight stumble.

"We have this, My Lord," a voice above Enki spoke. He looked up to see a hundred medics in the air, already descending to help the critically wounded. One landed next to him, checking the woman before snapping her fingers, making a few gestures. She stepped back as three techs rushed up and started working on the fallen. They helped the God of Magic take a few steps back, a bottle pressed into his hand. He took a quick drink.

"Ambrosia. Do not spare any for the wounded," Enki said as he tried to hand the bottle back.

"We are using it on the wounded, you have gashes along your tail, right arm, and other cuts. I can see a bone where the skin was ripped from it," the Head Harpy replied.

"Alright, Celaeno, I will drink," Enki agreed.

"Should we figure out how to rescue Lady Rhea and Hestia?" asked Krousses.

"It's not them. They were underground and then, with the evacuation to Elysium, they should have been sheltered from all of this. While we should plan a rescue, we are not able to deal with it now. We need to scout around the area if Celaeno can do that after the wounded," Enki instructed.

"We are on reduced staff due to the landslide in Alexandria.

We've sent most of our healers and Harpies to help with the rescue efforts. In-house, Hygeia is in surgery right now, Damu is providing triage at the pile of Giants, and Gula took the North Wall. The Harpies are providing most of the medical aid," Celaeno explained, her wings shifting uncomfortably.

"The wounded first. Krousses, I want every able-bodied individual building defenses. The walls need platforms to defend from. Tell Zababa I decreed that sSharuracred Sharur shall be handed out to the Guard," Enki commanded.

"Yes, milord," Krousses replied. She waited a moment for more orders before sharply turning and running into the city.

"Celaeno, you have until first light to clear the field of the living. Chronos will attack again then. I will assist in bringing the wounded from Triage," Enki said.

"So many have been wounded in ways that prevent us from moving them," Celaeno pointed out.

"If you can't move them by first light, they are dead anyway. It's not something I like, but it's a fact of how we were raised on proper warfare." As if to say 'I have spoken', he turned, walking away from the Medic.

Enki arrived at the mound of dead Giants, the smell of blood filling his nostrils. The dead Amazonians were loaded into a wagon. The living were laid out on the blankets on the ground. The worse someone was wounded, the closer they came to Damu's worktable.

"Fill it in," Enki ordered. They pushed rock into the hole left by the attack on the wall. The last few hours had been busy as they quickly built defenses. They couldn't do much about the shock wave slopes, but set defenders at the top of the wall. Large crossbows were placed along each wall, put in pairs to provide covering fire. They used arrows large enough to take down a Denisovan.

The Amazonian Guard manned the battle line, dressed in their leather armor and pistols strapped to their hips. Some Humans backed them up, but they were not in full armor. They also only had swords on their hips.

"Where is Amphitrite?" Enki asked.

"She is on the outer island, defending us with her priests from Oceanus," explained Celaeno.

"With Athena, Minerva, and Rascyra gone, this leaves our forces under your command, Celaeno. They know that they have numbers on us. We lost close to three thousand in that move. They lost about a thousand. I place the defense in your hands," Enki said, his voice tired.

"My Lord, when was the last time you ate or slept?" Celaeno asked.

Enki waved his hand slightly. "Breakfast yesterday."

"Then my first order is for you to eat and sleep. We will need your power when the walls are breached again. We have two more days before Enlil can move, so rest when you can," Celaeno instructed.

"Why would I rest? I need to keep the defense going," Enki replied. Celaeno patted his shoulder before the two separated. The Lord of Magic shook his head. "Wh- what did you-?" he started to ask but his eyes rolled back in his head as the medication sent him into dreamland.

Chapter 36:

"Wake up, milord. Here is some food. Eat quick," Celaeno instructed as she placed a plate next to the bed of hay.

"What time is it?" Enki asked as he moved to eat breakfast.

"It's just past noon. The Titans have been testing our defenses, but they brought out their own fliers half an hour ago. These new creatures have riders and spit fire," Celaeno briefed.

"Oh, Chronos brought back the Dragon riders of An. Well Riders of Chronos now," Enki said between bites.

"That is not all. Amphitrite has requested backup as she fights with Oceanus, as Tethys has arrived," Celaeno reported, handing Enki a diagram of the attackers.

"Is Elysium still secure?"

"Yes, Lady Rhea and her child are within. Chronos might leave if we ha-" Enki cut Celaeno off by slamming his tail suddenly.

"No, we do not give up our own," Enki proclaimed, his eyes narrowed.

"Just making sure we have considered all the mortal lives we are sacrificing to protect them," Celaeno replied, as she cleaned Enki's armor. "You should have taken this off so the Adama could clean it."

"Who would have done that? If they are staying safe, then they are on the line," Enki said as he cracked his neck, stretching himself out. "We have to protect ourselves from Chronos. He will not be a kind Lord. The Denisovans fear him and the other Titans. He would treat the Adama as slaves, beasts barely having intelligence. A treasured pet at best."

Enki took a long drink of Ambrosia before he continued. "The reason Chronos is so desperate to wipe his family out, the Adelphi Oracle said that he would die by one with male blood. He thinks if he is the Sky Lord that he'll be able to stop all threats."

"Why would he think that?"

"No idea. There is a reason my sister and I don't have anymore siblings," Enki said as he adjusted his armor. "I'm going to help fight Oceanus. Someone needs to find out where Hades is. He said something about investigating some caves a few days' walks away. I still haven't seen a full account of who's around. Try to get me the report before sunset."

"I'll get right on that, Milord," Celaeno replied.

"If there is nothing else, I am going to stop Oceanus," Enki said. He quickly left and found himself at the harbor. The fishing boats docked there, well, would have been docked there. Their wreckage was tossed across the beach, and the water break. They ripped the wooden docks out, even their pylons were used as weapons. In the distance, he could see a trio of tornados rotating around the next island in the chain.

The Annunaki Lord glanced at the distance he needed to cross before he flicked his wrist and whispered a word. A raft quickly formed with a small sail. He stepped onto it before twisting his finger, and the wind picked up to push him across. He used his tail to steer and crossed the distance in a few minutes. He shook his head. It must have taken more than a few minutes as the sun was setting. Stepping onto the beach, he could feel the vibrations from the fighting. He quickly headed for the battle. As he neared, he hid in the remaining vegetation.

On the beach was Amphitrite, her body clad in navy-blue armor, her hair floating in the wind. She hovered half a meter from the ground, her right leg raised slightly as she used it to direct one of the tornados.

Next to the Ocean Goddess was Aphrodite, wearing body armor covered in hearts and the beige color of the sand she was fighting on. Her eyes were glowing a soft white, while her hair had shifted from red to the same shades as the sand. She had a compound bow she was firing arrow after arrow, pulling from an invisible quiver.

Hades stood behind the pair, his hair lit blue, while flames hovered around his eyes. His scepter's head was the same blue flame. He wore dark red form-fitting armor that had been forged in the fires of An. He shot the rod forward, a beam of blue cutting through the air, striking a flying creature. Its head fell, while its rider fell the other direction. They landed in the water with a loud splash.

"What's going on?" Enki asked. The water retreated from the shoreline. It left behind fish and other creatures, flopping on the ground. The Lord of Magic could see the wave rising in the distance.

"By Anu's blood, thou shall not do that," snarled Amphitrite as she dropped to the ground. Her whole body glowed purple as she gripped the sand. The water rushed back halfway before it stopped. The wave in the distance did not appear to be getting closer, but looks could deceive with something that far away.

Hades fired several blasts at the Dragon Riders. They were dive-bombing the small group to distract or stop the Ocean Goddess. Aphrodite fired three arrows at a time. They would pepper a dragon from the neck, chest, and rear. The second round would drop the pair into the ocean. The problem had become that there were too many attackers.

Enki grabbed the rear tornado as he said words of power. He could feel Amphitrite's relief at someone taking the burden. He used the upper part of the wind column to manipulate the winds a few dozen meters up. It had the effect of pushing the Dragons out of range, and leaving the Olympians out of range of their breath of flame.

A Rider raised his bow and fired an arrow. It struck Hades in the left shoulder, right between the armor plates, causing blue blood to spray. He let out a grunt and broke the shaft. Using one hand, he returned fire. However, the Dragon Rider dove and the shot went wide. Enki tried to knock the rider off using a gust of wind, but the rider was experienced and wasn't knocked off his mount.

The Rider dove for the trio, his dragon weaving through the air as a fish would the water. As he neared the point of recovering, the dragon opened its jaws, flames forming within. With eyes only for the target, the Rider cackled right up to the point a wall of water slammed into him. Amphitrite's hand pulled the stream back before slamming the now riderless dragon into the ground. It hit with a thud, followed by the sound of bones shattering. The Rider crashed headfirst into a broken tree and slumped into a lifeless lump.

Enki let out a roar of pain as an arrow pierced his tail. Twisting in rage, he sent a blue jet of flame into the face of the dragon and its Rider. The dragon rolled his head to allow his flame-resistant chest to take it, but the heat was too much for the unexpecting Rider. He had his bow drawn, ready to launch another shot, when his face melted. His lifeless body fell to the ground.

Hades lifted his scepter in his right hand, his left arm still hanging useless thanks to the arrow, and fired several blue light beams. The problem for him was, he wasn't as practiced with his off-hand, so his shots were going wide.

Aphrodite was grabbing an arrow, drawing, and firing faster than Enki could track. The woman just couldn't miss it seemed. Every trio shot she fired dropped a dragon. Several didn't even need the second and third arrows as the headshot went right through an eye. "Two thousand and twenty-seven. Two thousand and twenty-eight," she mumbled, the count going up after each dragon died.

"Gotcha," whispered Amphitrite as she stood. Grains of sand languidly poured out of her fists as she lifted them to be level with the ocean. She slowly twisted her hands so that they were palm up. She opened them, slowly turning to the right, and threw the sand into the air.

In the ocean, a rush of water shot from the surface. It was a muddy mess as sand blasted Oceanus out. Enki reached out with the wind to catch the Titan and pulled him to the beach. Amphitrite grabbed the front two tornados, flinging both out to keep the flyers away from their Lord. Water jets shot from the ocean, trying to catch the Titan. Hades used his staff to blow the tops of the water away.

A dozen dragons dove for the sand bar, moving the Titan along. "No," Amphitrite growled, her hands clenching tight to wrap Oceanus with more sand, but the fliers cut the soil from the source of magic and flew away with the Grey. The remaining attackers soared away. Night had fallen during the fight.

"Thank you, milord," Amphitrite said before taking a long drink of Ambrosia. She dropped to her knees, panting. "I think I could sleep for a month. I had little left in me, that last move took the last of my reserves."

Aphrodite knelt next to Hades who had laid on his back. He was panting as he struggled to stay awake. "Hold still. The arrow has barbs."

"Just pull the damn thing out," Hades hissed. He let out a scream when Aphrodite cut one side, tossing the hooked arrowhead into the sand.

"The tip is poisoned, but it's not enough to kill you. You'll be sick for a few days and probably have minimal access to your powers," Aphrodite explained.

"What took you guys so long? We asked for backup two nights ago," Amphitrite said.

"We were busy defending the walls from the Denisovans last night," Enki reminded her.

"No, that was two nights ago. We just started the third night, finishing the second day since Chronos attacked," Amphitrite replied, her voice confused.

"Chronos must be using his powers as a Time Lord. That must

be extremely taxing on him. Not only does he have to bend space-time around the city, but he also must keep the place spinning at the same speed as the planet, to keep up with the orbit. The strain must be enormous. Which means we are probably going to have another plasma discharge in the next few days," Enki said.

"Why would he do that? Wouldn't it be easier to starve us?" Aphrodite asked as she cleaned the blood from her knife.

"Chronos wants the power of Sky Lord. Thus, he needs to kill the other claimants since it didn't go directly to him. He hopes he can slow Deacon Enlil's rebirth as Sky Lord. That's not how any of this works, but he still thinks he can stop it," Enki explained.

"Lovely. Perhaps the Underworld would be the best escape for us. We can live down there for years, more than enough time to carve tunnels," Hades suggested as he slowly stood.

"Chronos won't stop his attack. If he can't find us, he will tear everything apart to find us. He's doing this partly so he could keep Rhea in his clutches. That is a very unhealthy obsession," Aphrodite said.

"Why does he want her if he hates the Human Form so much?" Amphitrite asked.

"He's infertile. At least when it comes to the Great Lizard Form. The Great Mother has told him that if he takes a Titan as a wife, his line will end," Hades informed them.

"How do you know?" Enki asked.

"Because I'm the one causing the stillborn. No souls may return to his line," Hades said as they started walking for the city.

Aphrodite gave Hades a look. "You dare interfere with another's love?"

"I am protecting them from Chronos at the request of his dead children. He arranged for their deaths if they didn't match his ideal Annunaki. He is not a kind being. His idea of love is not love. He thinks love is someone obeying your every wish. If he wants your meal, you don't love him if you don't give it to him. The fist he gives you deserved," Hades hissed.

"Oh dear, no, that is not love. It will take a long time to correct that," Aphrodite replied.

"I plan on recommending Chronos for Tartarus if the Great Mother doesn't judge his deeds harshly." Hades' voice held judgment and truth within.

"Should we not worry about Oceanus recovering?" Enki asked.

"Eh, the tsunami was his last-ditch attempt. He knows we can match him, even go beyond his power. If he is going to help, he'll do it with Chronos or other Titans for backup," Amphitrite said.

The group came around a hill and froze as the sound of stone exploding hit them. Their city was on fire. Across the water, the Gods watched Denisovans rushing over the walls. The three main pyramids had their tops ripped off, laying to the side. The warehouses were burning, including the ones that held grain. That one had a flame that reached seven meters. The fire consumed the residential areas of the Humans.

"What-" Hades' voice cracked. Clearing his throat, he spoke again. "What happened?"

"Enlil has awoken," Aphrodite whispered. "His fury is like no other. They attacked his children." Just then, a thud sounded as a shock wave crossed the water. The Denisovans leaping over the wall were thrown back, followed by multiple water splashes as it flung attackers from the city.

"Yes, you can see that the damage to the Science center was from the inside out. Now, shall we cross?" Enki asked.

Amphitrite stepped forward, her hands moving. She spoke a word, causing everyone's feet to glow. "The spell will raise the salinity of the surrounding water. You cannot sink because of it."

"Won't this kill the species that live in the water?" Enki asked.

"No, you are only borrowing the salt. It also pushes the critters away from you," Amphitrite explained as she walked onto the beach, the waves rolling away from her. She took a deliberate step into the water. Her feet glowed green as she kept walking, small glowing footprints left behind. The Gods shrugged and followed her.

Hades placed his hand on Enki's shoulder. "Remember to trust yourself. Apparent failure today often will provide a lasting victory."

"Of course, young whippersnapper." Enki chucked as he stepped onto the water. "Oh, how odd. I leave purple footprints while the rest of you leave green."

"You are still of the Old Gods. We are the New Gods. We've been calling ourselves the Olympians," Aphrodite said, her hand gesturing to the other Humanaki.

"We do not speak of Cthulhu. He is of the OLD GODs," Enki snapped.

"Oh my, I can hear the capitalization of Old Gods," Aphrodite replied.

"If we stopped remembering him, he'd fade back into the whole cycle," Enki said.

"Well, actually, The Grandfather is an angry God. He is several planes of existence above us. He does not like having to give attention to individual cycles. He tends to destroy worlds that demand his attention," Hades said matter-of-factly.

"Wait, he's a real being?" Aphrodite asked, fear coloring her voice. "I thought he was a story to get children to obey their parents."

"Yes, he is. He observes many worlds," Hades explained.

"That's the Great Mother and Father." Aphrodite sounded confused.

"Yes, that's our Mother and Father. I am speaking of their parents, so to speak. They nurture our souls in the Great Cycle. The cycle for each race means that there is one pair per world. Galaxies are observed by the Grandparent Cycle, with four Grandparents. From there, it starts to get fuzzy, even for me. However, getting Lord Cthulhu's attention is hard, as he is as far above us as we are to the ant. If a colony of ants gathers our attention, it never works out well for the ants," Hades stated.

"Okay, he sounds like we shouldn't use that name at all. If we don't name him then..." Aphrodite's voice trailed off.

"Oh no, Lord Cthulhu will ensure that he is remembered. Besides, there is one already known as 'He Who is Not to be Named' among the Elder Gods. Whenever he's forgotten on a world, he gives a mortal a dream, and they end up telling stories about him," Hades explained.

"Anyway, what's the attack plan?" Amphitrite asked, changing the subject.

"Can you wash the area outside the walls with a tsunami?" asked Enki.

"It would affect our own," Amphitrite said.

"I can't feel our own beyond the walls," Hades informed her.

"Then yes. I'm done after, but I can do it," Amphitrite confirmed.

Chapter 37:

The darkness was suffocating. The sun had nothing to reflect; the light reaching the group was the stars and what little was bent around the planet. Flames flickered across the city, across water, reflecting upon the surface as it retreated. That was the only sign that the attackers had that something was happening.

Without warning, water slammed into the ground on the north and south sides of the city. The liquid took the attackers away in twenty meters of saltwater. The power carved channels into the ground, taking dirt and stone for a ride. The abrasive nature took more material with it as the semi-natural hills around the city trapped the water, blocking the passages between them. Around the town, a gap of thirty meters of water protected the village from the attackers.

Amphitrite collapsed to the ground at the south wall, her breath coming in heaves. Her eyes closed as she brought her hand to her chest. "My chest hurts. It feels like a Denisovan has sat on me."

Enki knelt next to the Goddess of the Ocean, whispering a few words. "You're fine. Just strained your heart by moving that much power."

The sky lit up for a few moments as several plasma lines appeared. That let the group see the damage that Amphitrite had brought. The water was brown from the dirt that it stirred up. Neanderthal bodies were floating to the surface. It looked like one could almost traverse the new moat just by walking across the dead.

"Tartar sauce," spat Hades.

"You mean Tartarus?" Amphitrite gasped.

"Have you had tarter sauce? That stuff is worse than anything I could serve as punishment." Hades chuckled for a moment. "That, however…" he let his voice trail off as he pointed to the sky.

"The last time this happened, I almost died," Enki warned, fear in his eyes as the plasma flashed again. "We are using too much power. The ambient energy produced by solar winds isn't enough. Nature abhors a vacuum, and we made a rather large one."

"Yet you survived two direct hits," Amphitrite reminded him.

"No, I survived creating the vacuum. As it was, we almost died from just the shock wave of the actual plasma burst. Then came the tsunami that almost drowned us. It is why we created Elysium to ride out the storms," Enki explained.

"My son," a grateful voice said behind the group.

Enki turned. "Father."

"Thank you, Amphitrite, for your actions. You have bought us the time we needed," Enlil thanked her with a bow of his head. He handed her a wineskin with Ambrosia. "Drink, my child." He paused for a moment to ensure she drank. "You've given us options. However few they are, this is more than we had at sunset."

"What? Surrender or starve?" Hades asked.

"Nay, my friend. We still have the growth tubes from the Nibiru, more than enough to feed those who are still alive. We just need to outlast Chronos," Enlil replied.

"What about Chronos' temporal slowdown?" Amphitrite asked.

"I am countering him right now, thus the sky," Enlil said as he pointed up.

Hades stood at the edge of the water, his eyes glowing grey as he looked over the dead. He shook his head at the senseless loss of life. "If only Chronos wasn't a controlling fool, none of you would have died. Dayan, you had potential to become a mighty Chief, creating the greatest of the Denisovan structures for thousands of years," he spoke to a specter he had made visible as the soul floated in front of him.

Enlil placed a clawed hand on Hades' shoulder. "My friend, we can only worry about the now. The what-ifs will drive us insane."

"I know, but I can't help but feel the sorrow at their lives being cut short," Hades replied before shaking his head. "What else can we do besides stay trapped?"

"We can dig our way out," Enki suggested.

"Dig our way out," Hades repeated, giving Enki a look of confusion.

"Well, we have the sonic diggers," Enki explained.

"Until they break like everything else from An," Amphitrite groaned.

"They don't break in the hands of the Adama," Aphrodite said, her eyes narrowed as she looked over the moat. "My Lord, is that Chronos?"

The group turned while Hades' eyes flashed red. "Yes, that is Chronos."

"Enlil, I see you," Chronos' voice carried across the water. "Give up, little brother. The eldest should inherit the power of the father, not the youngest."

"You know as well as I do, brother, that the Great Mother alone chooses who will lead us. It is by her divine will that I am the Sky Lord of the Olympians," Enlil called back.

"Pah, the Annunaki are the prime race here. If not them, then the Titans are the clear superior species. We are the ones blessed by the Lady," Chronos spat.

"How many times have we kicked your Titans' asses?" bellowed Amphitrite.

"Hush you," Enlil chastised with a bit of a laugh. "The Lady brings up a good point. Lady Tiamat tested you and found you wanting. Lizard, ape, dolphin, or space whale, flesh matters not. It is who we are that matters, my brother."

"The now is the only thing that matters. We are the first race. We roamed the Heavens for millennia. While we were ruling over the weak, these apes were still flinging their feces around. Our very will bends the fabric of reality," Chronos stated.

Enlil glanced at Amphitrite. "Did he not see what you just did? What the three of you did to his warriors?"

Amphitrite raised an eyebrow, shaking her head slightly as Enlil turned to speak. "Brother, do you not see what Amphitrite brought with her powers? In every way possible, their forms prove true."

"Never will a member of the Titans use those forms. No matter how many abominations Rhea keeps birthing," Chronos snarled.

"If you think she births abominations, why is she your queen?" Aphrodite demanded.

"Because what Tiamat brings together, no one shall break apart.

She bonded us in this life. She will belong to me for the rest of this life. You will hand her back to me, and perhaps I will not siege you," Chronos offered.

Aphrodite glanced at Enlil. "Is he trying to become the God of Lies?"

"Perhaps he is suffering from the long nam-tar?" Hades suggested.

"What's that?" asked Aphrodite.

"A sickness of the soul. That nasty virus slowly corrupts the inner-self until you become unrecognizable and removed from the Great Cycle. No one understands where it comes from or how it appears," Hades explained.

"That's only a tale to scare children into obeying," Enlil replied before looking back at Chronos. "What assurance do we have that you will leave us if we comply?"

"Oh, you have none. You just don't have another choice. Your city is in ruins, your food stores up in flames, your Warrior God locked away in my camp. Oh, and the greatest feat of all, we killed your Knowledge Goddess. You simply have nothing left to defend with," Chronos said.

"Can you give us until daybreak for a response?" Enlil asked.

"This I can do. This place once the sun appears in the sky," Chronos replied before walking off.

"My Lord, you know the suffering Rhea will experience-" Aphrodite started.

Enlil held up his hand to stop her. "Let's talk in the command center, away from any possible spies."

The group nodded before heading inside the semi-broken walls.

Chapter 38:

Fires flickered among the homes. Humans and Anunnaki lived among each other, reflecting from the few attempts to put out the flames. Sadly, they were fighting a losing battle. Amphitrite reached out, pulling a mist from the ocean, the wind pooling together before dropping over the burning structures and putting out most out-of-control blazes.

Hades ran to a collapsed building, pulling stone and wood out. Aphrodite lent a hand as she started to dig frantically. A few minutes later, the Goddess of Love carried a child out of the rubble. She carefully laid the limp form down. "Harpy!" she screamed.

Aphrodite didn't need to scream. Since the fires were out, the medics were already landing. One knelt next to the child as she opened the pack on her waist. The child's wounds were quickly bandaged after being cleaned. The Harpy nodded slightly before turning to look at the Goddess.

"Medic," Hades called as he laid a small woman next to the child. She was missing her legs from halfway down her thighs.

"There is nothing we can do," the Harpy replied, tears dripping from her nose.

"Her heart beats, her soul is still within. Save her," Hades demanded.

The woman's hand shakily reached out to her daughter. "Safe?" came the woman's weak voice.

"Yes, little one. Her father?" Aphrodite asked.

"De-dead," the dying woman shuddered, her body racked with a convulsion.

"I will take care of her," Aphrodite swore. Around the Goddess's hair, a blue light glowed for a moment. The dying woman closed her eyes and gave her last breath, knowing her child would be safe.

Hades stood and stomped over to another building. A wave of his hand removed every bit of stone, screaming in rage that he had failed to save one of his charges. The cleared area showed a family of three, the two adults laying across a child, protecting her from the harm. They slowly lifted their heads before hugging each other.

The sky had a warm glow over the horizon, catching Enki's attention. He glanced over at Enlil, who was facing the southern wall, his staff glowing. "Amphitrite, we'll need tsunami protection. Hades, start getting everyone who's left into the shelter. Harpy, what happened to the Amazonian attack force that we sent behind the lines?"

The medic glanced at Enki while checking the couple. "They fell back into the hill passages after Minerva went down. While the Titans can't pass through the air shafts like we can, they have blocked the holes with stone."

Enlil tapped the staff three times before thrusting it into the sky. Lightning reached out, grabbing hold of something that turned out to be a dark purple bolt of its own. The new Sky Lord snarled as he struggled to push the spark back into the sky. He let out a roar as he lifted the staff again, a green pulse going up the bolt. There was a bright explosion before the purple bolt faded into the rest of the sky.

Gasping, Enlil slumped to one knee. He placed one of his clawed hands on the ground as a Harpy rushed over to him. She handed him a bottle of Ambrosia, which he finished in one gulp. Then, tossing the bottle aside, he nodded to the medic as he stood.

Enki walked over to the Sky Lord. "Father, let us retreat and recover our strength. You are weak from the turmoil within your soul."

"I must defend everyone until we can retreat. You can help me the most by getting everyone underground," Enlil snapped as he spun the staff, a gust of wind developing to envelop a massive stone that had appeared above him. The rock slammed into the ground, taking out the wall it hit. "Go, my son!" he yelled.

"Come on, Hades, point me to the living. I'll lift the stone, you bring them out," Enki ordered as he started for another grouping of huts. Hades followed him, pointing to a house. The God of Magic spoke a word before grunting as he lifted his hands, the stone creeping up until Hades could run in. Moments later, he ran out with a man and child.

"That's it," Hades said. Enki dropped his hands, the stone slamming back to the ground.

The pair spent the next two hours going from house to house. They often skipped homes, only to save those who were closer to death. Finally, Enki dropped the last stone and his head dropped as he panted. "How many more?"

"That was the last one," Hades replied.

"Good, I need to rest," Enki said, his tail dragging along the ground as they walked for the Science Pyramid.

The sky lit up again as energy countered energy. The sky had three spheres with what looked like a stick figure, complete with a slight tail. Above the plasma structure was a purple ring. In the center was a four-point star, pointing at the cardinal points. From the ring were fifty-eight spikes that shot plasma at the stick figure. The plasma spheres absorbed the bolt before it flowed back at the ring.

"We evacuated everyone, milord," Enki reported.

Enlil nodded, his breath coming in gasps. He spat several words as he smashed his staff into the ground. The squatting man in the sky suddenly shifted into a long snake that struck the ring, splitting it before swallowing. The snake flashed purple and green, then red, before fading into nothing.

"It is done for now," Enlil said before his eyes rolled back in his head, collapsing in a heap.

Chapter 39:

Celaeno swore as she moved around Minerva, whose right leg was cut open. "Suction," she spat. Another Harpy placed a hose over the exposed bone. The lead Harpy drilled several holes so that she could attach several rods.

Enki turned from the observation and almost ran over a woman who stood over two meters, her brown hair pulled back in a ponytail. She wore a red sundress, and in one of her arms was a baby with charcoal skin and black hair.

"Lady Rhea. I am glad to see you are well. I take it they found the decoys?" Enki asked.

"Yes, they did," Rhea replied.

"Is this little Hestia?" Enki asked as he took a step back.

Rhea tilted her head slightly. "Yes, milord. You should turn us over. Chronos will rip this place apart to find me."

"I'd slit his throat if we were still on the Nibiru, as would Enlil. No one hits their family, period," Enki growled.

"My suffering is a small price to pay for the lives of the Mortals. They might be a part of the Great Cycle, they are young and have yet to have an awakening. It is a small price to pay to protect them. I know that the arms of the Mother await me, and she'll help me cope with this life. They will not," Rhea said as she shifted Hestia.

"You don't hit to show love. You don't mentally abuse someone if you love them. Family is sacred." Hestia let out a giggle, causing a slight flash of light.

Rhea shifted the infant again. "She seems to agree with you, milord."

"Do you like family, little one?" Enki asked. Hestia let out a loud giggle in response. "That sounds like a 'yes'."

"Back to the point. I'll give myself up to save the rest of my family," Rhea said.

"Think about it Rhea. Will Chronos leave Enlil alone? Will he leave us alone? He might despise the Elites, but you and your children are of his blood. That at least is the line he doesn't cross," Enki pointed out as he motioned for Rhea to follow him.

"No, he will wipe out everyone that might challenge him," Rhea replied softly.

"Or force them into slavery under his superior race," Enki growled.

"I can't sit here and do nothing," Rhea spat.

"You have one job, and that is to protect that little one in your arms. Let us worry about the rest," Enki said.

"This is my path. The Delphi Oracles have spoken," Rhea argued, her eyes narrowing at the God of Magic.

"Only possibilities. Prophecy is tricky to understand until after the events," Enki said with a chuckle. He paused mid-step as a memory flashed. "Oh. Were you told that you will birth the Gods that will guide the Adama to enlightenment?"

"Yes, milord," Rhea replied.

"Prophecy shed," Enki snarled. "This is real life, not some fantasy novel. I know I am a dream reader, but that's from your own brain tapping the Dimethyltryptamine it produces to access other planes of existence. You are interpreting someone else's memories or just having fun. Not some cryptic word vomit that sounds like nonsense that makes no sense to anyone until after events finish."

"Well, we know they are doing the same thing, but awake," Rhea chuckled.

"Yeah, and that makes them reclusive. Too much noise and it upsets the writers when their routines are disrupted. Are you sure that they didn't give you one of their fantasy novels?" Enki asked with a sigh.

"No, this was an actual Oracle, not one of the Holo-producers," Rhea stated. Enki paused and looked at Rhea. "Really, it wasn't the entertainment division that said it. Enlightenment will come from my personal suffering, then everyone dies."

Enki snorted. "What?"

Rhea snorted as well. "Everyone dies at some point. I just thought it odd that the seven Oracles kept talking about the Seven of Sevens of Seven Seals that will cause the Seven Seas to run red with the blood of the Great Beast. From the ashes, Seven will rise, with an Eighth to protect them from the Four and One. The Seven and Four shall part with the Ones. Eighth becomes the One."

"See, word vomit that makes no sense. Dreams are at least easy to explain. You can ask questions," Enki replied.

"Still, sometimes to win the war, you must lose the battle," Rhea pointed out.

"Why do I keep being told that? It's not a saying of our people," an exasperated Enki said.

"Because it's some-" a runner coming up to the pair cut Rhea off.

"My Lord, we have reviewed our food situation. We have a week's worth of food left. The destruction of the city reached down to our stores of both gel and grain. Primary power is also offline, with no hope of rebuilding," the runner reported.

"Why can't we rebuild it?" Rhea asked.

"It was taken from the Nibiru and requires metals we can't access anymore," Enki explained.

"Ah, right. We don't have the machines to make the machines that create the machines," Rhea recited.

"Correct. We know how to rebuild a lot of our things. We just can't thanks to that," Enki said as he handed the report back. "We can stretch the food out for longer. I didn't see a water report."

"We are fine with water. The ocean is still being filtered by the limestone"

"Could we use the ocean to escape?" asked Rhea.

"No, the harbor was obliterated, along with any ship we had there. Oceanus is also probably watching the bay now that we've fallen back," Enki said.

"Then what are we going to do?" demanded Rhea.

Enki grinned at her, showing his pointed teeth before explaining, "We get a stone eater."

"What do you mean we don't have a stone eater?" Enki demanded. "Two weeks ago, it was in perfect condition, with plans to extend the underground to Nymph Island. In the last twenty-four hours, you've already cleared a kilometer. How could it break now?"

"Because our stone eater burnt out an hour ago. We sent the other three to build the caverns so we could start building Athens, Sparta, and Troy," explained Ninurta. He stepped out of a ten-meter in diameter cylinder that was thirty meters long, most of it buried within the stone wall. The last five meters reached into the massive cavern.

"When did we send them out? Wait, I remember, last Tuesday. What about the scoopers?" Enki asked.

"They are good for fine work, such as carving out obelisks for wireless power transmission. We have about two dozen, but they need an eight-hour recharge after moving fifteen tons. We could get maybe thirty meters per day of digging through this rock. Our food stores are good for about a week, maybe two," Ninurta said.

"What about your powers? Can't you shape the rock?" Enki demanded.

"I was channeling my power through the stone eater, allowing the machine to scoop up the rock. Once it broke down, I tried reaching out to the stone, but I was countered. What they are doing is countering the infusion of energy I am using. I get the shape I want, but before it becomes a reality, the power is just diffused into nothing," Ninurta explained.

"Chronos probably blew the machine," Enki stated before pausing and running his hand over his face. "Wait, oh my Gods. We are under Chronos' camp. That's why it broke. They are directly above us."

Ninurta looked up. "You know, if we go back a hundred meters, we should be able to core an observation pipe."

"Do it," Enki hissed.

Raising his arm to his mouth, Ninurta spoke into his communicator. "Bring me- Gods dammit, comms are still offline down here. I'll get a drill team here." He quickly headed out of the area.

"Enki, I see you," called the stone.

The Lord of Magic turned to look at the distortion. "Hello there. Are you auditioning for the role of the God of the Underworld? I'm sorry, but I am not in charge of that department. You'll have to speak to Hades."

"What?" snapped the stone.

"I wouldn't dream of pissing off someone who could lock my soul away. Makes you think twice that he has that kind of power." Enki shrugged before turning to walk away. "Speak Chronos or piss off."

"I offer you one last time, hand over Rhea, and I'll let the Human Gods leave," said the Stone Chronos.

"Hand you the Mantle of the Underworld for Rhea. That's-" Enki was cut off as the wall spoke again.

"That is not the deal, and you know it, child. Hand me my slave woman, or I will kill everyone. You have nowhere to go. We've ruined all your food, and we've found your tunnels. Hand over my property, and some may live. Don't, and everyone will die," Chronos demanded.

Enki snapped his hand out, gripping the stone. Chronos grabbed at the hand that was choking him. "Counteroffer, you can die." Chronos faded before Enki let go. He let out a growl as he slammed his tail into the wall.

A runner appeared around the corner, entering the large cavern. "My Lord, Ninurta has a camera in place. He'd like you to observe."

"Lead the way," Enki commanded. He was quickly taken around the corner to find three Anunnaki and several Humans working to move a metal snake into a small hole in the overhead. The wall displayed the video feed.

"There doesn't seem to be that many here," Ninurta said.

"We might have killed more than we expected with the tsunami. Can you find Chronos? He is in this camp," Enki stated.

"Haven't seen him yet. We've seen Tethys tending to the wounded. Hyperion also leads a battalion of Denisovans. Prometheus, well, he was brooding in the corner. We left him helping Rhea and the kids," Ninurta reported.

"Oh, so that's where that assistant went," Enki commented.

"Prometheus is a Titan. Are you sure he worked for you?" asked a human servant.

"Yes. He has sworn fealty to Anu. He also was the one who discovered the Gods' connection to the Spirit World," Enki explained, shaking his head. "Anyway, how many troops have we counted?"

"More than enough to finish us," Ninurta replied.

Enki stared at the image for a few more seconds, mumbling, "To win the war, you might need to lose the battle." He shook his head before looking at Ninurta. "Seal the hole and bring the mobile to the cafeteria. I will address them after speaking with the Sky Lord."

"It will help calm a lot of the fear," Ninurta said.

Enki nodded and left, heading to find the Sky Lord. Thankfully, he was in the Sky Lord's chambers trying to meditate.

"Sky Lord, I come bearing bad news," Enki reported.

"Proceed," Enlil said.

Enki explained the forces above them, how they couldn't dig out fast enough for their food stores, and the latest taunt by Chronos.

"Why does he keep contacting us to demand Rhea? This is not like him at all. He has the upper hand. Why doesn't he come down here and get us? They have taken control of our exits," Enlil commented.

"Perhaps he also is lacking food to control his forces with. Perhaps he fears your power potential," Enki suggested.

Enlil lifted his hand, causing sparks to float above it. "My control is shot. The fight with Chronos cost me a lot. If we had not ended it when we did, it is possible he would have won."

"Maybe that's it. You've forced him to expend his will. You have power but no control. Perhaps he has no power or control," Enki wondered.

Pondering that for a few moments, Enlil nodded. "He's become a Sky Lord in his own right. His mantle is new, frail, and small in breath. The mantle I hold is old, strong, and wide. I do not know how to use it. It's like being thrown into the deep end and being told to just figure it out or die."

"He has to end it before you figure that out. Yet, he's managed to destroy all the food, which means you'll starve well before you can use your powers," Enki said.

"Fight and die or starve and die. Either way, he wins," Enlil lamented.

Enki looked at his father. "Are we not the Annunaki? Do we not know how to control the return of our souls to the Mortal plane? Sometimes to win, you must lose."

"Indeed," Enlil agreed with a raised eyebrow. "Call everyone."

"Already did," Enki said.

Chapter 40:

"I will not sugarcoat this. We are in a lot of trouble," Enlil said as he stood over the crowd. Annunaki, Neanderthals, and Sapiens looked to their new Sky Lord. "We have enough food to feed all of us for a week if we ration. We can't leave via the water, and we are surrounded. Amphitrite has bought us time, but that works to the advantage of our attackers."

Enlil took a few deep breaths as he looked around. "We can save the nursery and a few others to guard them," he paused, holding up a clawed hand. "Please, hold the outbursts. We are going to teach you our soul ritual to reinsert yourself into the Great Cycle. The Great Mother welcomes everyone who returns to better their lives. It is the goal of each Anunnaki to become the best they can be before embracing the Great Mother."

"We are not sure why Chronos thinks that smiting Mortals is a good thing, but here we are. To counter the abuse he is bringing upon us, I am adopting you into my family line. What this means to anyone who isn't Annunaki, you are invited to join the Gods. Drink our Ambrosia and be reborn among us. Tonight, the Annunaki Patheon dies in a ball of flames," Enlil paused again, his face showing a somber mood. He looked around the room, making eye contact with several Humans.

"From the ashes, the Olympians shall rise. We shall be reborn among the lands. We shall become one with each other, a pact between us that shall never be broken. Together, we shall guide all of Olympus. I am inviting you into my house to become my family, offering you immortality. In exchange for this, I am simply asking you to risk your Mortal form. To cast it off and join the Mortal world to the Immortal one for all time. Will you join me and become Gods?" Enlil yelled.

The crowd chanted "Olympus!" over and over. After a few minutes, Enlil raised his staff, causing the crowd to quiet. "Everyone, please report to your assigned primary common areas. One of the current Olympians will visit you and add you to the family with my blessing."

Enlil stepped off the platform as the crowd filtered out of the room. He walked over to Rhea, who was fussing with little Hestia. He bowed his head slightly. "Forgive us, Lady Rhea. We cannot protect you for a while."

Rhea waved her hand. "At worst, it will be a thousand years. That's like a day for us. I'll recover."

"Yes, but what happens to the little one in your arms? What harm will happen to her developing mind?" Enlil asked.

"I will protect my child," Rhea hissed.

"Even from her father?" asked Enlil.

Rhea narrowed her eyes. "Don't you have a family to add, milord?"

"Indeed, I do, Lady," Enlil said with a nod. He glanced around the nearly empty room. "Indeed, I do."

Enki nodded at his father before leading a group to a side chamber. The room was already set up for the ritual, with the candles at the corners of a pentagram carved into the floor. Inside each point, there were ten vials of purple liquid with three layers of green. Next to each bottle was a small ritual knife.

The Lord of Magic clicked two claws together, causing the circle to burst into flames. "This is your one and only chance to back out. Once started, we must complete the ritual. It will not be complete until the Sky Lord accepts your oaths. By drinking the blood of his blood, you will forever become bound to the house of Enlil. By your oath of family, you will seal the pact. You will be bound to assist your kin should the need arise. You will join arms with a family already sworn to protect each other. Does everyone understand the ramifications of this?"

A young woman holding a toddler in her arms raised her hand. "My Lord, what of the little ones? They are too young to understand the choice that is being forced upon them."

"Upon adulthood, it will be offered again to them so they can make the pact. Either in this life or the next," Enki informed the group. That calmed the assembled parents. "If there are no objections, we shall start the ritual." The Lord of Magic looked at each person, brushing their minds to ensure their dedication, providing assurance to them as he moved to stand in the middle of the pentagram. "I will speak in High Annunaki, the language of old. You will, however, still understand the intentions behind each word. Let us begin."

"Vilfac, blessed be the power of Tiamat," Enki started, reaching out to connect with the Humans before him. "We ask for your blessing upon these chosen few. We beseech you to accept these souls into the family of Enlil, son of Anu, Son of Anšar, Son of Tiamat. We beseech you to take these souls into the family of Enki, Son of Namma, Daughter of Kishar, Daughter of Tiamat. We ask that you take these souls from the River Okeanos and return them to the Mortal Realms as Gods."

Enki pulled out a ritual knife and pricked his scarred palm, letting his blue blood drip five times, one droplet into each point. The moment the last drop hit the ground, the star lit up, engulfing the drinks in a purple flame that only affected the liquid. The layers twisted, steadily mixing but staying separate at the same time. The Lord of Magic slowly spread his arms, breaking the planes of the pentagram, causing his clothes to alight with the same flame.

"Do you accept the flesh of our Father?" Enki asked.

As one, the group said, "Yes."

"Do you accept the Blood of the Son?" Enki asked.

Once more, the group said, "Yes."

"Then drink with the blessing of the spirit, the Great Mother," Enki commanded, his arms wide. The purple flames engulfed the group as each drank from a cup, parents feeding their young before drinking themselves. The fire slowly sank into their skin, causing the group to sway as they closed their eyes. They slowly dropped to the ground as their breathing slowed. A woman let out a cry of shock as her daughter's breath shuttered, and then she went limp in her arms.

The woman turned to face her God, rage forming across her

face. Her voice sounded hoarse and weak. "You swore to protect," she gasped as she fell to her knees, "us."

"This is the only way, my child," Enki said, his head bowed. He spoke again when the last person fell lifeless to the ground. "From birth to death, these souls have learned hardship. Blessed be Tiamat for accepting them into her heart. From the cleansing fires, they shall be reborn." The Annunaki Lord slammed his tail into the ground, cracking the pentagram with force.

Blue and purple flames shot out of the bodies, bits of green sparks appearing as the fire roared over the group. "Blessed be Tiamat. Let them be reborn!" Enki shouted. The flames became more intense, reaching two meters before they suddenly were pulled into Enki. His head arched up to the ceiling as he let out a roar of joy, the flames billowing from his mouth and through the stone above.

Slowly the little one who stopped breathing lifted her head. She started to poke at the body next to her. "Mama? Wake up, Mama."

The woman gasped before flinging her arms around her little girl. "Oh my word, you're still alive," she gasped between tears.

"Reborn you have been from the ashes of your past. Whatever you were before, that is now behind you. Gods you wished to become, Gods you shall be. Forever, I am bound to you as your Patriarch. The others among us shall have their own Patriarch and Matriarchs. The call to help those families will be less than our own," Enki informed the group after they woke.

Suddenly the circle's flames flashed blue, purple, then green before fading. "Enlil has accepted you within the family. Mothers of young children, please go see Lord Damu in the healing chambers. From there, you and your children will remain until the battle is over and Chronos' forces depart. Lord Ningišzida shall seal the chambers until then. He has sworn to protect each of you as if you were direct family. Everyone else, we are going to chase the invaders out of our lands or die trying. Report to Lord Ninazu as our Athena has been captured. We attack in two days," Enki ordered.

Chapter 41:

The sun crested over the horizon, barely visible from the lines of plasma filling the sky. The center was a circle, while streaks of purple-blue lines reached out beyond the visible parts of the sky. A figure rose just as the first light hit the spot from the rubble in the city center, highlighting him.

"Brother, I have risen. Thy challenge for the right to rule these lesser beings is accepted!" Enlil bellowed, his voice echoing over the area. "Face me, as tradition demands. If thou demands the Mantle, then come get it," he snarled as he slammed his staff into the ground, gold light rushing from him southeast before a light glowed in the distance.

"There you are, brother," Enlil mumbled as he ground the staff deeper into the rubnle. Blue and green lines appeared above the gold before both faded. He walked, following the path before him, and came to a stop at the collapsed wall.

"Chronos, are you too much of a coward to face me?" demanded Enlil, his voice echoing off the countryside once more. "You attack me and mine like a coward, but the moment I show up to face you, where are you? Hiding like prey from the Hunter. I am right here. Come forth and take my mantle of power from my cold, dead claws."

Enlil stood there, his arms wide as he waited for a response. He felt the tugs of power in response, causing him to lower his head slightly, a 'come and get it' expression forming on his face. The pull became greater, causing him to slide slightly forward.

"Oh, no, brother!" Enlil bellowed as his hands wrapped around the tri-color bands that connected the two and pulled. One hill slightly moved from the force of Chronos, followed by the sound of impact. Moments later, the Lord of Time clawed his way to the top.

"You have my attention, dear brother. Have you come to bargain for the lives of your Mortals?" Chronos taunted.

"They know the price of service," Enlil retorted, his eyes narrowing. "Why?"

"Why what? Why are we here in the Mortal World? The Mother demands it. Why are you so weak? So, I can take what is mine. Why am I attacking you? The Great Tiamat demands the return of your soul. She whispers in my ear, telling me I am the master of this planet and I need to take it back," Chronos said as he walked to the waterline.

"That is not for you to decide. That is only in the realm of the Mother and Father," Enlil corrected him.

"It IS for me to decide!" Chronos screamed in rage. He tapped his head with his free hand. "She tells me in here. She assures me that everything is according to her plan. Even now, you are too deaf to hear her will," he said as he paced back and forth.

"Look at you, brother. What happened to you that has made you act like this?" Enlil asked, his hand reaching out as if to place his hand on Chronos' shoulder.

The other Lord reacted as if the hand touched him, jerking his body back. "Traitors are not family, and only family is allowed such familiarity," he spat. "Nothing you say can cause my path to divert. We still outnumber you, even if you've killed two-thirds of my forces. Accept your death, and I shall spare the Mortal lives."

"As what? Slaves?" Enlil demanded.

"That is what the Adama and Eves were designed for, to become our servants, our slaves," Chronos spat.

"And yet, they are living beings. They are intelligent. They have souls."

"They are children, barely babes. They need our guidance and a firm hand so that they learn their place under our feet," Chronos snarled.

"Yet, you repeat the mistakes that lead to our expulsion from An," Enlil sighed.

"Because they thought they were our 'friends', not our cattle. This time, the herd will know their place from the beginning," Chronos said, his tone patronizing. He let out a sudden roar. "Why are you stalling our fight? Is it because you're scared?"

"Brother, I only wish to understand your pain. Why do you feel the need to lash out and destroy those around you?" Enlil asked sadly.

"You don't know me-" Chronos started.

"I know you, brother. We lived and worked together for thousands of years. You are not the same God that accepted me as Father's other hand," Enlil interrupted, his hand extended.

"Then you were not paying attention. This is who I've always been. You just never wanted to see it. We show up here, then your side of the family accepts abominations as family," Chronos slammed his tail in the ground as he snarled.

"What about your daughter, Hestia? Is she family?"

"She is of blood, even if she is an abomination. I will not drown her like she deserves."

"Why take one as a mate?"

"Because the Mother demands it. Our souls are connected, something a false Sky Lord like you wouldn't understand. I have hopes she will produce a proper heir, but alas, I will probably have to take a concubine to ensure this."

"You hate your children, but you will still have more? What kind of father are you?"

"Control, Enlil. It's all about control. By having the abominations in some fake power, it will help keep the slaves under control, as they will see their kind in apparent power."

"Then the brother I knew is gone," Enlil replied, steeling himself for the conflict.

"No, I am far better than that lum-" A bolt of lightning striking at him cut Chronos off. His reflexes barely let him move out of the way of the direct strike. "Finely figured out-" Chronos had to dodge another power strike, this one leaving a small crater behind. "So be it," he snarled, lifting his staff to attack.

As Chronos fired a blast from his staff, the tops of several hills exploded. The shrapnel from the rocks instantly killed several hundred Giants guarding the vents. Amazonians poured out of the now unguarded exits, their shields lifted to prevent the enemy's arrows from landing, if there were any.

The fierceness of the initial attack left the Titan forces in shock. It took several long moments before the other Giants and Neanderthals realized they shouldn't watch the pretty lights being thrown around the new moat. It took the cries of pain before they realized they were standing on a field of battle.

Enki leaped out of the exit, followed by Amphitrite and Hades. The Lord of Magic pointed at the water that was getting choppy and shouted, "Stop that! Hades, with me!" The personification of the sea nodded, her armored form already moving to fight Oceanus once more.

Hades let out a roar of defiance, his hands balling into fists at his waist. His hair went from a soft brown to blue flames, as did his hands and forearms. With a lunge, he struck a Neanderthal. As he pulled his arm back, his target fell to the ground, lifeless. His form blurred as a dozen more fell, blue flames left in his wake.

With quick strikes, Enki batted away the Neanderthal that moved close to Hades. A Denisovan sprinted for the pair, causing the God of the Underworld to leap sideways, sliding across Enki's back and jumping into the Giant's chest. His hands gripped the large man's ears before he ripped them off, dragging his soul with them. They hit the ground with a thump that shook everything within five meters.

"The Harpies completely underestimated their numbers," Hades called over the sound of battle.

"Good thing we have the Gods on our side," Enki chuckled. He let out a snarl as he lifted his staff like a rifle and let lightning bolts fly out of the head.

"Well, it's a good day to die. I have fresh real estate in the Underworld to work on." Hades chuckled as he grabbed two by the skull and reaped their souls. The sky sparked as solar plasma increased as the fighters drew upon their powers to keep up with battle demands.

One of the Guards snarled something that Enki didn't quite catch, but the result was that every one of her fellow Amazonians' blades lit up in a green fire. The woman's other hand had the same green light wrap around her fist that impacted the chin of a Denisovan. His head jerked back with a loud snap before he fell back.

The Guard leaped over the dead man as he hit the ground, her fist slamming into another Giant's hand. She snarled as she pushed back despite the size difference. She spun her flaming sword to shove it back into a Neanderthal that had tried to stab her in the back before she yanked it in an underhand arc that took the Denisovan's arm followed by his head.

Enki spun his staff, causing a strong wind to blowback arrows as his tail slammed into a Neanderthal, bones snapping like twigs being stepped on. He snarled as he ducked a Giant's fist; the wind directing the arrows into the Denisovan's back. As the large man roared in pain, the Lord of Magic leaped and slammed his feet into the chest of the other, causing him to fall and drive the shafts deeper into the Giant's body.

Snarling, Enki smashed his staff into the neck of another

attacker. He heard someone shout, "Enemies everywhere!" causing him to snort that such a thing had to be said. Glancing around, he surveyed the battle. "Krousses, Phalanx Seven."

"Roger!" came the bellow from the Commander. She started barking orders for the Guard to set up a shield wall. As the last shield slid into place, she turned slightly and shouted, "Kulla, rip it!"

The enormous God ran in front of the shields, dragging his claws along the ground. He quickly cut two long trenches that were three meters wide and a meter deep. They had used every remaining shield to make the wall, but the Olympians had secured a beachhead for the rest of their forces once more. As he went behind the hill and the rest of the troops, Krousses lifted a horn and let out a long blast, followed by two short and another long sound.

From behind the fight for the mantle of Sky Lord, several hundred beings burst out of the ground, their figures blurred by how fast they moved. It was like being shot out of a cannon or like a beehive emptying the entire hive to attack the bear trying to eat their honey. The Harpies came like a wave breaking over the shore across the enemy forces. Arrows tipped with flames of multiple colors shot from their bows, the streaks of light tearing through the daylight into targets with deadly accuracy.

Another part of the wave flowed into the beachhead, quickly moving among the wounded. Others started grabbing bodies from the battle. Shouts of blood, bandages, and saw were among the loudest of the Harpies doing triage and battlefield surgery. There was already a pile of dead being stacked.

After the initial pass through the center of the battle, the Harpies split into four groups. Two started for the back lines of the enemy, while the other two split the battlefield. When one of the Olympian forces went down, one would act as a medic, and a medic would return from triage. This had the added benefit of resting the aerial forces.

"Enki, where are the Riders?" demanded Krousses.

"They were with Oceanus. Perhaps we killed the few that he was able to create?" wondered Enki before knocking the legs out of a Neanderthal and smashing his tail into the man's neck.

By the city, the sky grew bright before a large plasma bolt slammed into the ground, knocking everyone off their feet from the shock wave. Those without proper headgear slapped their hands over their ears as they screamed in pain. Boulders crashed back into the earth as a twelve-meter crater was left in the ground.

The Harpies tumbled in the air. Some of them had wrapped their wings around to ride the shock wave, while others slammed into the ground from broken wings. Many died upon impact, their heads at impossible angles or severed. In an instant, most of the flying force was wounded or dead.

"Or," Enki groaned as he healed his ears. "Chronos expected that and didn't want to waste his forces. Krousses, get the Harpies on the ground. Restrict flight to recovery operations. We can't afford to take such losses."

Krousses nodded as she gave the signal via horn calls. The remaining Harpies quickly dove for the triage area to provide a defensive line when the sky erupted in a green and orange ball of fire. Another bolt struck the ground, this one was green, and an orange strike deflected back into the sky at a shallow angle.

Everyone had learned from the prior strike and had dropped to the ground the moment it started forming in the sky. Hands covered their ears in a vain attempt to protect themselves from the shock wave. Those closest to the plasma were the unlucky ones. The heat of it vaporized them. The surrounding foliage turned black. A few hundred meters away, bodies exploded from the shock wave pressure.

Enki waved his hand in a complex gesture with a snarl as he screamed a word of power. His hand shot out, solidifying into a honey cone sloped shield made from the bedrock over himself and the nearest forces. The shock wave was deflected around both troops.

The Amazonians dropped behind their shields, letting them angle back. They used their swords and spears to secure the barrier. Harpies were a blur as they practically tossed the wounded behind the wall before diving on top of them to protect their charges. The shock wave also was deflected into the air and around them.

Enki scrambled to his feet, helping a Denisovan to his feet. "Come on, let's get behind the shield wall."

"But we are to fight each other," the big man rumbled, eyeing the dead near the fight.

"We can fight after the Titans finish their fight unless you want to explode, too?" Enki asked as he scooped up a Neanderthal with a head wound. "Grab her. Careful, I think her spine is broken."

The Denisovan nodded as he scooped up an Amazonian, taking the dirt with her. "Polybotes, Sub-lieutenant of Lord Hyperion."

"Enki, God of Magic of the Olympians," the Lord replied as he escorted the group up the hill, helping where they could.

"Da, this is good," the Denisovan said with a toothy grin. "The Fates say that I will die at the hands of the Ocean Olympian. So, I will help you all tonight and live."

"Or, you could try to take our heads off," Krousses snapped as she let the group past the wall line.

"Nidya," the Giant said softly when he looked at Krousses.

"Keep the walkway clear! Duck!" Krousses bellowed as another bolt formed. Enki dropped the person he was holding, caught by a Harpy. He threw both hands forward, snarling the exact words he had used when they first landed on the planet eons ago.

Snaking around the purple bolt was a green spark that seemed to crawl around the forming pillar. It lashed out and stuck around the hilltop, projecting from the old shields and forming a dome. Enki fell to the ground, gasping for air, his body looking much thinner than it had a few minutes prior.

"Enki, what did you do?" Krousses demanded.

"I activated the Kalth," Enki groaned. His voice sounded like he was barely awake.

"What in the name of Anu is that, and where did you learn about it?" Krousses snapped as she helped the Lizard-God drink some Ambrosia.

"It was a story." Enki coughed harshly, blue blood spraying from his mouth. "The Amazonian lore," he gasped out as he coughed again. "Among the lore, Athena and I read about. It was about a battle that they could survive by activating the shield of Kalth." Enki's eyes rolled back in his head as he let go.

Krousses checked Enki's vitals, a grim expression crossing her face. "He's alive, but barely. Harpy, get your ass over here," she snarled as she pulled the Lord of Magic to the triage center.

The sky darkened again as multiple plasma bolts struck the moat area; the shock waves passing over the shield. Sparks of hot pink flowed from the pulse into the shield wall. Enki groaned as the same sparks ran through his body. He gasped for air for long moments before his breathing went back to normal.

"That bastard," snarled Celaeno. "That spell is linked to his life force. He is literally the shield protecting us." She turned to face her helpers. "Get an IV in him. We need to get fluids into him now."

Chapter 42:

"What is going on?" Gaia asked as she watched the lines forming in the sky.

Aamira glanced up. "Oh, no. The sun is about to have a CME event. This matches the recordings of the last time this happened."

"What should we do, Aamira?" Khione asked.

"Head to the nearest coast and find a cave to hide in," Aamira instructed. They all jumped as the sky flashed white, bright as the noon sun. The sky had erupted in sparks as a magnetic band broke.

"Can we sail between Asia and its southern islands?" Gaia asked.

"Probably not. We are several days out to sea. Khione, can you give us a strong wind to send us to those islands?" the captain requested.

"I can, but it will take a lot out of me," Khione said, her eyes flashing white as the wind picked up.

"Helm, due west, keep her steady," the captain ordered. The ship turned, slowly gaining speed. Waves cut from the bow, slamming the craft into the waves.

"For the love of," Aamira groaned as she darted out of the wheelhouse, retching sounds following shortly after her departure.

"Can you make an island to shore us?" asked the captain.

Gaia closed her eyes, moving them around as if looking at something only she could see. "Not easily. We are near some of the deepest parts of the ocean. If we were closer to the shore, probably."

"Captain," the aft lookout called.

"What is that?" the captain asked as he saw a shape above the water that looked like a red jellyfish rising from the surface.

"I have no idea," Gaia replied. "I think we need to go faster. Khione, more wind."

The Goddess of Winter nodded, her eyes turning entirely white. The winds picked up, but storm clouds formed. Lightning stretched across the sky. Plasma suddenly ripped through the clouds, riding a strike into the water. A shock wave slammed into the rear of the ship, sending everyone crashing to the deck.

"Captain, we have a problem," Gaia called over the roar of the wind.

"You think?" the captain spat as he picked himself up. "We have a hole in the back of our ship. The sails are ripped, and we have a plasma storm trying to kill us."

"Anything we could do?" Gaia asked.

"Unless you could make us go faster, then no," the captain said.

"What about the lifeboats? Would they-" a sailor bursting into the wheelhouse cut Gaia off before she could finish her query.

"Captain, we are taking on water. The lower deck has flooded already," the sailor breathlessly reported.

"Launch the rafts. It's the only thing we can do. Hopefully, being that low to the water will protect us," the captain ordered, his sailor following him out. He rang a bell, calling everyone to the main deck. The ship was listing as sailors appeared on deck. "Abandon ship."

Everyone immediately dropped the lifeboats into the water, all two of them. They were designed to take a shore party ashore, not for long-term survival. The three Humanaki took the same boat. They dropped four oars into the water, trying to take them away from the rapidly sinking Gaia's Rest.

"Can't you do something about the storm?" Gaia shouted to Khione over the roar of the rain and wind.

"This isn't my storm. The plasma is heating the ocean, causing a flash storm," Khione said, her hair sticking to her face. "Oh, no," she gasped as a large wave crashed over the other life raft. As the wave dispersed, a few wood planks floated in the water.

Across the water, in Olympus, another fight continued. "Think, brother," Chronos spat as he used his tail to bat away a bolt, sending it into the wall behind Enlil. The wall exploded in a shower of stone shards. "It is with a firm hand you raise the young and dumb animals."

"They are not dumb animals," snarled Enlil as he twisted his hand to start a breeze over him. The pair panted for a few moments to enjoy the breeze off the shore.

Chronos swiped his staff at the moat, causing a wave to wash over Enlil. The target of the water attack simply planted his feet and tail, opened his arms wide, and took the saltwater blast. Steam rose from the Olympian Lord's body.

"Think, Chronos, we're huge Lizards. We barely regulate our body heat as it is. You think dumping water over me is a good idea?" laughed Enlil.

The Lord of Time let out a roar of frustration before his body shot across the water, a white glow left in his wake. Enlil barely had time to bring his arms up to deflect the right hook and the tail slam. His hand snapped to his waist before slamming his fist into his attacker's tail and batting it away. As the arm reached back to strike again, the Sky Lord caught Chronos' right arm in his teeth and bit down hard.

Screaming in pain, Chronos slammed his left hand into Enlil's chest and cried out a word that caused a burst of power to explode into his attacker's chest. The Olympian instantly slammed into the rubble behind him. The Titan let out a roar of pain as he looked at his stump of an arm.

Enlil spat out the useless appendage as he stood, pain lancing through his tail and up his spine. His chest smoked from the burn that the blast had left behind. "Are we becoming physical now? What happened to power only as per tradition?" he asked as he rolled out of the crater, crouching as his muscles tensed like a flattened spring.

Ignoring his brother, Chronos let out a scream of rage, pain, and determination. The air around the Titan warped as he roared. The grass under him, what little remained, filled an area under his feet before turning green and growing longer. The grass reached to his knees before it went to a mix of green/brown, and seeds formed. The Lord of Time let out a roar of frustration as he shook his now scarred stump of an arm.

"Oh, are you trying to regrow your arm?" Enlil laughed as he reached into a pocket and removed a vial. "Good luck with that. I coated my blade with this. What is this, you wonder? Well, this blocks your ability to regenerate forever. If you had let the healers help you, they would have been able to cure you. This virus removes regeneration from your DNA." He tossed the bottle to his brother. "Hope you don't spread it to the rest of us. Oh wait, we have made the Olympians immune to that virus. Guess that's a problem for the Titans. Oh, and it only affects Annunaki, not the Humanaki or anyone else on this planet. Maybe the chickens as well, seeing as they are us."

"We have nothing in common with those stupid, flightless birds," spat Chronos.

"Science says otherwise, brother. They are what would have happened if the Gods hadn't helped us leave Olympus the first time," Enlil said.

"We're the Gods," Chronos snarled as his left hand reached out to grab the staff he had left behind. It shot across the water and hit his palm with a thud.

"There is always someone better than you, stronger than you, and more experienced than you. Just because we are as Gods doesn't make us the only Gods in this universe. We were like the Adama on An and here, so the stories say. From the stories, we were elevated to Gods, much like we've done to the Humans now that we've returned," Enlil informed him as he twisted his own staff, readying a defense.

Chronos let out a defiant roar as his staff shot out a purple bolt. Enlil shifted slightly out of the way. "Finding it hard to aim one-handed? Perhaps you should have taken those drills back on Nibiru," Enlil taunted.

"Die," Chronos spat as the rubble lifted behind Enlil. With

several quick strikes by Enlil, the stones exploded, preventing the Lord of Time from using them.

"Chronos, you'll have to do better, or else you won't kill me," Enlil said as he shouldered his staff. "Take aim, release your breath, and fire," he instructed as he snapped off three red bolts.

The Lord of Time spun his staff, absorbing the red bolts. He brought the head to swipe at Enlil with his good hand, speaking a word of power as he returned the bolts but in a solid beam. Enlil dove out of the way, but he was slightly too slow. The beam severed the man's tail, causing him to scream.

Enlil rolled, leaving a blue streak across the ground. He snarled, his hands snapping up, shooting bursts of power at Chronos. The Lord of Time was too busy laughing at the tail damage when two white bolts slammed into his face, knocking him onto his back. He spat several teeth out as he picked himself off the ground.

"Unlike my stump, that's going to keep bleeding," Chronos said with a laugh. He stepped to the side as power passed. "And will bleed faster the more you move. Are you going to flee?"

"Not until your body is gone," Enlil snarled as he leaped, his feet slamming into the Lord of Time's chest, sending him flying. He slammed into a wall remnant, leaving a massive crater behind.

Chronos coughed from the dust around him as he stood. "Let's end this." He spat blood to the side as he spun his staff before slamming the end into the ground, sending a slight ripple through the earth.

Chapter 43:

Behind the shield, Enki awoke with a start. "Tighten that tourniquet. We gotta slow the bleeding," Celaeno snapped. The Lord of Magic's head snapped over to the medic. She was working on a Denisovan with a large hole through his forearm. Slowly, he stood and took a step to help. The IV yanked his arm back, which he promptly removed.

Kneeling next to the wounded man, Enki looked at Celaeno. "Cauterize it," he instructed, his voice barely above a whisper.

"All the iron is in use," Celaeno said, as she sewed the big man's arm from the center of the wound.

Enki placed his claw into the wound, causing Celaeno to hiss angrily at him. A word later, the Denisovan screamed in pain as the air filled with the stench of burning flesh. As quickly as it appeared, the smell was gone. He removed his claw, the wound no longer bleeding.

"Don't do that again," Celaeno snapped. "The shield almost killed you."

"Enki!" a bellow ripped through the area. "Face me, usurper. Lord of Magic, my tail. You are the Lord of Science if anything."

"Who's that?" Celaeno whispered to Enki.

"Asalluhe, my old friend," Enki said as he stood to look at the newcomer.

"Asshole?" asked Krousses. "Who names their child, Asshole?"

"It's Asalluhe, not Asshole," snarled Asalluhe. Enki looked over at the Grey Titan. He was hunched over, his skin a sickly grey, almost translucent verses the living grey of his kind. His right arm was deformed, like it had been broken and healed crooked. He held a silverish staff with a snakehead in his left hand.

"Finally crawled out of the bowels of the Nibiru?" Enki cackled.

"You know full well that by the orders of your Lord, everyone had to leave whether they wanted to or not. You claimed what is not yours when you stepped on this planet. I am the true Lord of Magic. Usurper, fraud, false God," snarled Asalluhe. "Step out there and face me, thief."

"In case you haven't noticed, there is a Sky Lord battle over there," Krousses pointed out.

"True Gods-" he started before his staff twisted, deflecting a shock wave from another plasma strike into the shield. "True Gods know how to avoid the issue. Come out here and face me as my Lord is doing with your false Sky Lord."

Celaeno placed her hand on Enki's shoulder. "You will die if you go out there."

Enki looked at the medic, taking her in as if he were memorizing her. "Sometimes, to win the war, you must lose the battle. We are bound to the house of Enlil. His family is many and will remain in the Great Cycle. If even one remains in the mortal realm, we will return. Not the same, but we will still walk among everyone once more." He placed his hand on the Harpy's shoulder. "Remember, you are an Immortal now. What would kill a mortal is but a flesh wound. If Enlil somehow loses, take who you can and fly away as fast as you can. You will find Gaia and help her hide."

"Yes, My Lord," Celaeno agreed.

Turning sharply, Enki levitated himself out of the shield area, passing through the electrical field as if it didn't exist. His staff snapped into his hand from where he had dropped it as he landed. "You wanted a fight, old man? Let's fight," the Olympian snarled as he swung the staff, the head slamming into Asalluhe's lower jaw. Bone audibly shattered from the impact, causing half the Lizard's mouth to hang.

Asalluhe let out a roar of rage, a blue flame appearing in his mouth. A burst of power fired at Enki even as the other dodged. The Titan cut the flow of energy, drawing a stick figure in the dirt. With a push of power, a column of soil rose around the weakened Lord of Magic. Earthen fists took slow swipes at their target.

"Really? A slow dirt creature?" Enki laughed before he snapped his hand out, gripping at the air. The water in the moat rose before the power slipped from his hands and slammed into Enlil, washing him away from Chronos.

"Clearly better than your Water Man," Asalluhe laughed. Drawing a dagger from his waist, he snapped it at Enki. The Olympian had his head turned slightly, trying to control the water when the blade sunk into his left side. He let out a cry of pain before trying to dodge the golem. He was too slow, and the creature picked him up with both hands, the staff dropping from the former Anunnaki's hand.

"Smash," Asalluhe commanded. The golem slammed Enki into

the ground. His bones audibly broke, including his snout when it bounced off the dirt.

The former Magical Lord of the Annunaki could barely lift his head, much less his hand. However, he still managed to do so and let out a burst of power, ripping the dirt arms from the golem, causing it to drop him with a sickening crunch. Asalluhe laughed as he limped over to Enki.

"Think, Enki. In what world did you think you could defeat me? Someone who was a master practitioner before your worthless father donated his sperm. The spirits of judgment will find yo-" Asalluhe's bragging was cut off as a blade appeared out of his chest, blue blood dripping from the tip. "Wh-what is this?" he gasped as his good hand wrapped around the blade.

"Your death," snarled a wrathful Celaeno. She withdrew the blade and decapitated the Titan Lord. She dropped to a knee as she felt the Mantle of Magic shift to her. "Three days of being stuck here?" she ground out from the pain.

"N-no, you mus-" Enki was cut off by a hard cough and a cry of pain. "Must be in your sanctum."

Celaeno knelt next to Enki, her eyes glancing at his wounds. "I can't save your body."

"I name thee the holder of Lady of... of Ma-Magic," Enki barely got out as he placed his broken hand on her cheek. The hand fell with a thud after a soft glow entered Celaeno's hair, life leaving the Annunaki Lord's body, a streak of blue blood left on her cheek and staining her hair.

"Move out!" Celaeno screamed, already taking to the air. A woman was thrown into the air, who she caught as she flew over the shields. A hundred Harpies leaped into the air behind their leader, flying as fast as their powers let them. Each held one of the less wounded, their equipment left behind.

As the Harpies passed the waterline, Celaeno took her horn and gave three mournful bursts. This caused Amphitrite to wrap the few remaining defenders on the beach with water and wash them out to sea, protected from the Titans.

Chapter 44:

Chronos let out a belly laugh as Enlil turned once more to face the Titan. "You feel that? That was your pathetic spawn dying and his powers being absorbed by my champion. You've lost everything, Enlil."

"I have gained everything," Enlil gasped as he lifted himself out of the tsunami his son had caused. He found his footing and walked across the surface.

The Lord of Time let out another laugh. "You have nothing. I've destroyed everything that is yours. You can no longer reach the Nibiru. Your home here is devastated. Even the limited repairable gear you had left is scattered to the winds. I alone still hold anything of An."

Enlil stepped onto land, glancing back at the line of the blue he had left. Shaking his head, he reached up as he snarled a word. Lightning appeared in his hand before he flung it into Chronos' face. The bolt knocked the Lord of Time back. A clawed hand came up to the side of the Titan's face.

"Blinding me will not save you," Chronos spat as he lowered his hand. The left side of his face was black with burns that sparked out from his cheek, across his eye, and face. The Lord slammed into Enlil so fast that he was simply a blur of light. It sent the new Olympian flying back, landing with a thud and a snap of a bone. Enlil's thigh ripped open as his skeletal structure broke apart.

"Pathetic," Chronos intoned as he slowly moved closer to Enlil.

"You are dead, your body just doesn't know it yet. I can see in your eyes you've accepted your fate."

"Go to Hel," Enlil spat through gritted teeth. The Lord's staff leaped to his hand, firing a blast that Chronos deflected with ease. With a bellow of frustration, his staff was thrust into the sky that darkened as power was drawn from the magnetic sphere. Sparks of plasma appeared again above them, bending slowly down.

The air above them protested with thunder. Clouds formed from the steam being created as the humidity heated beyond boiling. Suddenly, the plasma slammed into the ground, covering Enlil with its heat and power. He slowly rose, his tail sizzling as the wound cauterized. His leg sparked, power arcing through the injury as it slid back into place and then sealed.

Rising from the ground, Enlil lifted his head and opened his arms. Power gathered around his hands as the staff drifted into them. Suddenly the plasma was drawn within the golden rod, the dragon at the head coming to life. "Kaaaaaaaaaaaaaaaaaaaa!" he bellowed as the energy exploded from the staff. The head melted from the heat while blue smoke started to flow from cracks in the gold.

Chronos shook his head at the flashy and long power draw. It had taken long moments that allowed him to prepare a defense. The bolt flew for him, only for him to spin his staff three times before tapping it on the ground. Coming within a meter of him, the electrical charge bent and slammed into the ground.

"Flashy displays of power are all you have left," Chronos taunted.

"Flash this," Enlil spat, flicking his cracked staff's end across the ground in front of him. The dust exploded out, along with the discharging plasma that he was the conduit for. The wind and dirt exploded out, slamming into the deflection. It shoved Chronos back as the air still had to go somewhere after it hit the ground.

Enlil's staff crumbled as the discharge faded, but he was already moving. He was a blur as he moved forward, slamming into Chronos' back to push him into the air. Jumping, he used both hands clenched together to punch the Lord of Time in the stomach. The impact as he hit the ground left a small crater.

Rolling, Chronos came to a knee before using the momentum to fling himself into Enlil. The pair exchanged blows with such force that the impacts echoed through the hills. They began to fall as they reached the top of the arc. Chronos twisted as he tried to slam his tail into his target's stomach.

With a quick movement of his hand, the Olympian caught the tail before using his free elbow to slam into it. A snap and a scream from the Lord of Time happened as Enlil broke the other's tail. Taking the opening caused by the pain, the Sky Lord punched both fists into Chronos' stomach, sending him towards the ground with explosive force.

Chronos slowed before coming to a stop a few meters from the ground. Twisting, Enlil used a power blast to change his trajectory and land on the ground with a loud thud. He barely had time to roll as the Time Lord's shots missed.

Blue flame shot out of Enlil's mouth, trying to trap his attacker within, but Chronos simply flicked his hand, freezing the flames as he touched down. He walked through them, laughing at the attempt. "Really? Flames against the Lord of Time? Pathetic."

Enlil collapsed to the ground, his breath coming in heaves. His hand rested on his thigh, his body twitching from exhaustion. Chronos walked up, his staff returning to his hand. He barked a word before the head shifted into a long blade. With one hand, the Lord of Time and Titan Sky Lord beheaded the old Annunaki Lord.

"It is done," Chronos panted as he dropped to his knees. Sparks wrapped around him as the Mantle shifted. He did not know how long it had been before one of his servants came up to him.

"We've found Rhea and the child. There were about a thousand underground. Families mostly. We think they sent their entire Guard force after us. Nothing to worry about," reported a man in a simple cloth.

"Prepare to return home, Adama. I need a rest," Chronos said exhaustedly. Using his staff, he brought himself to his feet and walked from the devastation. "So ends the Annunaki. Sixty-five million years as a species, ended by a pathetic leader who was in charge for a week."

"Milord?" asked the man as he let Chronos use him as a crutch.

"A plague is coming for the Titans. Unless we can solve it, this is the last generation of the Titans," Chronos explained. "Where is Oceanus?"

"Right here, milord," the God of the Ocean said as a wave placed him onshore.

"Did you get your hands on your target?" Chronos demanded.

"No, she had backup and then fled with the Harpies. I will find her soon. She will join us or die," Oceanus replied with a clenched fist.

Cronus slammed his staff into Oceanus' stomach. "You failed me again. Why should I not slice your head off right here, right now?"

Oceanus picked himself off the ground, clutching his stomach with one arm. "Be-Because I am the only educated Titan that can control water."

The Sky Lord narrowed his eyes and nodded. "Good enough for now. Drag anyone still alive back to camp. If they are the enemy, chain them. We are returning to the temple." He turned to his servant. "Put Rhea on the flagship. Make sure she's chained so she can't leave my quarters."

"By your command," the Adama replied with a bow before he ran to complete the order. Throughout the rest of the day and night, Chronos watched his followers load the ships with captives. Once they finished, the sun had risen to mid-morning. Chronos finally moved from his command tent and returned to his flagship.

"Take us home, Admiral," Chronos commanded. The fleet pulled away from the shore and sailed off towards the horizon.

Across the ocean, Gaia's head fell as she felt the death of her father and grandfather. "Something's happened. Olympus is under attack," she whispered.

"Do you think that caused the plasma attack?" Aamira asked.

"Probably. Hard to starboard, the land is that way, about four hours away. We'll all take turns rowing. Hopefully, we'll be safe there," Gaia said.

To be Continued

CPSIA information can be obtained
at www.ICGtesting.com
Printed in the USA
BVHW092254150822
644633BV00002B/5